**Praise for the Novels
of Vicki Lewis Thompson**

The *Babes on Brooms* Romances

Chick with a Charm

"Thompson again gives readers a charming, warm, humorous, sexually charged romance with likable characters, a magical dog, and a feel-good ending." —*Booklist*

Blonde with a Wand

"Extremely readable . . . terrific writing and great character development. . . . Readers will fully enjoy this confection." —*Romantic Times* (4 stars)

The *Hexy* Romances

Casual Hex

"Ms. Thompson weaves a romantic tale that's sprinkled with magic and reinforced by love . . . a fast-paced read, and a great addition to the enchanting world of Big Knob. Readers will be looking forward to seeing who falls under the spell of the town's magical matchmaking duo next." —Darque Reviews

"An enjoyable lighthearted story . . . Fans will enjoy this jocular jaunt." —*Midwest Book Review*

continued . . .

"Vicki Lewis Thompson sure delivers with *Over Hexed* . . . a lighthearted tale that won't soon be forgotten."　　　　　　　　　　—Fallen Angel Reviews

"With her wonderful talent of lighthearted humor, Vicki Lewis Thompson pens an enchanting tale for her amorous characters, steeping it in magic and enough passion to scorch the pages."　　　　　　　　—Darque Reviews

Further Praise for
Vicki Lewis Thompson and her Novels

"Count on Vicki Lewis Thompson for a sharp, sassy, sexy read. Stranded on a desert island? I hope you've got this book in your beach bag."　　—Jayne Ann Krentz

"Wildly sexy . . . a full complement of oddball characters and sparkles with sassy humor."　　　　*—Library Journal*

"A riotous cast of colorful characters . . . fills the pages with hilarious situations and hot, creative sex."　　　*—Booklist*

"Smart, spunky, and delightfully over-the-top."
　　　　　　　　　　　　　　　—Publishers Weekly

"[A] lighthearted and frisky tale of discovery between two engaging people."　　　　　*—The Oakland Press*

"Delightfully eccentric . . . humor, mystical ingredients, and plenty of fun . . . a winning tale."—The Best Reviews

"A funny and thrilling ride!" —Romance Reviews Today

"A hilarious romp."　　　　　　　　—Romance Junkies

"Extremely sexy . . . over-the-top . . . sparkling."
　　　　　　　　　　　　　　　　—Rendezvous

"A whole new dimension in laughter. A big . . . BRAVO!"
　　　　　　　　　　　　　—A Romance Review

Also by Vicki Lewis Thompson

A Werewolf in Manhattan
Chick with a Charm
Blonde with a Wand
Over Hexed
Wild & Hexy
Casual Hex

A Werewolf in the North Woods

A WILD ABOUT YOU NOVEL

Vicki Lewis Thompson

A SIGNET ECLIPSE BOOK

SIGNET ECLIPSE
Published by New American Library, a division of
Penguin Group (USA) Inc., 375 Hudson Street,
New York, New York 10014, USA
Penguin Group (Canada), 90 Eglinton Avenue East, Suite 700, Toronto,
Ontario M4P 2Y3, Canada (a division of Pearson Penguin Canada Inc.)
Penguin Books Ltd., 80 Strand, London WC2R 0RL, England
Penguin Ireland, 25 St. Stephen's Green, Dublin 2,
Ireland (a division of Penguin Books Ltd.)
Penguin Group (Australia), 250 Camberwell Road, Camberwell, Victoria 3124,
Australia (a division of Pearson Australia Group Pty. Ltd.)
Penguin Books India Pvt. Ltd., 11 Community Centre, Panchsheel Park,
New Delhi - 110 017, India
Penguin Group (NZ), 67 Apollo Drive, Rosedale, Auckland 0632,
New Zealand (a division of Pearson New Zealand Ltd.)
Penguin Books (South Africa) (Pty.) Ltd., 24 Sturdee Avenue,
Rosebank, Johannesburg 2196, South Africa

Penguin Books Ltd., Registered Offices:
80 Strand, London WC2R 0RL, England

First published by Signet Eclipse, an imprint of New American Library,
a division of Penguin Group (USA) Inc.

First Printing, October 2011
10 9 8 7 6 5 4 3 2

To Claire Zion, whose perceptive comments always result in a better story. Thank you, Claire!

ACKNOWLEDGMENTS

As always, I owe much to my agent, Robert Gottlieb, my trusty assistant, Audrey Sharpe, and the terrific editorial, art, and marketing departments at Penguin. I'm also blessed with wonderful readers whose cheerful and warm e-mails make me smile. I treasure my connection with each and every one of them.

Chapter 1

Maybe Bigfoot is watching me.

Abby Winchell had loved imagining that from the time she'd been old enough to wander alone on her grandfather's property about thirty miles outside Portland. As she trudged through the early-morning mist, damp leaves squished under her hiking boots and the evergreens dripped in a steady, familiar rhythm. Otherwise the forest was quiet, but she kept her hand on the camera tucked inside her jacket pocket, just in case she saw something big and furry.

Ten days ago, after a lifetime of fruitless searching, Grandpa Earl Dooley had seen not one but *two* big furry creatures. A Bigfoot mated pair! But his evidence was maddeningly inconclusive. His single grainy shot could easily be a picture of two very tall hikers wearing hooded sweatshirts. Two exceedingly smelly hikers. Grandpa Earl claimed the stench had been overpowering, even from a hundred yards away.

While Earl had struggled to attach his zoom lens, the creatures had loped off. Earl's arthritis had kept him from giving chase, and a heavy rain had washed out any footprints. That left Earl with only one bad picture to corroborate his story.

It had been enough for the Bigfoot faithful. Earl had made the trip to town and told everyone down at his favorite bar, Flannigan's. News had spread quickly among the cryptozoology crowd. As happy as he'd been about finally realizing his dream of a Bigfoot sighting, Grandpa Earl hadn't been all that pleased with the consequences.

With the exception of Abby, his family down in Arizona thought he was losing his marbles. Curiosity seekers had trespassed on his property. And his wealthy neighbors, the Gentrys, had flown in some big-deal NYU professor to label the sighting bogus. Having Dr. Roarke Wallace challenge Earl's claim had cut down on the trespassers, but Abby's grandfather smarted under the insinuation that he was either gullible or a nutcase.

Abby had volunteered to take a week off from her job as an insurance claims adjuster in Phoenix to check on Grandpa Earl. She'd promised the rest of the family that she'd convince him to sell the land and the general store with its attached living quarters so he could move to the desert, where his loved ones could keep an eye on him. He might have agreed to do it, too, now that he'd seen Bigfoot and possibly Bigfoot's mate.

But that damned professor had gotten her grandfather's back up and he wanted to prove the stuffed shirt wrong. Grandpa Earl was also convinced the Gentrys were smearing his reputation on purpose because they hoped he'd leave and then they could buy his land. He didn't want to give them the satisfaction.

Abby didn't blame him. The Gentrys had been trying to buy out the Dooleys for at least seventy years. Both pieces of property backed up to a wilderness area, so if the Gentrys got Grandpa Earl's land, they'd be sitting on one of the most secluded private estates around.

And the Gentrys loved their seclusion. She could imagine how horrified those high-brows must have been to hear about the Bigfoot sighting. Flying in a PhD from some Eastern school fit the Gentry mentality. No doubt the guy was a condescending jerk.

The Gentrys were like royalty in Portland, and as a kid Abby had often climbed a rocky promontory on Dooley land because it provided a view of the obnoxiously huge Gentry mansion. She decided to do that again this morning for old-time's sake. The estate was off-limits to all but a select few, so spying on them had always appealed to her sense of mischief.

Other than this view from the promontory, the heavily wooded estate couldn't be seen except from the air. A tall iron gate at the main road barred anyone from driving up to the mansion unannounced, and a sheer rock wall dropped fifty feet below the promontory. The steep cliff continued along the property line for about half a mile, neatly dividing Gentry land from Dooley land.

Grandpa Earl's property ended at a rushing stream that tumbled over the cliff in a beautiful waterfall. The far side of the stream marked the beginning of the wilderness area. That's where Grandpa Earl had spotted the Bigfoot pair.

Abby was puffing by the time she reached the top of the outcropping, which meant she'd spent too much time sitting at a desk lately. Looking across to Gentry land, she noticed lazy curls of smoke rising from two of the Gentry mansion's six chimneys. Trees hid a good part of the building, giving it an air of mystery.

Abby trained her camera on the mansion and zoomed in to admire the stonework and the massive bulk of the place. Surely a family this powerful wouldn't sabotage some old guy's reputation in order to get what they wanted. They already had plenty of holdings in the Portland area.

Standing on the rocky outcropping looking down at the mansion, she wondered why the Dooley land was so important to the Gentrys. Maybe they knew something Grandpa Earl didn't, like the presence of mineral deposits. Or what if the prize was this very spot? What if they hated the idea that someone could watch them from here?

Fascinated by that thought, Abby began scanning with her zoom to evaluate how much she could see of the place. A cherry-red Corvette convertible sat in the circular cobblestone drive, but no people were around. Slowly she panned toward the back of the house, with its formal gardens, neatly trimmed hedges, and a large collection of marble statuary. As she did, she caught movement in the trees.

Focusing on that spot strained the limits of her little camera, but she managed to identify what looked like a large dog. It behaved more like a wild animal than a domestic dog, though, as it glided through the trees. A coyote, maybe? No, it was too big, and its coat was an unusual pale blond.

The body shape reminded her of a wolf, but that was impossible. There were no wolves on the west coast of Oregon, and even if one had somehow migrated over here, it wouldn't be this color. She'd heard of white wolves, but not blond ones. Knowing the Gentrys, the animal could be some sort of exotic hybrid.

Grandpa Earl wouldn't be happy if the Gentrys had decided to keep dogs on their property. Her grandfather and great-grandfather had always avoided adopting any because they didn't want dogs around to scare off Bigfoot. In all her visits to her grandfather's place, she'd never heard the sound of barking dogs coming from the Gentry estate, either.

She snapped a couple of pictures, even though she knew they wouldn't be very clear. Grandpa Earl would want to know about this. Maybe the wolf-dog was another tactic to annoy him.

As she considered that, she deleted the pictures. No sense in stirring up her grandfather even more. That wouldn't fit with the plan that was gradually forming in her mind.

Much as she'd love her grandfather to stick it to the Gentrys and stay on the land for another ten or fifteen years, that wasn't in his best interest. His arthritis wouldn't bother him nearly as much in Arizona and she sensed that Grandma Olive's death a year ago had left him lonelier than he'd admit.

Therefore she needed to contact the stuffed-shirt anthropology professor and convince him to change his tactics. If the professor would support Earl's belief in Bigfoot instead of challenging it, everyone might get what they wanted. Grandpa Earl would relax, sell his land, and move to Arizona, and the Gentrys would get her grandfather's property. Grandpa Earl said the professor was staying with the Gentrys. But Abby didn't relish driving up to the gate in Grandpa Earl's ancient pickup with the battered camper shell on the back and asking for admittance to the estate. Too demeaning. But she was a member of Rotary Club International, so she could attend their meeting today at a hotel in Portland, where the guest speaker just happened to be Dr. Roarke Wallace.

Taking one last look through her camera's viewfinder, she was startled to notice that the blond animal was staring at her. Then he wheeled and ran into the trees, moving with a fluid grace that looked far more wild and wolflike than doglike.

What in hell had she seen down there?

Damn it. Roarke hadn't seen her until the last minute, but he was positive she'd seen him. Seeking thicker cover, he prayed he hadn't caused a problem. At home in upstate New York he could roam the isolated property without fear of discovery and he'd made the mistake of thinking he could do the same here. No wonder Cameron Gentry wanted the Dooley property with its rocky overlook of the Gentry estate.

Irving Gentry, the alpha who'd bought this land in the early 1900s, obviously hadn't been the brightest bulb in the chandelier. There was some evidence that Irving had enjoyed his whiskey a little too much. That might explain why he'd purchased this low-lying acreage with a vantage point right next door.

The woman standing on the rocks hadn't been worried about being seen. Anyone with hair that red would have to wear a stocking cap if she expected to sneak around. He didn't think she was into sneaking. With luck she was a tourist trespassing on Dooley land in an attempt to find Bigfoot, and a canine creature wouldn't interest her.

Roarke made sure the woman was gone before he loped back through the formal gardens and headed for the tunnel entrance into the mansion. Whoever had devised this entrance had been a werewolf genius. A fake piece of granite swiveled at the touch of a paw, allowing Roarke to enter a tunnel.

Once inside the tunnel, Roarke took the branch that led to a stone stairway. Bounding up those steps, he nudged open a revolving panel and was standing in his guest room. All the bedrooms had the same arrangement, which allowed Weres to enter and leave without having to navigate doors and locks.

Stretching out on the bedroom's antique Aubusson rug, Roarke shifted to human form before hitting the shower. In moments he was downstairs for the breakfast being served buffet-style in the immense dining hall.

Cameron, the pack alpha, was the only member of the Gentry family sitting at the table. A slim man who was beginning to gray at the temples, he looked every inch the aristocrat. As a wolf, though, he had more trouble looking noble. Most Weres were powerfully built with luxurious coats, but Cameron shifted into a scrawny wolf with dull gray fur and a furtive look in his brown eyes.

Come to think of it, he had a furtive look as a human, too. The way he lingered over his coffee and darted glances at Roarke suggested he'd stayed in the dining room in order to give his guest the third degree. Roarke wished Cameron good morning and headed for the sideboard loaded with food. He was starving.

"The surveillance cameras picked you up this morning," Cameron said. "Find anything?"

"Unfortunately, no." Roarke considered telling Cameron about the woman and decided against it. Cameron was already paranoid about the overlook and seemed willing to do almost anything to get his hands on that property and eliminate the potential security risk.

That was one of the reasons Roarke was here—to make Earl Dooley look like a fool in hopes that he'd decide to sell out and leave town. In the Were community, Roarke was an expert on megafauna cryptids such as Bigfoot and the Loch Ness Monster, but in his university career he was known as a prominent myth buster. The good people of Portland would take his word that Earl's sighting was bogus.

It hadn't been, of course, and Roarke had also agreed

to quietly track down the Sasquatch mated pair and relocate them out of Were territory. Gentry didn't fancy having Bigfoot seekers tramping around the countryside anywhere near his estate. More people increased the likelihood that someone would accidentally learn that werewolves lived here.

Roarke hadn't warmed to Cameron, unfortunately. The Were had a ruthless streak, a dangerous trait in a pack alpha. But he was now the guy in charge, having taken over from his father, Gerald. Gerald and his mate, Tabitha, had moved up to Alaska, where Gerald could indulge in his fishing hobby.

Roarke thought Gerald would have been a whole lot easier to deal with than Cameron. Now that Roarke understood his host's lack of empathy, he planned to make sure that the Sasquatch pair was relocated far away from Cameron Gentry.

Roarke respected the Sasquatch tribe and wanted these two moved to safety without incident. He was afraid Cameron just wanted them gone and would choose the most expedient method. Roarke wasn't about to have Sasquatch blood on his conscience.

Cameron drained his coffee cup and stood, shoving back his chair. It moved smoothly on the polished oak floor. "You're at the Rotary Club today, right?"

"Right." Roarke found the lectures increasingly difficult to give. When Cameron had called asking for his help, he'd thought busting the myth of Bigfoot wouldn't bother him even though he knew damned well the creatures existed. If a werewolf pack was in danger of being discovered by Bigfoot-happy trespassers, Roarke was happy to fly to the rescue.

But he was a teacher at heart, and dispensing false information, even to keep people from discovering that a werewolf pack owned half of Portland, was distasteful.

Because of his degrees and his position at NYU, his audiences tended to believe everything that came out of his mouth. He deliberately enhanced his scholarly image by wearing plaid vests, a bow tie, and corduroy jackets with elbow patches.

The outfit was an Indiana Jones kind of cliché, but it inspired confidence in his scholarly opinions. Dressed in his professorial duds, he looked less like a college quarterback—which he'd been ten years ago—and more like a man with multiple degrees.

"I won't be able to make this one." Cameron braced his fingertips on the dining room table. "I have an important business meeting."

"No problem." Roarke would prefer not having him there.

"How many more are scheduled?"

"Two. Tomorrow and Friday."

"I think that should do it." Cameron looked pleased with himself. "Lately I've heard people joking about Dooley and his wild imagination, so the plan seems to be working."

"I can't help feeling sorry for Dooley, though."

Cameron straightened and adjusted his cuff links. "Hey, I'm doing him a favor. He's old and he has arthritis. Selling to me and moving to a dry climate would be the best thing for him."

Roarke wondered what it would be like to be so sure of everything. Alphas were naturally confident, but Cameron's arrogance set Roarke's teeth on edge. "If you say so."

"He's been a thorn in our side for years. Stubborn old goat just laughed at my dad's offers, which were, by the way, more than generous. So it's time to try something new."

"Meaning public humiliation."

Cameron gazed at him. "Whatever works. That overlook is a security threat and I'm tired of worrying about it. I *will* get that land. In any case, I have to go now. Good luck with your talk."

"Thanks." Roarke couldn't argue that the Gentrys needed to own that promontory. A pack of Weres required privacy. He thought again of the redhead and hoped to hell she wouldn't become a problem.

Three hours later, when she walked into the Rotary Club luncheon in the banquet room of a downtown hotel, he had a hunch she was going to be a very big problem, because the first thing he noticed about her was the way she smelled. Scent was all-important to a Were, and this woman's aroma filled him with a longing so deep he lost his place in the conversation he'd been having with a couple of club members.

Absorbed as he was by her scent, he wasn't immune to her visual appeal, either. A tiara of raindrops glittered in her bright red hair, a white trench coat was belted around her tiny waist, and her stiletto heels drew his attention to her shapely legs.

As she unfastened the coat to reveal an emerald-green knit dress, his gaze traveled back upward and he felt a visceral tug. It wasn't that her figure was spectacular, but something about the fit of the dress made him long to peel it off. Not good. He wasn't in Portland for any sexual conquests, no matter how much a woman appealed to him.

Other members greeted her politely, but no one acted as if they knew her, so she must not be a regular member. She leaned close to someone as if asking a question. Then her gaze swept the room and she headed directly for Roarke's table, bringing all those lovely pheromones with her.

He stood, noticing that he didn't tower over her the way

he did with most women. Even taking her heels into account, she had to be at least five-nine in bare feet. Thinking of her in bare feet was an erotic exercise in itself.

God help him, he did favor tall women. They were built for so many interesting sexual positions that weren't possible between a tall man and a short woman. Not that he needed to be thinking about sexual positions in the middle of a Rotary Club luncheon.

Her blue-eyed glance traveled over him and her freckled cheeks grew pink as if she liked what she saw, too. He'd have to be made of ice not to react to that kind of obvious feminine approval. Roarke was a lot of things, but stoic he was not. He gave her his best winning smile.

She smiled back, revealing an adorable little gap between her two front teeth. Then she held out her hand. "Dr. Wallace, I'm Abby Winchell."

The name wasn't familiar, but her hand in his felt perfect—warm, soft, and slender. He breathed her in and barely kept himself from groaning with pleasure. "When someone calls me Dr. Wallace I always feel as if I should be wearing a stethoscope," he said. "Plain old Roarke's fine."

She beamed at him. "All right, Roarke. I'm looking forward to your talk."

Despite struggling with sensory overload, he managed to say something halfway appropriate in response. "So you're interested in cryptozoology?"

"I was as a kid." She glanced down and gently extricated her hand from his.

Great. Apparently he'd held the handshake longer than the socially acceptable two seconds. At least he hadn't hauled her into his arms. "Would you like to sit down?" *Would you like to leave with me right this minute and check into a hotel room upstairs?*

"I'm afraid your table is already filled."

He glanced at the head table and sure enough, every seat but his was taken. He should be glad of that because he needed to nip this instant attraction in the bud for many reasons.

He wasn't forbidden to have a romantic liaison with a human, but he had to be careful about it. If a woman got too close and began to suspect that he was not quite the man she'd bargained for, that was a potential security breach for the pack. Roarke's brother, Aidan, had landed in exactly that fix and there'd been all kinds of trouble, even if he was now married to a human.

Roarke had no intention of following in Aidan's paw prints. He didn't believe Weres should mate for life with humans. It was just too complicated. That issue aside, Roarke had two important assignments here in Portland, and allowing sex to overrule duty was frowned upon in the Wallace pack. Translated, that meant he didn't have time to fool around on this trip. He had a mated Bigfoot pair to find, and no telling how long that would take.

"I'd better find a seat before they start serving the meal," Abby said. "I just wanted to introduce myself and see if you'd be available after your talk in case I have some questions."

Now there was a really bad idea, but his libido trumped his brain. "Sure, I have some spare time."

"Great. There's a quaint little bar called Flannigan's in this hotel. I'll buy you a drink."

He heard himself agree to that suggestion, too. But it was only one drink. One harmless drink with a beautiful redhead. A beautiful, tall redhead with eyes like sapphires, *who had spied him roaming the Gentry property as a wolf.*

Maybe having a drink with her was actually a good idea. He could plant some story about the Gentrys offering to dog-sit for a friend. That would solve any lingering issue over what she might have seen this morning. So meeting the willowy, wonderfully scented Abby for drinks was okay. Provided, of course, that he kept his libido under control.

But as he watched her walk away, her hips swaying gently, he realized his libido had been in charge all along.

Chapter 2

She was in luck. Under that cheesy getup, Dr. Roarke Wallace was one hot guy. Give him a surfboard and a wetsuit and he could be a California surfer dude, complete with the sun-streaked blond hair and killer green eyes. She'd love to see what those eyes looked like minus the wire-rimmed cheaters.

Even better, Roarke had reacted well to her quickly created outfit. She'd packed only jeans and sweatshirts, her usual Portland gear. Consequently she'd had to spend the morning on a power shopping spree at Pioneer Place, change in a public bathroom, and then stash her other clothes in Grandpa Earl's pickup.

But Roarke's expression as she'd walked into the meeting had justified all the trouble plus the damage to her credit card. Here she'd expected to work her wiles on a pudgy, middle-aged scholar with an attitude, and instead she'd been blessed with Roarke.

Spending time over a drink in Flannigan's would be no hardship at all. And unless she'd read him wrong, he'd be willing to listen to what she had to say about Grandpa Earl and his dedication to the Bigfoot myth.

She found a seat at a table populated mostly with real estate brokers. First she identified herself as an insurance claims adjuster visiting her grandfather, and everyone was fine with that. The conversation flowed easily through the salad course and the main entree.

But right before dessert, someone thought to ask whose granddaughter she was. The name Earl Dooley apparently left them all at a loss for words. Abby guessed that they'd bought into the current theory that her grandfather was a kook.

Abby pushed aside her chocolate cake, no longer hungry. "I don't know what he saw, but he's studied Bigfoot for years. I'm willing to believe this was the real deal." She wasn't quite as convinced as all that, but Grandpa Earl deserved to be defended and nobody else was volunteering for the job.

A balding man in a gray suit cleared his throat. "I'm not calling your grandfather a liar, Abby. But everyone's eyesight gets worse as they get older. Earl's what . . . seventy-eight?"

"Seventy-seven." Abby's jaw tightened. "But the picture proves that something was out there, and whatever it was stunk something terrible. No hiker would smell that bad, no matter how many days they'd skipped a shower."

"But maybe a skunk was in the area," said a blond woman in a purple turtleneck. "When our dog flushed a skunk, I thought we'd never get rid of the smell."

Abby didn't want to admit she'd thought of the skunk angle. Or that Grandpa Earl's fierce yearning to see Bigfoot might have influenced his description of the sighting. "All I know is that my grandfather has lived in this area all his life, and I think he'd recognize the smell of a skunk."

A brunette dressed all in black with silver jewelry

frowned and started to say something, but the table was spared her opinion when Roarke was introduced. Abby didn't expect Grandpa Earl to get any better treatment from Roarke's lecture, but at least he was yummy to look at. She was digging those broad shoulders and his square jaw.

He needed someone to dress him, though. His lack of a wedding ring and the dopey outfit suggested he wasn't married. His corduroy jacket wasn't bad, but the plaid vest and bow tie were ridiculous. If she didn't know better, she'd think he was channeling Professor Henry "Indiana" Jones Jr.

"The idea of a mystical creature living in the Pacific Northwest originated with the indigenous tribes." Roarke touched a button on his laptop and the screen behind him lit up with a crude drawing of Bigfoot. "Humans have always fantasized about megafauna cryptids like the Yeti and Bigfoot."

Even if Roarke was about to rain on Grandpa Earl's parade, Abby thought he was unbelievably cute as he threw out terms like *megafauna cryptids*. She had a weakness for brainy guys who spouted jargon, especially when they looked like Roarke.

He showed the audience a few more slides reputed to be of Bigfoot. "We seem to have an innate need to imagine something larger than life." He glanced at Abby.

She had the urge to laugh. There was no chance in hell he'd made a sexual reference just now, but that's where her mind was at the moment. Although she had zero intention of seducing the bodacious professor, she amused herself by wondering what sex with him would be like and whether certain parts of him would be larger than life.

Roarke hesitated. "But wanting to believe in something doesn't make it so. These creatures are not real."

She met his gaze and had the craziest impression that he didn't believe what he was saying. But that couldn't be right. He was a man of science, brought here specifically so he could blast this myth out of the water. She must be imagining things.

"Purely in biological terms, the existence of Bigfoot is an impossibility, especially in this area," Roarke continued. "Climate and food supply issues would preclude establishing a large enough breeding population to guarantee survival. And, as most of you know, no one's ever found the remains of a Bigfoot specimen. That alone is enough to convince any thinking person."

As Abby listened to him, logic warred with loyalty. His argument was convincing, and he looked damned good making it, too. If he'd come to Portland on his own, motivated by scientific curiosity, she might be more willing to accept what he was saying. But the Gentrys had sponsored his visit, so in her view, his argument was tainted by the Gentrys' desire to get Earl Dooley's land.

Nope, she was still going to believe in Grandpa Earl's sighting. The kid in her wanted it to be true, even if the practical adult she'd become agreed with Roarke. Thinking of Bigfoot as real brought back the magic she'd felt as an eight-year-old walking through those mysterious woods.

Grandpa Earl was the dreamer of the family, and her parents used to worry that she'd take after him, partly because she was the only one who'd inherited his red hair, although his was now snow white. She hadn't taken after him, though.

To the great relief of her mom and dad, she'd picked a solid career in insurance, one that fit in well with the rest of her relatives. Her mother and father ran an auto-parts store. Her brother, Pete, was an accountant. Her aunt and uncle owned several fast-food franchises and both her cousins were in business school.

Last year Abby had almost married an insurance agent she'd met through work. She'd broken up with him over what everyone else called a stupid reason. He didn't think kids should be encouraged to believe in Santa Claus. Abby knew Santa Claus wasn't an actual person who flew all over the world delivering toys, but for the first six years of her life she'd thought he did, and she wasn't willing to rob her children of that innocent joy.

She wondered if Roarke had believed in Santa Claus when he was a kid, or if he'd been a child prodigy who'd always been as mercilessly scientific as he seemed now. He continued with his PowerPoint presentation by showing a photograph that looked very much like her grandfather's, except that only one Bigfoot was pictured instead of a pair.

"The person who took this photo up in Washington near Mount Rainier was positive he'd seen Bigfoot," Roarke said. "It was an honest mistake, not an attempt to defraud. But soon afterward a hiker came forward and identified himself as the one in the photograph. The hiker agreed to pose in the same area in similar weather and at the same time of day, and this is the result." Roarke showed another shot almost identical to the first.

Abby noticed her tablemates sneaking glances at her, and she had to admit the evidence was damning. But what about the smell? Grandpa Earl had been very specific about the smell, and he wouldn't confuse skunks with Sasquatch.

It was as if Roarke had read her mind. "Our local celebrity Mr. Dooley, who claims to have seen a mated pair, says the stench was unmistakable. Unfortunately for the veracity of his story, that stench could be any number of less exotic things—a skunk, a dead animal in the underbrush, even a colony of feral cats."

With a sigh, Abby acknowledged that could be true. Roarke wasn't destroying her grandfather's claim with ridicule. Instead he was quietly dismantling it with clear and unassailable logic, which was much more effective. She'd been faced with that kind of reasoning all her life, which was why she'd given up on tales of unicorns, frogs turning into princes, and Bigfoot.

If Grandpa Earl's cherished Bigfoot really existed—and Abby wanted to believe that for her grandfather's sake if for no other reason—then more evidence was needed. One grainy picture and a report of an offensive smell didn't cut it. Grandpa Earl wanted that evidence, but his arthritis kept him from spending hours hiking through the woods.

She wasn't scheduled to leave for another five days. Once she convinced this professor to lay off his campaign, she'd buy a better camera and devote the rest of her visit to combing the woods. She wouldn't tell her parents about it, though, because they'd probably want to fly up and stage an intervention.

Roarke finished his presentation and invited questions, but he didn't get many. Judging from the comments at Abby's table, everyone was convinced that her grandfather had seen a couple of tall hikers wearing bulky sweat suits. They'd left quickly because they'd known they were hiking illegally on private land. Case closed.

Gathering her coat and purse, Abby exchanged pleasantries with the people leaving her table and assured them that she wasn't offended by their doubts about her grandfather's claim. And she wasn't. The evidence was inconclusive and even Earl probably knew that. But he'd been there, and he believed.

If Abby found better evidence, she'd enjoy parading it in front of the skeptical professor Wallace. She should be sure to get his card before they parted ways. The thought of continuing a debate through e-mail sent a zing of excitement through her.

As she approached the small group of people surrounding him, her heart rate spiked. Okay, so she was attracted to him. Any woman would be who managed to look past his clothing choices. He might not be married, but there was a good chance he had a girlfriend back in New York.

Maybe his girlfriend was a geek who preferred her man in plaid vests and bow ties. Or maybe she was a smart cookie who realized that turning her honey into a *GQ* guy would only increase his hottie quotient and cause her more problems with other women. Maybe . . .

Abby blew out a breath, impatient with herself. Debating Roarke's availability was distracting her from her goal to help restore Grandpa Earl's reputation in the community. She'd come here to assess the enemy. Whether or not he had a girlfriend was completely beside the point.

She waited until everyone else drifted away from Roarke before stepping forward. "Interesting talk."

He smiled. "You weren't bored out of your skull?"

"Not at all. Still have time for that drink?"

"Sure. Let me shut down my laptop and I'll be right with you." He turned and tapped a few keys.

He looked as handsome from the side as he did straight on, and she allowed herself to admire him in profile. He had very sensuous lips. That didn't guarantee that a man was a good kisser, but it was a fine start.

"Did I convince you that Bigfoot is a myth?" He closed the laptop and disconnected it before stowing it in a carrying case.

"You convinced me that Earl Dooley's evidence doesn't prove anything."

"Nobody's evidence has ever proved anything." Grabbing a tan raincoat, he hoisted the carrying case strap over his shoulder.

"Yet." She couldn't resist.

"Ah." He smiled at her as they started out of the banquet room. "You're a believer."

"I'm a semi-believer. I'm also Earl Dooley's granddaughter."

He stopped to gaze at her. "Oh."

"Is that a problem?"

"Not for me, but I'm curious why you'd want to buy me a drink, all things considered."

She laughed. "Afraid I'll slip some arsenic in it?"

His worried expression relaxed into a grin. "Would you?"

"Nah. Too obvious."

"In that case, where's this quaint little bar you mentioned? I could use a beer."

"Follow me." She led the way to Flannigan's and soon they were seated opposite each other in a cozy booth surrounded by gleaming mahogany paneling and jeweled light from Tiffany shades.

The place was nearly empty at this time of day, which meant Abby could actually hear the Irish ballads on the bar's sound system for a change. She'd been in here with Grandpa Earl and Grandma Olive on summer nights when the noise level had made conversation impossible. Both her grandparents, Irish to the core, had enjoyed sipping a pint of beer served in a publike atmosphere.

After Grandma Olive died last year, Grandpa Earl had stopped going to Flannigan's. But then he'd sighted the Bigfoot pair and had headed to the bar with his pictures and his story. Abby's heart squeezed as she imagined how excited he must have been to share his discovery.

Roarke ordered a Guinness and Abby did, too. Being in Flannigan's always brought out the Irish in her.

The beer, served in glass mugs, arrived quickly. Abby lifted hers in a salute. "Here's to scientific inquiry."

"I'm for that." Roarke touched his mug to hers. Then he took a sip and set the mug on its coaster. "I'm going to guess you have some ulterior motive for coming to the meeting today."

"Of course." She savored the tang of the dark beer, which she drank only when she was in Flannigan's. "Have you known the Gentrys long?"

An emotion flickered in his green eyes. "No. My dad knows Cameron Gentry's parents."

"The Gentrys have wanted Dooley land for years."

"I'm aware of that."

Damn, but he was good-looking, which made it tougher to concentrate on her mission. "You're a smart guy, Roarke. You also must have figured out that Cameron Gentry wants to make my grandfather into a laughingstock so he'll give up and sell." She waited, wondering if he'd try to deny it.

He gazed at her for a long time before sighing. "Yes, I know."

"That's not very nice."

"You're right, it isn't, but there were other issues, like concerns about trespassers. Once your grandfather made a public announcement of his supposed discovery, the Gentrys had to deal with unwanted curiosity seekers. That wasn't fair to them."

"Come on. Don't tell me that was a huge problem for them. With all their money, I'm sure they have a security system to end all security systems."

"They have a surveillance system, but—"

"Roarke, if I tell you something, can you promise not to take it right back to the Gentrys?"

He hesitated, as if weighing that. "All right."

"I'd like to see my grandfather sell that land, too."

"You would?"

"Absolutely. He's all alone up here now that my grandmother's gone. That little general store he runs out by the main road is a lot of work, but he doesn't make enough to justify hiring help. The rest of his family moved to Arizona years ago, and now we want him to come down there. It would be so much better for his arthritis and we could keep an eye on him as he gets older."

Roarke frowned. "So why hasn't he done that?"

"Bigfoot. He wanted to see that creature just once."

"And now he thinks he has."

"Right. And he might have sold out after that, except the Gentrys brought you in to rain all over his parade. Now he says the only way he'll leave is feetfirst."

Leaning back in the booth, Roarke scrubbed a hand over his face. Then he began to chuckle.

"It isn't funny."

"Oh, but it is." Shaking his head, he picked up his mug and took a swallow of his beer.

"Not to my grandfather."

"No, I suppose not." Roarke returned his mug to its coaster. "Abby, I regret making your grandfather look foolish, but in a way, he left himself open to it with his flimsy case."

She felt compelled to defend Grandpa Earl. "If you'd searched for something all your life, and then you found it, wouldn't you tell people? Wouldn't you show them the picture, even if it wasn't a very good picture?"

His green eyes filled with compassion. "You love him very much, don't you?"

"Yes. That's why I'm asking you to help repair the damage you've done to his self-esteem."

"How could I do that?"

She took a deep breath. "I don't suppose you'd give a talk saying you've studied his picture more thoroughly and have decided it could be a legitimate shot of Bigfoot."

"I can't do that."

"Because of the Gentrys?"

"Partly, and partly because it wouldn't be true." His glance flickered slightly. "Anyway, Bigfoot doesn't exist."

If she hadn't been fascinated by his gorgeous green eyes, she might have missed that flicker. In her experience with insurance claims, a flicker like that meant the subject wasn't giving her the whole truth.

She sensed an opening and decided to try a different tack. "I'm willing to agree that it's unlikely that Bigfoot exists, but the world's an amazing place, where new discoveries are made every day. I would think as a scientist you'd want to leave yourself open to the possibility."

"But all the hard evidence—"

"Screw the hard evidence, Roarke. My grandfather saw something, and he doesn't believe for one minute it was hikers. I challenge you to come by Dooley's General Store and talk to him about it."

"He'd probably throw me out on my ear."

"Not if I'm there to stop him. Come tomorrow morning around ten. Please. This is a delicate situation, but you and I might be able to make it end well for all concerned."

Roarke turned his mug around in his large hands before glancing at her. "You'll be there?"

"I'll be there. I'll admit that Grandpa Earl has a stubborn streak, so somebody needs to hang around and referee. But I think if you hear him tell the story of what he saw and smelled, you'll find that ridiculing his sighting won't be so easy."

"It's never been easy."

She leaped on that. "Because you think Bigfoot is a possibility?"

"Because I don't like poking holes in somebody's cherished dream."

"So why did you?"

He finished off his beer. "It's complicated. I—" A cell phone chimed and he pulled a BlackBerry from inside his corduroy jacket and checked the number. "Sorry, but I need to go."

"No problem. But your call reminds me. Would you give me your cell number? I think my grandfather will be available tomorrow, but something might come up and I'll need to call you."

"Sure thing." He took a cream-colored business card from a different inside pocket of his jacket and handed it to her. Then he levered himself out of the booth and picked up his coat and laptop case. "Unless I hear from you, I'll be at your grandfather's store tomorrow at ten. I owe him that much."

"Thank you, Roarke."

"Don't thank me yet. It could turn into a shouting match that won't solve anything."

"It won't be a shouting match." She gazed up at him. "I'll prepare him for the visit. I'll tell him you're actually a good guy."

He smiled at that. "You're making quite an assumption on such brief acquaintance."

"I'm an insurance claims adjuster. It's my job to separate the white hats from the black hats. Until today, I thought you were in the black hat category, but now I've changed my mind."

Roarke held her gaze. "I wouldn't be too quick to do that if I were you."

A shiver of sensual awareness ran through her. "Are you saying you're a bad boy?"

"I've been known to be."

She gulped, unable to come up with a single snappy comeback.

"See you tomorrow."

Her heart racing, she turned to watch him walk away. *Oh, baby.*

Chapter 3

Although technically the Gentrys lived next door to the Dooleys, it was a couple of miles on the main road from the Gentry mansion to Dooley's General Store, so the next morning Roarke drove his rented Corvette. There was enough misty rain to need the wipers every couple of seconds and the asphalt was shiny and wet. So far this week the convertible top had been a waste. He had yet to see a sunny day.

Still, the Corvette was a sweet car to drive on a temporary basis. He'd always prefer his Ferrari, but the Corvette hugged the curves and purred like a contented cat. Growing up he'd longed to be a race car driver, but drivers spent too much time in crowds and on camera. A Were needed a certain amount of privacy because sometimes, shift happened. *Ha, ha.*

As he neared the general store, he thought about his phone message yesterday afternoon, which had turned out to be a text from his brother, Aidan, announcing that Emma was pregnant. So Roarke had spent the rest of the afternoon on the phone with Aidan, Emma, and his parents as they all celebrated the news. Although it was too soon to tell whether the baby would be a boy or girl, Roarke doubted that was the question on everyone's mind.

Instead of mating with a Were as he'd been expected to do, Aidan had mated with Emma, a human. Would their kid be Were or human? Nobody knew. The baby would look like a human child until puberty, so the family would have to wait for the verdict until then. At puberty a Were child began showing signs of being able to shift.

Aidan's choice had rocked the Wallace family to its foundation, and although Roarke liked Emma, even loved her as a sister-in-law, he still didn't approve of Aidan's decision. Weres mated with Weres, and that's what Roarke would do. He hadn't found anyone yet, but he wouldn't turn thirty until next year. Aidan hadn't married until he was thirty-two. Roarke had time.

His immediate concern regarding females, Were or human, was what to do about Abby Winchell, who made him think of cool sheets and hot sex. She was here visiting and so was he, which made for a potential fling, a shipboard romance minus the ship.

Except, as he'd determined yesterday, he didn't have the time. He sighed as he pulled into the gravel parking lot in front of Dooley's General Store. Maybe he'd luck out and find the Bigfoot pair this afternoon, arrange for their relocation before dinner, and be free to party with Abby tonight. *Dream on, Wallace.*

Climbing out of the low-slung car, he took a deep breath of pungent, rain-soaked earth before surveying the store in front of him. Yes, it was a little run-down, the gray siding a tad bit weathered, but Roarke felt welcomed by the covered front porch complete with four rocking chairs. True, the chairs were wet with rain that had blown in. But if Portland ever had a sunny day—and Roarke had been assured there were many sunny days in Portland—those chairs would provide a relaxing spot to watch the world go by.

A row of stained-glass sun catchers hung in each window on either side of the door. Roarke wondered if anyone ever bought them or if the display was evidence of wishful thinking. Personally Roarke didn't mind the constant light rain, which created such beautiful and werewolf-concealing foliage and washed away incriminating wolf tracks. But he did miss being able to drive with the top down.

A mechanical bird twittered as he opened the front door and stepped inside. True to its label of "general store," Dooley's seemed to stock a little bit of everything. Roarke smelled coffee brewing, wood smoke, and the musty odor of canvas. A quick scan of the shelves revealed camping gear, groceries, fishing tackle, kids' toys, and Portland souvenirs.

At first Roarke thought the place was empty, but then his Were senses picked up Abby's distinctive aroma. A second later she appeared from the back room and walked toward him. Today she looked more like the woman he'd seen on the outcropping than the one who had appeared at the Rotary meeting. She'd pulled her bright hair up into a ponytail and she wore jeans and a green *Kiss me, I'm Irish* sweatshirt.

The sentiment on the sweatshirt made him wonder if she was throwing out hints. No need for that. He'd be happy to kiss her whatever nationality she was. But he didn't have time. Damn.

She looked him over with an impish smile. "I almost didn't recognize you without your vest and bow tie."

He glanced down at his jeans and black sweatshirt with the NYU bobcat mascot on it. "You're disappointed. I should have known the vest and bow tie were a turn-on."

"Oh, yeah. Especially the vest." She laughed and glanced out the window. "Is that your red Corvette out there?"

"It's my rental."

"I see." She pursed her lips and gazed at him. "So who's the real Roarke Wallace? The geeky professor or the laid-back guy driving a red ragtop?"

"Geeky? I'll have you know that's my Henry Jones Jr. look."

"So you did that on purpose! I wondered."

"I'm an anthropology professor. I recognize the value of costume."

Humor flashed in her blue eyes. "So is this your indolent rich boy costume?"

"Something like that. I'm a man of many parts." Boy, wasn't that the truth. If she knew about his third costume, she'd freak.

"And a man of your word," she said quietly. "I appreciate this, Roarke. Grandpa Earl will be out in a few minutes. He didn't want to appear too eager, so he's dawdling around back there pretending to be very busy."

"Just so he's not very busy loading a shotgun."

Abby shook her head, which made her ponytail dance. "I think he's secretly flattered that you want to meet with him. We have a little area in the far corner of the store with a pot-bellied stove and a couple of wooden armchairs. Why don't you wait for him over there?"

"That's fine." Roarke followed her down a store aisle and caught himself enjoying the way her jeans fit her backside as she walked. He should look away. He didn't.

From the corner of his eye he noticed a small display of condoms on a top shelf, out of reach of little kids. So Dooley's General Store helped promote safe sex. Good to know. Except buying condoms from her grandfather might not be the smoothest move he'd ever made.

Besides, he wasn't buying any, because he didn't have time to have sex with her. He would talk with her grandfather and hear his story. Maybe Earl Dooley would tell him something that would help in his own search. In fact, he should have thought of that earlier.

Abby turned and gestured toward the two battered chairs sitting on either side of an old-fashioned woodstove. A fire crackled behind what was probably the original leaded glass in the door. "Can I get you something? A cup of coffee? Hot chocolate?"

"Coffee would be great, thanks."

"How do you—"

"Black."

She nodded. "Coming right up." She headed for the door leading into the back of the store. "I'll see if I can move Grandpa Earl along."

The wooden chair creaked as Roarke settled in. He figured it was an antique, too, and he hoped it could hold a two-hundred-twenty-pound werewolf. Sitting in the chair beside the fire and surrounded by the organized clutter of the store, Roarke wondered if Dooley would be happy retiring to Arizona, after all. A man needed something to do with himself, an identity of some kind. And clearly he had one here.

But that wasn't for Roarke to worry about. He had plenty on his plate dealing with the Gentry pack's crisis. That was his ultimate priority, no matter what he thought of Cameron. Exposing one werewolf pack meant all of them were in danger—the Wallaces in New York, the Hendersons in Chicago, the Stillmans in Denver, the Landrys in San Francisco.

Roarke smelled Abby before he saw her come out from the back room holding a steaming mug of coffee. Every whiff of her was more enticing than the last. He'd be wise to limit his exposure.

She was followed by a tall, thin man with a head of thick white hair. He wore glasses, but they didn't soften his piercing blue gaze a bit. If Roarke had been hoping for a guy with failing eyesight, Earl Dooley wasn't about to accommodate him.

Roarke stood.

"Here's your coffee." Abby handed him the mug.

"Thank you."

"And here's my grandfather." She stood aside. "Dr. Roarke Wallace, meet Dr. Earl Dooley."

Roarke's eyebrows rose as he stepped forward to shake Earl's hand. "I didn't realize that you—"

"Ah, I never use the title." Earl's handshake was firm. "My degree's in mythology."

"That explains your interest in Sasquatch."

"Actually, Sasquatch explains my graduate studies. I've been stalking Bigfoot all my life, just like my father did before me." Earl gestured to the two chairs. "Have a seat. Abby says you're willing to hear my side of the story, so you might as well get comfortable. Abby, you take the other chair."

"Let me get your stool first."

"I'll get it. You sit."

"Okay." Like an obedient child, she sank onto the other wooden chair.

"Be right back. Talk among yourselves. Drink your coffee, Dr. Wallace." With a chuckle, Earl ambled down the aisle toward the front of the store.

Feeling a little like an obedient child himself, Roarke sipped his coffee. "You could've told me he's a PhD."

"As he likes to say, it's window dressing. He got the degree because his father insisted that he have one since he's so darned smart, but the only thing Grandpa Earl ever wanted was to help run the store and look for Bigfoot."

"And with all that time spent studying folklore and legends, he never began to doubt?"

She shook her head, and her ponytail swayed again. "Nope. His father saw Bigfoot once, but he didn't have a camera at the time. The Irish are great story-tellers, though, so he described the event in vivid detail to anyone who would listen. Grandpa Earl listened a *lot.*"

"I'm beginning to understand his dedication to the cause."

Abby smiled. "That was the idea."

He was also beginning to understand that Abby didn't do much of anything without a reason, which led him back to the question of why she'd worn a sweatshirt inviting someone to kiss her. It also invited someone—in this case him—to focus on her breasts.

Under different circumstances, Roarke would have been happy to follow up on Abby's broad hints. Knowing he didn't dare was making him cranky. He couldn't remember the last time a woman had affected him this much, and what bad luck that he wouldn't be able to do anything about it.

So he drank his coffee and tried not to think about kissing Abby.

"Okay, kids." Earl returned with a tall stool and placed it in front of them before perching on it. "You might think I'm doing this so I'll have a superior position in the discussion, but my damned knees make low chairs booby traps."

"This climate must not be helping any," Roarke said.

Earl's glance sharpened. "Now, don't you start in on me. I suppose Abby told you that she wants me to move to Arizona."

"She mentioned it."

"Your friends the Gentrys would just love that. I've

often wondered if they sit over there with a voodoo doll and a box of pins."

Roarke stared at him. "Surely you don't believe in voodoo?"

"I do, and don't call me Shirley." Earl chuckled again. "Sorry for the cornball joke, but it still makes me laugh. Anyway, I guess you don't believe in voodoo."

"I can't say that I do." He couldn't say that he didn't, either. The power of suggestion had always fascinated him.

"'There are more things in heaven and earth, Horatio, than are dreamt of in your philosophy.' That's Shakespeare."

"I know."

Earl shifted on the stool. "You're a physical anthropologist, right?"

"Right."

"And you graduated *magna cum laude*, plus you were asked to take part in the New York Consortium for Evolutionary Primatology."

Roarke was impressed. "You've been reading my online bio."

"I wanted to know the credentials of the man who planned to shred my Bigfoot evidence. At least you're brilliant. That helps me deal with the hatchet job."

Guilt stabbed him as he thought of how arrogant, and how hypocritical, his talks had been. He had no doubt that Earl had seen that mated pair, and regardless of Earl's evidence, he'd made a terrific scientific discovery. As a reward, his name had been dragged through the mud.

"Hell, I know the evidence is bad. My camera's old and my arthritic fingers don't work as well as they used to. But can I give you anecdotal evidence instead?"

"Sure." Roarke leaned forward and cradled the warm mug in both hands. "I'd love to hear about what you saw."

Earl launched into his tale, and Abby hadn't been

kidding about the Irish gift for storytelling. Roarke sat spellbound, his coffee forgotten, as Earl described the early morning, the apelike roar of the creatures, the gag-inducing smell, and the camera that refused to cooperate. When Earl finished, Roarke had absolutely no doubt that this was a Bigfoot sighting of massive importance to cryptozoology.

"I think they're still out there." Behind his glasses, Earl's blue eyes shone with excitement. "I couldn't say for sure, but I thought one had a belly on her, as if she might be pregnant. I think they're looking for a place to have that baby."

Roarke did his best to look unaffected by that news, but he was struggling.

"I want to throw out a challenge to you, Dr. Wallace."

"Hey, call me Roarke."

"Roarke is an Irish name. Are your folks Irish?"

Roarke shook his head. "Russian, if you go back far enough. My mom just likes Celtic names, I guess. My brother is Aidan."

"I like your mother's taste in names. At any rate, I challenge you to spend some time in the wilderness area beyond my property looking for that Sasquatch pair. I want to make a believer of you."

Roarke would be spending time in that area, all right, but he'd do it as a wolf. He could travel more efficiently, and the pair would be less likely to run if they saw him. Besides that, when he found them he'd be able to communicate telepathically, one mythical creature to another.

"You're hesitating," Earl said. "Are you afraid that you'll find something that blows your pet theories out of the water?"

"No." Roarke searched for a way to reject the challenge without sounding like a pompous jerk. "But I have . . . a paper that I need to be writing, so I'm afraid I don't have time to spare."

Earl looked as if he didn't believe a word of that excuse. "You could take Abby with you."

Abby made a soft exclamation of protest.

Earl turned to her. "What's wrong with that idea?"

"You can't just spring something like that on people, Grandpa. Even if Roarke wanted to look around, he might not want to take me, and now he's in the awkward position of having to say so."

"At my age you don't worry about etiquette, sweetheart. He should go and you should go with him because your knowledge of the woods could save him some time."

Roarke imagined sharing a tent with Abby and almost reconsidered. But then he'd never find his quarry because he'd be too busy enjoying the charms of Abby Winchell. "It's a thought," he said, "and I appreciate the motivation behind it. But I really can't afford the time."

"I would go myself, but my arthritis is driving me nuts lately. Still, I may have to ignore that and head on out."

"That's a bad idea, Grandpa," Abby said.

"Probably, but it really frosts me that no one believes what I saw. Even Roarke doesn't believe me. Am I right?"

Roarke fell back on his canned response. "It's highly improbable that a large, bipedal humanoid could survive in this climate."

"Bullshit. If bears can, then Bigfoot could. I sure wish you could see that. I must be losing my storytelling skills, because if you believed what I told you, you'd be out combing those woods. A brilliant scientist like you wouldn't be able to resist." Earl's shoulders slumped.

"It's a great story," Roarke said. "But my scientific training tells me—"

"You can't rely solely on your training. 'To know is nothing at all; to imagine is everything.' Einstein."

"I've heard that," Roarke said.

"But . . . I can't force you to go out there and look." Earl stood and held out his hand. "Thanks for coming, Roarke. It was worth a shot trying to convince you."

Roarke stood and gripped Earl's hand. "I wish I could say you changed my mind." He wished he could say a lot of things, including that.

"I wish you could, too."

Glancing at his watch, Roarke grimaced. "Sorry to cut this short, but I need to take off."

"That's some watch you have there." Earl peered at it. "Doesn't look like a Rolex. Judging from that fancy car outside, I'd expect you to wear a Rolex. What is it?"

"A Louis Moinet Magistalis."

"*Huh*. Never heard of that before."

Abby got up. "I'll walk you to the door, Roarke."

"Which is my cue to let you two young people have a private conversation," Earl said. "Thanks for listening to an old coot."

"It was a pleasure."

"And tell Cameron Gentry I will see him in hell before I'll let him have this land."

Roarke couldn't help smiling. The guy had spunk. "I'll tell him. Take care, Dr. Dooley."

"You, too, Dr. Wallace."

Still smiling, Roarke walked with Abby to the front door. He wouldn't mind continuing a friendship with Earl, but that would be impossible given the situation.

"I watched your face during Grandpa Earl's story," Abby said when they reached the door. "You were digging it."

Roarke glanced down at her. "Of course I was. You

were absolutely right. Nobody can tell a story like an Irishman."

"Yes, but I think it was more than that. I can't shake the feeling that a part of you believes in Bigfoot."

Gazing at her, Roarke longed to give her the satisfaction of knowing he'd changed his mind. But because he'd never doubted her grandfather in the first place, he couldn't claim an about-face. "Let it go, Abby."

"I can't. He's so frustrated."

"Then tell him this." Roarke pictured Gentry's fury at this decision, but he didn't much care. "I haven't changed my mind, but I'll cancel the rest of my talks. He can spin that information any way he wants to."

Abby's eyes glowed. "Thank you, Roarke." Placing both hands lightly on his shoulders, she stood on tiptoe and kissed him.

Her kiss was quick but potent. Her lips tasted like warm coffee, and the imprint of her velvet touch lingered long after she'd pulled away. It took all of Roarke's willpower not to kiss her back. Somehow he managed to get out the door and into his car, but he had no memory of the drive back to the Gentry estate.

No doubt about it, Abby was big medicine. He remembered the way his brother, Aidan, had behaved after meeting Emma, and Roarke had a really bad feeling he was heading down that same path. He needed to find the mated pair and get the hell out of Portland before he did something really stupid.

Chapter 4

After Roarke left, a customer came in for some crackers and a couple packs of gum. Abby gave them too much change for their twenty and didn't realize it until they'd driven away. That's what she got for kissing Roarke Wallace. Now her brain was mush.

Worse yet, he hadn't kissed her back. Instead he'd stood there like a bump on a log. Then he'd left in a hurry, as if he couldn't wait to get away from her. How demoralizing.

Yesterday he'd seemed interested, but yesterday she'd been wearing a killer outfit. Maybe he was just that shallow. Now she was embarrassed for choosing to wear her *Kiss me, I'm Irish* sweatshirt. She'd thought doing that would be flirty and fun, when in fact it had only added to her humiliation when Roarke turned to stone at the touch of her mouth on his.

Grandpa Earl might deserve some of the blame for that. His suggestion that Roarke take Abby camping had been a blatant attempt at matchmaking. Roarke probably had a girlfriend back home and he'd only shown interest yesterday out of courtesy or habit. When he realized her grandfather was ready to welcome him into the family, he'd slammed on the brakes. God, she wished she could take back that kiss!

"Abby," Grandpa Earl called from the back room. "Come look at this."

With a glance toward the parking lot to make sure nobody had driven up, she started toward the back room. Business had fallen off lately, which Earl attributed to the Gentrys' smear campaign but Abby thought might be due to the convenience store that had opened about four miles down the road. It offered longer hours and served soft drinks from a dispenser. People liked that.

She walked into the back room. A door to the right led to the living quarters, which must have been cramped for a family of four back in the day, but were about right for a widower and his occasional guest, Abby.

Grandpa Earl sat at the desk in an armless swivel chair that he could get out of without struggling. He was hunched over his aging computer staring at the monitor. "Come look at what that watch of his sells for," he said without looking up.

She didn't have to ask who he was talking about. Obviously he meant the nonkisser, Roarke Wallace. "Grandpa, I know he has money. His parents are friends with Cameron's parents, so it stands to reason that he'd be wearing a pricey watch."

"I guess pricey describes a watch worth eight hundred and sixty thousand dollars. I assume that's before they add tax."

Abby gasped. As a claims adjuster she'd dealt with some expensive items, but she couldn't remember ever hearing about a watch in that price range. No wonder Roarke hadn't wanted to get involved with her. She was from the wrong side of the tracks.

Grandpa Earl punched a few more keys. "Here's some information on his family." He gestured toward the screen. "I gather that the Wallaces are to New York City what the Gentrys are to Portland."

"That explains a lot." Abby flopped into an old easy chair beside her grandfather's desk. Her Grandma Olive used to sit there with her knitting while her husband researched Bigfoot on the Internet. Olive's knitting basket still sat beside the chair and no one had ever suggested moving it.

"It does, but it makes me sad." Earl sat back in his chair and glanced over at Abby. "He may be a rich boy, but he's a professor at a prestigious university. As such, he should keep an open mind and not allow other considerations, like loyalty to the Gentrys, to interfere with scientific inquiry."

"You gave it a good try, Grandpa."

"Not good enough, obviously."

"I don't think it helped that you practically threw me at him."

Her grandfather blinked. "Who was throwing? I just thought—"

"That he should take me camping? That's a very intimate thing to do."

"Not if you sleep in separate tents! Did I say you should share a tent? No, I did not. I said he should take you along. Men and women go on scientific explorations all the time without having sex, Abby."

Her cheeks warmed. He was right. She was the one who had jumped to the conclusion that if Roarke took her camping, they'd sleep together. Her mind had been on sex, but her grandfather's mind had been on creating a team of two people for scientific exploration.

Come to think of it, Roarke probably went on trips like that in his field work as an anthropologist. He might not have interpreted Grandpa Earl's suggestion as matchmaking, after all. He simply hadn't wanted to go.

She understood that, in a way. He'd been flown here to take care of a problem—Grandpa Earl's supposed sighting of Bigfoot and his mate. Going out to search for the very thing he was supposed to discredit wasn't in his job description. He took the chance of alienating the Gentrys, who were friends of his family.

Viewed that way, Roarke's decision not to tramp through the woods with her became less personal. Still, she would have liked to see some sort of reaction when she'd kissed him. But she hadn't, and that was that. End of story for her and the gorgeous Dr. Wallace.

"Abby, I need to ask a favor."

"That's why I'm here. To help."

"I want you to watch the store so I can go back out and find Bigfoot and his mate."

Abby thought carefully about her answer. She didn't want her grandfather to think she considered him incapable of that, but she couldn't let him go out by himself and wander around in the woods. He didn't move very well, and he could trip.

Maybe if he'd been willing to carry a cell phone, she'd feel better about his hiking alone, but he wasn't. The computer he'd bought ten years ago was as far into the electronic world as he wanted to go. Besides, cell phone reception wasn't very reliable in the woods.

"You don't think I'm up to it," her grandfather said quietly.

"You'd probably be fine, but I would spend the whole time you were gone worrying about you. At some point I'd probably close up the store and come after you, which wouldn't be a good thing for business. If you want more evidence, and I don't blame you for that, then I'll go."

"I wish we'd been able to talk Roarke into searching. It's better if two people go. Then even if the camera malfunctions, you have a witness to what you've seen."

"But Roarke doesn't want to go, Grandpa. So you'll have to make do with me."

His expression was adorably serious. "I couldn't ask for a better person than you, Abby."

"So do we have a deal?"

"How would you feel about camping out by yourself?"

Abby hesitated. She'd never actually done that. Pitching a tent in the backyard wasn't quite the same as hiking into an unspoiled forest and setting up camp all alone. A person would be pretty damned isolated out there.

"You don't have to stay overnight," he said gently. "It was only an idea. Hiking in a different area every day will probably accomplish the same thing."

Abby nodded enthusiastically. "I'm sure it will. In fact, I'll take a short one this afternoon. I'll do a grid search over the next few days and chart where I've been. This'll be great. I'll take my camera, and . . . damn. I probably need a better camera than my little digital."

"Take mine."

"I hate to tell you, but I don't like yours. With the zoom attached, it's awkward and heavy."

"But it's far better than that little toy of yours, Abby. Maybe I should go, after all. I know that camera, and if I keep the zoom attached instead of carrying it separately, then I won't have the same problem that—"

"Let me try it this afternoon." She dreaded hauling that monster zoom around, but her grandfather was right about the quality of the pictures it took. She'd have to spend a bundle to get a small camera that would come anywhere close.

He brightened. "Good. I'll bet once you've worked with it awhile, you'll come to appreciate what a great camera it is."

She doubted it, but now that she'd volunteered herself to go on a Bigfoot search, she was determined to do it to Grandpa Earl's satisfaction. Hearing him repeat his story to Roarke had impressed her all over again. He might not have convinced Roarke, but he'd convinced her. Bigfoot was out there. Although her chances of spotting the creature were slim considering she had only limited time to look, she had to give it her best shot.

Many hours later, as she trudged through the forest with her grandfather's camera looking like an AK-47 concealed under her jacket, she began to doubt again. Maybe she'd secretly thought that agreeing to carry the big-ass camera would give her the reward of an immediate sighting today. Instead, she was sick to death of hauling the damn thing with nothing to show for it.

Out of sheer boredom she'd taken some outstanding close-ups of a squirrel. While zooming in on the squirrel, she'd realized that Photoshop might be able to transform a squirrel into a Sasquatch. Who was to say that any of the photos used to prove Bigfoot existed were legitimate? Even if she stumbled upon an actual creature, what kind of proof would that be without a witness swearing she hadn't doctored the shot?

Although the rain had stopped earlier in the afternoon, the drizzle had returned and the light was fading. She pictured herself wrapped in a quilt, sitting in front of the potbellied stove and drinking hot coffee laced with Baileys. Maybe it was time to give up for the day.

She was so intent on her image of a warm fire and a hot drink that she almost missed seeing movement about a hundred yards away. There. Somebody . . . or *something* was walking through the trees.

Heart pounding, she raised the camera and zoomed in. What she saw made her blink in surprise. Had Roarke changed his mind about looking for Sasquatch on her grandfather's land? She couldn't imagine any other reason he'd be there.

Gradually surprise turned to anger. Obviously Earl's story had put some doubts in Roarke's mind and he'd decided to investigate, after all, but damn it, why couldn't he have said so this morning? An admission that he was rethinking his position on Bigfoot would have meant the world to Grandpa Earl. Apparently Roarke was too proud to make it, and the sexy professor instantly dropped several notches in her estimation.

Focusing on him again, she took a couple of pictures. Maybe she'd print them up and present them to him over another drink at Flannigan's. *So, Dr. Arrogant Bastard, if you don't believe a word my grandfather said, what were you doing prowling around in his woods,* hmmm? *Is this or is this not you, Dr. Pompous Hypocrite?*

She would do exactly that. He deserved to be found out, and she was just the woman to do it. She snapped off a couple more pictures for good measure. What a prince. And she'd thought he might be worth pursuing. *Ha.* He was . . . he was *taking off his clothes?*

That made absolutely no sense whatsoever. Abby stopped clicking the shutter. Roarke was quickly going from hot prospect to strange weirdo. He could be a nudist, but he'd have to be one totally dedicated nudist to strip down in a cold drizzle.

Apparently he expected to put his clothes on again, though, because he was stuffing them into a nylon backpack as if he wanted to keep them dry. Through the zoom lens, Abby could see . . . everything. Too bad he was a total nutjob, because he was one of the most beautiful men she'd ever had the privilege of viewing naked.

Michelangelo would have loved to sculpt this guy. A girl didn't usually see this kind of muscle definition in a college professor. True, Abby had dated only one of those in her life, but he'd been sort of soft in the middle.

Roarke was the exact opposite of soft. He turned his back to her, and her mouth went dry. She hadn't meant to take a picture, but her finger had a mind of its own. It pushed the button. Now, whether she wanted it or not, she had a shot of his powerful back, narrow hips, and tight buns. Oh, darn.

Hey, what the hell. She'd make sure her grandfather never saw these pictures. But his legs were concealed behind some foliage, so she still didn't have the complete man preserved for later viewing.

Then he moved away from the foliage and she snapped another shot of his muscled thighs and strong calves. Yes, she was acting like a voyeur, but no woman in America would blame her. She willed him to turn around. She wasn't planning to take a full-frontal picture, but she wasn't above using the zoom to get a better look.

Then he turned, but he'd shifted his position so that a fern became a very effective fig leaf. Damn. She held her breath and waited. *Step away from the fern. Step away from the fern.*

Which he eventually did. *Omigod*. Now *that* was a package. If she'd been shivery and cold before, she imagined steam coming off her now. What a shame that such a well-endowed man was several slices shy of a loaf.

As she congratulated herself on making the best of what had previously been a boring afternoon, Roarke surprised her once again. Zipping the backpack containing his clothes, he got to his knees and then stretched out on the carpet of wet leaves and pine needles.

Whew. Anybody who would decide to sleep naked in the woods in the rain was seriously in need of a shrink. Maybe she should call 911. A loony appeared to be on the loose.

Except Roarke wasn't sleeping. Something was happening to him. When she began to understand what that something might be, she pinched herself hard. The pinch hurt, but that might not mean anything. She could still be in the middle of a nightmare.

She had one way to know for sure. She'd keep taking pictures. If she was dreaming, she'd wake up. If she wasn't, she'd have proof of what her eyes couldn't believe was happening—Roarke, esteemed NYU professor of anthropology, was becoming a wolf.

And not just any wolf, either. She'd seen this animal from the granite outcropping yesterday, its pale blond coat glowing in the early-morning light as it prowled the Gentry estate. She'd known then it was no dog.

She began to shiver and had to concentrate on holding the camera still. Assuming she was awake, the pictures she was taking now would change everything.

Belatedly she realized that she could be in danger, assuming this was real. If she remembered her mythology correctly, a man who could change into a wolf was called a werewolf. Werewolves didn't have a very good reputation. In movies they ran around biting people and generally causing problems.

She had her pictures, and she might want to leave now, before the wolf caught her scent. In fact, it was strange that it hadn't done so yet. The breeze might have something to do with that. She could feel it on her face, which meant it was blowing toward her, carrying her scent away from the wolf.

She was downwind of the wolf. The term hadn't been anything she'd needed to use before, but it was important in this case because it might give her a brief reprieve.

She'd been standing partially hidden behind a large pine. Slowly she backed away, stepping carefully so she didn't trip and make noise. Inch by torturous inch, she put distance between herself and the wolf.

Oddly enough, it didn't seem to be aware of her. In fact, it turned in the other direction. She paused to see what it would do.

Fortune smiled on her as the wolf sniffed the air and began trotting away. Apparently it had caught the scent of something upwind. Or rather *he* had caught the scent of something. She needed to remember that the wolf was Roarke. And Roarke was a wolf. A werewolf.

At least she needed to remember it for the length of this dream. She still wondered if she was sound asleep in the spare room at Grandpa Earl's place. The smell of coffee brewing would rouse her and she'd laugh about her overactive imagination.

Turning, she started for home, pausing every few yards to glance over her shoulder and make sure a wolf wasn't stalking her. Any minute now she might wake up, but even in dreams she liked to make it home safely.

The trip home seemed to take forever, but finally she could see the back door of Dooley's General Store. Grandpa Earl's pickup was parked under the overhang beside the store, and smoke from the potbellied stove curled into the evening sky.

Everything looked perfectly normal and not the least bit dreamlike. She stood gazing at the familiar scene and thought about Grandpa Earl waiting inside for a report on her adventures. Of all the people she knew, he might be the only one who would believe her if she described what she'd encountered.

And yet . . . now that she was in sight of a safe haven and was beginning to accept that what she'd seen was real, the ramifications became clear. A werewolf was as much of a mythical creature as Bigfoot. Therefore, if a werewolf had just appeared in front of her eyes, the other was no longer in doubt.

And Roarke was out there looking. If that was the scent he'd picked up, he might have already found the mated pair that Grandpa Earl had seen. But why would he want to find them? Did the Gentrys know they'd hired a werewolf or was she the only person in Portland with that information?

Come to think of it, she might be one of the few adults in Portland who could accept the fact that a man had transformed himself into a wolf. Someone else might offer a rational explanation having to do with shadows and poor eyesight. But she'd believed in fantastical creatures as a child, and judging from her instant recognition of a werewolf, she still believed in them.

Still, she had no idea what she'd stumbled onto. Maybe she should find out before involving Grandpa Earl. For one thing, he'd never allow her to confront a werewolf alone, and yet she didn't want to expose him to potential danger, either.

She clutched his camera, protected under her jacket. The camera was old, but not so old that it used film. Her grandfather had loved the idea of digital cameras and had bought one soon after they'd come out. When her grandfather went to bed, she'd be able to download the pictures and print them on his aging printer.

Then she could arrange to meet Roarke in broad daylight in a public place. Lunch at Flannigan's would be perfect. She'd take it slow and rely on her instincts as to whether he would harm her if she revealed what she knew.

He didn't strike her as a violent kind of person, but he wasn't a person, exactly. She wasn't sure how he'd react when he found out she wanted him to take her on the hunt for the Bigfoot pair. She'd use her pictures as leverage. It was the one sure way to prove her grandfather was right, so he'd move to Arizona.

The plan wasn't without risk, which was why she had to do it without telling Grandpa Earl. But she hadn't been this excited about anything in years. Essentially, she hoped to blackmail a werewolf into giving her the evidence she needed to vindicate her grandfather. Cool.

Chapter 5

Roarke had hoped finding the Sasquatch pair would be easier, but they must have been spooked by the recent large number of hikers in the area searching for them. If they would simply leave the area permanently, that would solve the Gentrys' problem. But Roarke wasn't convinced they'd cooperate.

Assuming the female was pregnant, she might be returning to her place of birth to have her baby. That theory had been advanced many times, although the evidence was scanty. Roarke couldn't ignore the possibility that the pair could move in the other direction for a while and then turn around and come back.

They hadn't done so yet, however. Roarke had followed several faint trails that led nowhere and had finally given up for the night, shifted back to human form, and dressed in the clothes he'd left stashed in his backpack.

Shifting out in the woods wasn't his idea of fun, but he'd been in a hurry to leave the Gentry mansion and hadn't wanted to linger even long enough to shift. Cameron Gentry was fast becoming a pain in the ass. He'd discovered late in the day that Roarke had canceled his last two talks, and Cameron had taken that as a slap in the face.

The Gentry alpha's ego knew no bounds. Roarke had tried to explain, without revealing anything Abby had confided in him, that the talks were having the opposite effect Cameron had hoped. After being attacked, Earl Dooley wasn't cowed at all. He was more determined to stand his ground and prove his case.

Cameron didn't get it. He'd launched a campaign to humiliate Dooley and he intended to keep up the pressure until he succeeded. He had all the subtlety of a sledgehammer.

The discussion had eventually turned into a heated argument, and Roarke had decided to leave before he said something he'd regret. After all, his parents were good friends with Cameron's parents. He was supposed to be out here on a goodwill mission, not to stir up controversy.

If he could find the Sasquatch pair, then he could relocate them and leave Cameron to stew in his juices. Roarke hadn't promised to deliver Earl Dooley's head on a platter, and he'd be damned if he'd continue that campaign. But the Sasquatch needed protection, maybe even from Cameron Gentry.

Too bad he hadn't found them tonight. But they were large and able to cover quite a bit of ground in a day. These two seemed to be diurnal instead of nocturnal. That was another misconception about Sasquatch—that they were all nocturnal. Like humans, some were night owls and some were larks. These two apparently moved around during the day, which was why Earl had spotted them in the first place.

Hungry and frustrated by his lack of success, Roarke didn't notice the message on his BlackBerry until he was back in his room at the mansion. Abby. She wanted to meet him for lunch at noon at Flannigan's.

Despite knowing that he shouldn't have anything more to do with her, he texted an acceptance. Lunch in the city would break up his day and cut down on the number of hours he could spend looking for the Sasquatch pair, but Abby was the only bright spot so far on his Portland trip. A simple little lunch wouldn't compromise the whole program.

It was a testament to his eagerness that he arrived at Flannigan's early the next day. But that meant he could watch her walk toward the booth where he was sitting. He soaked up every second of that experience.

Her outfit was urban chic—gray slacks with those strappy high-heeled sandals guaranteed to drive men crazy, and a roomy black jacket worn over a tight white T-shirt. She'd piled her red hair on top of her head and added some large silver hoop earrings to the mix. He wanted to eat her up.

Her color was high as she slid into the booth opposite him. "Thanks for meeting me on short notice."

"Happy to." In fact, *happy* was too mild for the emotion he was feeling at seeing her. And smelling her. Once again, her scent grabbed him by the gonads. The two of them were meant to be lovers—but when?

That sort of thing took time to develop, at least in his estimation. He couldn't just invite her to join him in one of the hotel rooms conveniently located above them and expect her to go along with that. Any woman worth having was worth the trouble of wooing with a long, slow seduction. But he didn't have that luxury.

She asked how he'd been as they both consulted the menu. He gave the automatic response that he'd been fine, but busy. Then he continued the conversational tennis match by asking how she'd been. Fine, but busy. He smiled at her response.

Eventually she'd tell him why she asked him to lunch. He wouldn't push. His ego wanted to believe that she was as intrigued by him as he was by her. She was aware they didn't have much time together in Portland, but maybe she wanted to make the most of what time they had. He wasn't free to do that, but it would be nice to have her say it.

After they ordered—steak sandwich for him and a bowl of vegetable soup for her—she leaned forward, as if not wanting to be overheard. He took that as a sign that she had something intimate to discuss. He mirrored her by leaning forward, too.

Her eyes really were incredibly blue. He could gaze into them for hours. Her scent surrounded him, and his groin tightened.

She moistened her full lips with her tongue. "I saw you in the woods late yesterday afternoon."

For a brief moment he didn't get it. Then he did. But maybe it wasn't as bad as he feared. "I went for a short hike."

"Not exactly."

Uh-oh. It was bad. "Abby, I don't know what you think you saw, but—"

"Professor Wallace, you are a hypocrite." Her blue eyes lost their friendly sparkle and bored into him like twin lasers. "Not only do you believe a Sasquatch pair is out there, you're looking for them."

So maybe she hadn't seen him shift. Maybe she'd just noticed him walking in the woods. He'd take the lesser charge any day. "You found me out, Abby. Your grandfather's story was so convincing that I decided to check out the situation for myself."

"You have an interesting method for doing that."

His heart pounded. Looking into her eyes, he saw what he'd been afraid he'd find there. She knew. Worse yet, hours had passed since then, hours when she could have spread the word about him to half of Portland. Any second a pitchfork-wielding mob could descend on Flannigan's.

But that wasn't the worst part. He'd compromised werewolves everywhere. He'd failed not only the Gentrys, but every werewolf in the world. If he'd shifted at the mansion, which would have been the sensible thing to do . . . but no, he'd let his temper rule. And now this.

He could tell by her determined expression that trying to convince her she hadn't seen him shift into wolf form was pointless. "All right," he said quietly. "Where do we go from here?"

She took a deep breath. "First of all, did you find anything last night?"

"No."

"Why were you looking in the first place?"

"I'm here to make contact and relocate them. But before I say anything more, please tell me if people will be arriving soon to take me away. For all I know, you invited me here so I could be captured, studied, put on display."

She cringed. "No."

He relaxed a little. She'd seemed genuinely dismayed by that idea. But she still could have told her grandfather. Or maybe not. If she'd told Earl, he would be sitting here with her, both to protect her and to satisfy his scientific curiosity.

Slowly the hope grew that she'd told no one. If that were the case, he still had a problem, but it wasn't a global one, at least not yet. They were involved in a very delicate dance. He had to step carefully.

"I know you have no reason to trust me," he said.

"None whatsoever. But I might have to take my chances and trust you, anyway."

"Why?"

"Despite everything, I think we have the same goal: to find that Sasquatch pair. My motivation is to validate my grandfather's claim. What's yours?"

He glanced around the restaurant. It was crowded and nobody seemed to be paying much attention to them, but that could change if someone happened to catch part of this conversation. "Look, you've said you may have to trust me, and if so, that needs to start now. We can't have this discussion here. I'm too much at risk."

She hesitated. "Where would you like to have it?"

"In my car would be good."

She looked nervous about that.

"Okay, how about this. My car's in a public garage. We can go sit in the car and talk. I won't drive anywhere."

"And you'll give me the keys."

"All right." He fished in his pocket and handed over the keys to the Corvette. Then he took out his wallet and put enough money on the table to cover lunch. "Let's go."

They didn't talk on the way to the parking garage. Roarke spent most of the time beating himself up for having shifted in the woods where Abby had been able to see him. The rest of the time he listened to the sexy *click-click-click* of her high heels on the sidewalk. And here he'd thought she'd asked him to lunch because she was hot for his body. Too bad he'd been wrong.

She clicked the locks open as they approached the red car and waved him away when he started to help her in the passenger side. "I've got it. Thanks."

He climbed behind the wheel and scooted the seat back as far as it would go so he could stretch his legs.

They closed their doors in a perfectly synchronized move, and then they were alone in the small cockpit of the sports car.

It could have been an erotic moment, considering how the tiny space was instantly filled with her compelling scent. But he was too worried about what this would mean to him and the Were community to be turned on.

He cleared his throat. "First let me explain something to you regarding my . . . kind. We don't have the best of reputations among humans." He glanced at her to see how she reacted to that.

She paled slightly, the first sign that she might not be as brave as she appeared. "So you're not human?"

"Not in the strictest sense."

"But right now you look like it."

"Right now there's not a single thing about me that isn't human. My eyesight and sense of smell are better than the average person's, but no one realizes that besides me. To the casual observer, I'm just a man."

Color bloomed in her cheeks. Then she glanced away.

That's when it hit him that she'd not only watched him transform into a wolf, she'd also seen him take off his clothes before the shift. "I guess you know exactly how human I am," he said.

She met his gaze. "I suppose I do." During a moment of silence, her eyes revealed the fascination she wouldn't acknowledge. She cleared her throat as if struggling to remain aloof. "You mentioned a brother, and parents. Are they also—"

"No, just me," he lied.

"Do they realize you're a werewolf?"

"Abby, you already know more than it's safe for you to know. Don't make me tell you things that will only make this worse for both of us."

"Can you explain that?"

He studied her, weighing the risks. "I can try. The usual reaction to my kind over the course of history has been fear. Fear makes people dangerous."

She tucked the car keys in her oversized black purse and zipped it closed before settling it on her lap. "I managed to sneak in a little Google time this morning. It sounds as if *your kind*, as you call it, can be dangerous, too."

He noted her choice of words—*I managed to sneak in a little Google time*. That reinforced his belief that she hadn't told Earl yet. "I won't lie to you. We—"

"Too late. You've been lying to me, and a bunch of other folks, ever since you arrived in Portland."

"Out of necessity."

She traced the stitching on her purse with one finger. "I guess I can understand that, but I still don't see how you could stand up there at those service club meetings and trash Grandpa Earl's sighting." Her glance was accusing. "He saw them, didn't he?"

"I'm sure he did."

Her fingers tightened over the strap of her purse. "Damn it, Roarke, he needs to know that. He's dreamed about making contact his entire life, and although he clings to the belief that the sighting was legitimate, I know you've made him doubt himself. That's not right."

Roarke sighed. "There are bigger issues than fulfilling your grandfather's lifelong dream. Unusual creatures like Bigfoot need to be protected, not exploited."

"He wouldn't exploit them!"

"Wouldn't he? The minute he printed that picture, he was down at Flannigan's telling the world about it."

"He was just excited. He didn't mean any harm."

Roarke sat in silence and waited for her to realize that excuse didn't cut it.

Finally she rolled her eyes. "Of course you're right.

He didn't stop to think about the repercussions of broadcasting his discovery. I'll admit that waving the picture around wasn't a very good idea."

"No, it wasn't. Luckily the search parties weren't well funded or well organized. If they had been, that Sasquatch pair would be on its way to a zoo somewhere, or worse, a laboratory."

Abby shuddered. "That makes me sick to my stomach."

"As well it should. They're very sweet animals, but they're not particularly smart. They wouldn't have understood what was happening to them, and if the people in charge decided to separate them ... They mate for life, and I'm afraid they both would have died of broken hearts."

"I don't want any of that. And neither would my grandfather, if he realized the problems he could cause. He didn't stop to think, but he's not totally insensitive. I just wish he could know that he really did see them."

Tension coiled in Roarke's gut. She held his fate in the palm of her hand and he wondered if she knew that. "Are you considering telling him ... about me?"

"I can't."

"Why not?" He held his breath as he waited for her answer.

"Because then I'd be putting you in the same danger as the Sasquatch."

The tension in his stomach eased. "I'm not quite as vulnerable as a Sasquatch."

She smiled. "And I'm sure you're a whole lot smarter. But as you talked about what could happen to them, I couldn't help thinking that most of it applies to you, too."

He was so fortunate that compassion was part of her personality. If he had to accidentally show himself to a human, at least it had been someone he might be able to work with.

"Some of it applies to me," he said, "but my ability to shift back to human form makes a huge difference. And I don't have a mate to be separated from, so that's not an issue." He didn't know why he'd felt compelled to add that piece of information.

She picked up on it, too. "Nobody's waiting at home?"

"No."

"Confirmed bachelor?"

"Not that, either. I just haven't met anyone who inspires me to settle down. It's a big deal with us, because we also mate for life. I know humans *say* they do, but when you get right down to it . . ."

She nodded. "Yeah, it's more like mating for the time being, to see if it works out or not. I suppose knowing that you're signing on for life would make you more cautious about making that commitment."

"It does." He wasn't about to tell her that she smelled the way he imagined his mate would smell, or that the very sight of her brought him joy. That didn't matter, because she was not Were, and he had no interest in a mixed marriage. Let Aidan be the trailblazer in that regard.

"Naturally you'll choose another . . . of your kind."

"Yes, I will."

She nodded. "Of course."

He watched the silver hoops in her ears sway as she moved. "Why did you arrange this meeting, Abby? What is it you want from me?"

"With all those degrees, I would think you'd have it figured out by now."

"I have some ideas, but unless you want to play guessing games, why don't you tell me and save some time?"

"All right." She turned to gaze at him. "If you didn't

find the Sasquatch pair yesterday, I'll assume you plan to keep looking."

"I do. The female may have picked this area because she was born here and wants her baby to be born here, but they need to change the plan. I hope to find them and convince them that another spot would be far better."

"Take me with you."

He'd expected this, but it was impossible. He shook his head. "I'm sorry, but that wouldn't work. I'll be moving quickly." *And in wolf form.*

"But if I go with you and I see them, then I can report back to Grandpa Earl."

"Who is liable to sound the alarm."

"Not if I tell him what you just told me about their vulnerability. He's a good man, Roarke. He wouldn't knowingly cause them harm, not after all these years of studying them."

"Abby, I really can't take you. You'd slow me down and potentially spook the Sasquatch. I can come back and report what happened, but—"

"You have to take me."

"No, I don't."

"I have the goods on you, Roarke."

"Nobody will believe you. They'll think you've spent too much time listening to your grandfather."

"They might, except for one thing." She patted the black leather purse. "I have pictures. I took them with Grandpa Earl's very powerful zoom lens. They're not fuzzy."

Chapter 6

The situation was serious, and not without risk, but still Abby felt giddy with triumph. Judging from Roarke's expression, she'd shocked him with her mention of the pictures. She'd never blackmailed anyone before, let alone a werewolf, and apparently she had a flair for it.

"Pictures." His green eyes narrowed. "Of *everything*?"

"Everything."

His face turned a dull red. "I see."

"Just so you know, I erased them from Grandpa Earl's camera, but I loaded them all on a flash drive first. I've hidden it, but if anything should happen to me, that hiding place would be the first spot Grandpa Earl would look for clues."

He nodded, as if finally realizing she'd thought this through. She could thank her logical parents for that ability, plus several years at a job that required her to use her analytical skills. She might be a dreamer at heart, but she'd had plenty of practice using the left side of her brain, too.

She'd put the flash drive in a small cedar box with *Portland, Oregon* burned into the lid. Grandpa Earl sold those boxes in his store, and he'd given her one when she was a little girl. The box had a hidden compartment, and he'd told her she could keep her secrets in it.

She'd been thrilled with the box, but she'd left it on a shelf in the spare bedroom at her grandparents' house because she'd been afraid her brother, Pete, would try to mess with it if she took it back to Arizona. The box was still there, and she and Grandpa Earl had joked about it just the other day.

She glanced at Roarke, whose blush was fading. She'd thought that blush was cute. "Would you like to see the pictures, so that you know I'm not bluffing?"

"Oh, I know you're not bluffing. But yes, I'd like to see them."

Opening her purse, she pulled out a five-by-seven manila envelope and passed it across the console. "I printed them last night after Grandpa Earl was asleep. I really don't want him to know about this. If he realized that you were . . . different, he'd never let me go with you."

Roarke unfastened the envelope's metal clasp. "He wouldn't have let you meet me for lunch, either, I'll bet."

"Not without him."

He glanced at her. "You did take quite a chance, meeting me today."

Her pulse quickened. It had seemed like a grand adventure when she'd planned coming here, but maybe she had been a little naive, a little foolhardy. Cars came and went in the garage, but would anyone hear her if she yelled for help? Would anyone respond?

Roarke pulled out the pictures and glanced at the first few, which were of him fully clothed. Then he came to one of him in his birthday suit. He flipped through the rest quickly and shoved them back in the envelope.

Then he sighed. "Yes, I'll be taking you with me."

But now she wasn't so sure she wanted to go. She'd be all alone out there in the woods . . . with a werewolf. What had she been thinking?

"This whole situation is unfortunate," he continued, "but I'm going to do my best to see you through it safely. Please don't ask too many questions along the way, because if I give you the answers, then—"

"Then you'll have to kill me?" She said it lightly, trying to make it into a joke, but still her chest tightened with fear. She'd thought she was so smart; yet if Roarke didn't want anyone to know he was a werewolf, he had one way to guarantee that she wouldn't tell.

But his expression softened. "Abby, it's not your fault that you saw me shift. It's mine. Because of that . . ." He paused and when he spoke again, his tone was resolute. "Because of that, I will protect you with my life."

That knocked the breath right out of her. Her hand to her chest, she struggled for air. "You . . . sound as if that might be necessary."

"Not if we're careful. I don't want to frighten you, but you've stumbled into something you don't understand."

"Then I need to understand."

He shook his head. "The less you know, the better. Your best bet is to destroy these pictures, wipe that flash drive clean, and stay out of the woods while I take care of business."

"Unless you have one of those gizmos from *Men in Black* that wipes out my memory, I just can't do that. I'd feel that I'd let down Grandpa Earl."

"That was a handy little item Tommy Lee Jones had." Roarke gave her a wry smile. "Believe me, if I had one, I would have used it on you by now."

"Lucky for you I can be trusted not to blab."

His gaze intensified. "Everything depends on that, Abby."

In for a penny, in for a pound. She'd come this far, so she might as well see this through. "But in return for not blabbing, you have to take me on your Sasquatch hunt."

"Looks like I do."

"Then let's get going." She reached for the door handle. "We could make some progress this afternoon. Where should we meet?"

"At Dooley's General Store. I want to accept your grandfather's offer of camping supplies so we can stay out there. That would increase the chance of finding the Sasquatch pair and decrease the chance that the Gentrys will know you're with me."

"You don't want them to know?"

"I think it's better if they don't. They'd think I was fraternizing with the enemy by taking Earl's granddaughter along on a Sasquatch hunt."

"Sure. Okay." She squashed the uneasy feeling in her tummy. Better not to think about the fact that she'd just agreed to spend at least one night in the woods with a werewolf. "Small matter, but do you ... ah ... shift every night? I mean, it's okay if you do. I'm totally cool with that. Don't worry about me freaking out or anything, but it might be good for me to know what—"

"I only shift when I choose to."

"Oh." What a surreal discussion. "So that whole full moon thing is not an issue?"

"Not anymore. We've— *I've* evolved to the point where the phase of the moon or time of day doesn't matter."

"Good to know." But she'd caught his little slip with the *we* part of that sentence. He wasn't the only werewolf in the world.

"So in other words, I'm in full control of my shift, so you don't have to worry about ..." He smiled. "Spontaneous fur."

"I do believe you just made a joke." She lowered her voice. "A werewolf joke."

"You were looking a little tense."

"I think that's perfectly understandable, under the circumstances, don't you?"

"Yes. In fact, I think you're handling this amazingly well."

"Thank you. I do have one question." A car with the sound system blaring drove past and she waited until the noise died down. "Let's say we're out in the woods, and you feel the need to shift. And then let's say you bite me, either by accident or on purpose."

"I won't, either by accident or on purpose."

"Pretend that you did, for the sake of argument. Would I become one of *your kind*?"

"No. That's a myth."

"Yes, but *you're* a myth. If you're real, then anything is possible, including the stories about bites turning the human into . . . you know. Those stories must be based on something."

"They're based on fear and superstition."

"So if you don't make new werewolves by biting people, then how do you become one?"

"Born that way."

She knew a little something about genetics. If Roarke had been born a werewolf, then he had others in his family tree. And she suspected that the Gentrys did, too. It was a lot to assimilate. She took a shaky breath and told herself to stay calm.

Roarke crossed his forearms over the steering wheel and glanced at her. "You don't have to go with me. I can come back and tell you what I saw. Wouldn't that be enough evidence for you to relay to your grandfather?"

She shook her head. "Not if I can be an eyewitness."

Obviously he'd picked up on her nervousness. "I was just trying to get an idea of what to expect."

"No biting."

Taking another deep breath, she studied him. "I believe you because your eyes didn't flicker."

"What?"

"When you were giving your talks and you insisted Bigfoot was an imaginary creature, your eyes flickered. I've learned at work that people do that when they're falsifying a claim."

"Are you saying that I need some practice at lying?"

"No, I'm saying that you might as well tell me the truth, because I'll know when you don't."

He met her gaze. "Fair enough. So how did you get here?"

"In my grandfather's old truck. It's parked on the next level."

"If you'll give me the keys, I'll drive you there."

She unzipped her purse and took them out. "I suppose if you'd really wanted to harm me, this little ploy wouldn't have mattered." She handed him the keys.

"No." He took the keys, put them in the ignition, and started the car. "Confronting me today was a reckless thing to do."

As the truth of that sank in, she leaned back with a sigh. "Guess I'm lucky you decided to be nice about this, *huh*?"

"Yes." He checked the rearview mirror and backed out of the parking space. "Yes, you are."

Roarke texted Cameron that he was heading out into the woods and wouldn't be back until he'd located the Sasquatch pair. Cameron's return text was short and to the point. *C that U do.*

After gathering up a change of clothes and some toiletry items, Roarke tossed them in a backpack and set out for the general store. He would have loved to drive the red Corvette, but he couldn't risk parking it anywhere near the store, so he walked the two miles separating the Gentrys' front gate from Earl's place. The ever-present light rain settled on his shoulders, but he wore a waterproof jacket and an NYU ball cap, so he didn't get very wet.

The mechanical bird noise twittered when he opened the door, and Earl came to greet him, all smiles. "Abby's in the back getting her stuff together. This is terrific, Roarke, just terrific. When Abby told me you wanted to mount an expedition to hunt for Bigfoot, I felt like dancing a jig, although I decided against it because I might fall down."

"That story of yours was very persuasive, Earl."

"But you had to take time to let it sink in." Earl's blue eyes were bright behind his glasses. "I understand that. I'm the same. Don't like to jump on the bandwagon until I've had a chance to assimilate the information. I admire that kind of caution in a man."

"Maybe I'm just dense." Roarke slipped off his backpack and left it by the front door.

"I don't think so." Earl clapped him on the shoulder. "Let's go pick out some camping gear. And before you even offer to pay, I want you to know the supplies are on the house."

"That's not right."

"Of course it is. I feel as if I'm mounting an expedition, sort of like when Queen Isabella sent Christopher Columbus out to find the New World. She couldn't go herself, but she provided the wherewithal. That's my position right now, and the least I can do is finance this trip."

"But—"

"I know that you can afford to pay me. Anybody who wears a watch as valuable as yours could probably buy the entire contents of my store without putting much of a dent in your checkbook."

"Earl, I—"

"But your ability to pay is not the issue. You're going out on a mission that could settle the Bigfoot question once and for all. You can't imagine how much that effort means to me. Now let's go look at tents."

Feeling guilty as hell because he didn't deserve Earl's goodwill, Roarke followed him to the shelves stacked with various types of tents. If Earl knew he was sending his granddaughter out in the woods with a werewolf, he wouldn't be so eager to outfit this expedition.

"I favor this one, myself." Earl patted a box containing a one-person nylon tent that resembled the kind Roarke used himself on research trips.

"I have one like that at home."

"Good. Then you'll be used to it. You might as well take the same type for Abby. I doubt she's been camping in a good long while, so she's not familiar with the new models. She'll like this one. It's light enough that she can carry it and a sleeping bag."

Tents. Sleeping bags. Roarke had been trying not to think of the night to come, when he and Abby would be alone in a secluded part of the forest. He had a special fondness for sex in a forest setting, and that, added to his growing fondness for Abby, could create a perfect storm of lust.

The irony wasn't lost on him. Several months ago he'd lectured his big brother, Aidan, for getting into a similar fix with Emma. Casual sex with a human was one thing, but when the chemistry was this strong, the Were community advised against sexual involvement.

Of course, in Aidan's case, Emma hadn't known he

was a werewolf when they first had sex. Abby already knew, so Roarke no longer had to worry about revealing that particular secret during pillow talk. But Abby's knowledge was still very limited, and he needed to keep it that way, which meant staying out of her tent and her sleeping bag.

"These sleeping bags are great, too." Earl pulled a couple of small packages from a different shelf. "They roll up into practically nothing, but they're warm as toast."

Roarke eyed his backpack propped by the front door. "We'll need some food, too—enough for a couple of days, anyway. I don't think my backpack is going to be big enough."

Earl gestured toward a row of packs and frames hanging on the wall. "Take your pick."

"Do you have one I can borrow rather than taking one that's new?"

"Sure, I do, but—"

"Then let's do that. You may not get to go, but your backpack can."

Earl grinned. "I like that. Man, I wish I could tag along! Abby offered to call me from the trail, but from what hikers tell me, the reception's no good out there."

"Probably not." Roarke took his BlackBerry out and wondered if he should have left it back at the Gentrys.

Just then Abby walked out with a medium-sized pack over her shoulder.

He held up his BlackBerry. "Are you taking yours?"

"I'm taking it, but I doubt it'll get reception." She hefted her backpack. "I just realized this pack might be too small for what I need to carry."

"No problem," Earl said. "Roarke and I have that covered, don't we, Roarke?" The old guy sounded like a kid with a new best friend. "I'm loaning him my big pack. I'll have it out here in a jiffy. Abby, help Roarke pick out some food."

"Be glad to." Abby walked toward him, bringing her delicious scent with her.

She'd opted for a navy Lycra sweat suit. Its dark color was a stark contrast to her bright hair, which she'd pulled into a ponytail. But mostly Roarke noticed how the stretchy material hugged her body, making him aware of every tantalizing curve.

"Grandpa Earl is so excited," she said in a low voice. "Having someone with your background agree to go on this expedition is a dream come true for him. I wish he could go instead of me, but he's just not up to it."

"I wish he could go, too." For many reasons that he wasn't going to share with her.

"But of course that wouldn't work, both because of his arthritis and because . . . he doesn't know about . . . you know." She moved closer and spoke in a soft whisper. "Are you bringing clothes?"

The jolt of excitement that shot through him stirred him in places that needed to stay calm, very calm. What in hell was she implying with that question? "Yeah, I am." His voice had taken on the husky tone of arousal and he couldn't seem to do much about that. "Why?"

She edged close enough that they were almost touching. "I figured out that you can probably search better in wolf form, so all this camping gear isn't necessary for you, but I understand why you're playing along."

Oh. She wasn't thinking they'd run naked through the woods together. She was thinking he'd spend most of the next couple of days wearing his fur coat. "This will be a normal camping trip," he said. "Or as normal as possible, considering what we're looking for."

"But what about—"

"Hey, you two!" Earl came out of the back carrying his pack. "Quit gabbing and get ready to go!"

"The man's right." Roarke stepped away from Abby, which slightly reduced his urge to haul her into his arms and kiss her until they were both breathless.

Getting on with the program should help. Once they left the store and were striding through the forest, each of them intent on their purpose for being there, he'd be better able to tuck away this inconvenient attraction.

Then Abby leaned over to take something from one of the lower shelves and the action presented him with a perfect view of her round, firm bottom. He coughed to cover the groan that rose from his throat. What was it about this woman that affected him so?

Yet he knew, and he didn't want to know. From the first time he'd caught her scent, he'd understood on some level that he was in trouble. He would *not* complicate his life the way his brother had by falling for a human female. But that was exactly what his body was telling him to do.

Chapter 7

Abby was more familiar with the trails than Roarke, although it had been a while since she'd hiked them. Still, she offered to lead the way for the first couple of hours. Out of pride she kept up a good pace, which didn't leave her much energy for conversation.

Roarke didn't seem inclined to talk, either, so they moved along in silence through the misty rain. Toward the end of the second hour, she was forced to admit that she was woefully out of shape. Her legs hurt and an ache had developed between her shoulder blades from carrying the pack, although hers was half the size of Roarke's. If he hadn't volunteered to take more than his share, she'd have been toast.

About the time she was questioning whether she'd made a mistake in coming on this trip, Roarke suggested a food break.

"Sounds good." *Thank God*. Grandpa Earl had packed turkey sandwiches once he'd realized neither of them had eaten lunch, and she was carrying them. That would eliminate one thing from her pack. It might not make a huge difference, but she'd take any lightening of the load, no matter how small.

She didn't plan to let Roarke know that, though. After blackmailing him to take her along, she couldn't very well complain that she couldn't handle the hike. Unfortunately for her, the trail had been relatively level up to this point, but soon it would grow steeper.

Glancing around, she noticed a somewhat dry spot under a large fir. "Let's go over there."

Roarke followed her under the tree and slid his pack from his shoulders. The rugged look of his tan windbreaker and worn jeans had banished the nerdy professor entirely. In his place stood a guy who would make any woman's heart beat faster. Abby had tried to be nonchalant about the transformation, but damn, he was serious eye candy. She could imagine that if he walked into a classroom looking like this, his female students would be too distracted to learn anything.

Fishing inside his backpack, he pulled out a small tarp before spreading it on the ground. "I think you have the sandwiches."

"Yep." She lowered her pack to the ground and clenched her jaw to keep from sighing in relief.

"How are you doing?"

"Great!" She unzipped her pack and pulled out the sandwiches. "How are you doing?" She handed him a sandwich before taking a seat on the tarp.

"Okay, but I'm used to this. I'm out in the field a lot with my work. Earl didn't think you'd been hiking or camping lately, so I wondered if the pack is bothering you."

"Not at all."

He smiled. "Your eyes just flickered."

"A bug flew in my face."

"It's too rainy for bugs. Is your back getting sore?"

She decided to admit to the crick between her shoulder blades but not the ache in her legs. "A little."

"I can take some of your stuff in my pack."

"No way. You're already loaded, starting with Grandpa Earl's camera." She ticked off the other items. "Sleeping bag, tent, the mini camp stove, fuel canisters, cookware, and all the food except for our sandwiches. Once we eat these, I won't be carrying anything except my clothes, my sleeping bag, and my tent."

"Which is a lot if you're not used to it."

"I'll be fine."

He looked as if he wanted to argue the point.

"Seriously, Roarke. Don't baby me."

He gave a slow nod. "All right." Respect flashed in his gaze before he turned his attention to his sandwich. Unwrapping it, he took a bite. *"Mmm."* He chewed and swallowed. "Food always tastes better out in the woods." He took another bite.

"It does." Or it would, if she had the energy and inclination to lift her sandwich. Instead she found herself dreamily focused on his beautiful mouth.

The line of his upper lip dipped into a classic Cupid's bow that she longed to trace with her finger . . . or better yet, her tongue. After that she'd explore the small crease in the middle of his full lower lip. Yesterday's kiss had been too brief. Roarke's mouth invited a woman to taste it slowly, savoring every part of the experience.

"Are you going to eat that?"

She blinked and hoped to hell he hadn't caught her gawking at him. Then she realized he was focused on the sandwich still in her lap. "Yes."

She dutifully started eating. She needed to keep up her strength and it gave her something to do with her mouth since she obviously wouldn't be kissing Roarke anytime soon.

He appeared to be all business so far on this trip, which was as it should be. They each had a one-person tent and sleeping bag. Judging from the way her body felt after only a couple hours of hiking, she'd be in no condition to do more than crawl in and conk out, so the solo sleeping arrangements were just as well.

Roarke picked up his stainless-steel water bottle and took a drink. "One good thing, we don't have to carry water on this trip. I love being able to refill my bottle from a stream. Water bottles get really heavy."

"That's probably why I've fallen out of the habit of taking long hikes." That was her excuse for being so out of shape, and she was sticking to it. "In the desert you have to take so much water that it weighs you down."

"But you like it there?"

"I do, although I've lived in the Phoenix area all my life and lately I've been thinking I should experience something else." Right now she'd like to experience a full-body massage, which wouldn't be happening, either. But prolonging this topic of conversation meant she wouldn't have to get up yet. "How do you like New York?"

"The city or the state?"

"Both, I guess. I've never been there. You get a fair amount of snow in the winter, I would think."

"We do. I don't mind the snow."

"You must live in the city if you're a professor at NYU." She was almost finished with her sandwich, so she slowed down to prolong the break.

Roarke didn't seem to be in a hurry to leave, either. "Mostly I do live in the city," he said, "except when I'm out in the field. But my normal routine is to stay in the city during the week and then head out to the family place on weekends. The city's all hustle and bustle, but the country is relaxing. It's a nice contrast."

Of course. It all clicked into place. His family, which she assumed was wealthy given the extravagant watch he wore, had a place in the country. She'd already concluded that Roarke's family tree included other werewolves like him.

The Gentrys were also wealthy and owned a place in the country. Maybe she was making too big a leap, but she had a hunch that some of the Gentrys were werewolves, too.

A chill traveled up her spine. In all these years, the Gentrys hadn't been a problem to Grandpa Earl, but still ... she'd feel so much better if he sold out and moved to Arizona.

Roarke gave her a questioning glance. "You're quiet all of a sudden. What's up?"

"Nothing. I was just wondering what it would be like to live where it snowed all winter."

"Sorry, but your eyes flickered. Try again."

So much for small talk. "I just wondered if any of the Gentrys are werewolves."

He met that statement with stony silence. But he didn't deny it.

A second chill shot up her spine. "So some of them are?"

"Abby, it's better if we don't discuss this."

"Just answer me one thing. Is—is my grandfather in danger?"

"No."

"Are you sure?"

"Yes, I'm sure. Werewolves avoid calling attention to ourselves. Harming your grandfather would be a very stupid move on Cameron's part, and he's not stupid."

She thought of something else. "Don't wolves live in packs?"

"Generally."

"Do you?"

"You know what? We should probably get going. It's late."

"Your family is a pack, isn't it? And so are the Gentrys. Are there more werewolf packs in other cities?"

"Abby . . ."

"There are, aren't there? Are all the families wealthy, too?"

Roarke sighed and looked out over the damp forest. "I had some crazy idea that during this trip we might be able to have simple, normal conversations, but that's ridiculous. Every conversation will wind back around to this subject, won't it?"

"Well, excuse me all to hell, but how can it not? Show me the woman who could carry on a simple, normal conversation with a werewolf and I'll show you Malibu Barbie!"

His mouth twitched, as if he might be trying not to laugh.

"I mean, really. I didn't try to spy on you, but it happened, and now I can't help thinking about it. You've told me not to ask questions, but if I were in your shoes—or in your *paws*—I'd want the person who knew the big secret to at least draw the correct conclusions."

He gazed at her. "So you think I should give you more information about Weres?"

"I do. The cat's out of the bag, the horse is out of the barn, and the werewolf's out of the woods. I think at this point the more I know, the better chance I'll have of avoiding disaster."

"Or the more ammunition you'll have to blackmail me."

She rolled her eyes. "I'm not naturally a blackmail kind of person, Roarke. I did it this one time so you'd have to bring me along on your search. If you're worried

I'll milk you and your rich werewolf family for the rest of my life, forget it. That's not me."

"I know, and I shouldn't have said that."

"Apology accepted. Besides, I don't need more ammunition to blackmail you if I were so inclined, which I'm not. Those pictures say all there is to say. Anyone who's met you would recognize you, and the news would be out."

He seemed to consider that. "You have a point. The pictures are pretty damning." He glanced at her. "You are so lucky it was me you saw and not someone who would have a . . . different response to the threat of exposure."

"Are we talking about Cameron Gentry?"

"He's not someone to mess with."

"You said werewolves wouldn't harm humans."

"No, I said we don't like to call attention to ourselves. But if a human learns about us, the potential for unwanted attention already exists and we have to initiate damage control in whatever way we see fit."

She became aware that she was alone in the woods with a werewolf who saw her as a threat to his kind. She told herself not to panic. "Do you have a damage control plan for me?"

"Don't look scared, Abby. I've promised you that you'll be okay. This is my fault, my problem." He balled up the sandwich wrapper and leaned over to tuck it in a pocket of his backpack.

"I still need information." She put her wrapper in her backpack, too. "I think it's ducky that you've sworn to protect me with your life, but unless you plan to hang around twenty-four-seven for the next fifty or sixty years, I'm not sure how you'd do that."

"I'm working on it."

"Okay, but in the meantime, if you'd give me a crash

course, sort of an Idiot's Guide to Werewolves, I'd be better able to protect myself."

"The thing is, I'm not supposed to tell you—"

"I realize that. But you weren't supposed to allow me to see you change into a wolf, either, were you?"

"No. That was a careless mistake I regret more than you can imagine."

"Oh, I can probably imagine more than you think, and that's the crux of my argument. I have a whale of an imagination. If you don't tell me how the werewolf world actually works, I'll concoct my own version. Is that what you want?"

He met her gaze and held it. "No, that's not what I want." His kiss-worthy lips tightened into a grim line of determination.

"What do you want?"

He stared at her in stoic silence. But gradually his green eyes warmed, and emotion thickened his voice. "Use your imagination."

Desire rose in her, hot and fast, touching her in intimate places, making her ache in ways that had nothing to do with hiking.

His gaze smoldered for an instant longer. Then he blew out a breath and got to his feet. "We need to push on. So far I haven't detected any evidence of the Sasquatch, so we'll have to go deeper into the forest."

"That's fine." She was still slightly dazed by the realization that he wanted her, even though he was fighting the attraction tooth and nail. *Ha.* That phrase took on a whole new meaning when referring to a werewolf. Still, knowing Roarke was attracted to her would keep her ego warm for a good long time.

But it didn't do much for her stiff muscles. She winced as she got to her feet and hoped he'd missed seeing that.

A quick glance in his direction confirmed that he was watching her and frowning.

"I suppose you'll argue if I suggest redistributing the load," he said.

"You suppose right." She picked up her backpack and ignored the jab of pain between her shoulder blades as she put it on. "I invited myself along on this search and I intend to be an asset, not a liability."

He chuckled. "Good luck with that."

"Hey!"

"Face it, Abby. No matter what your stated intentions, your very presence here fries my brain. I'm afraid you're a liability whether you *intend* to be or not."

She liked the idea of frying his brain, but she didn't like being labeled a handicap. "I'm handy with a camp stove. I'll cook our dinner."

He glanced at her as he hoisted his pack onto his shoulders. His very broad shoulders. "Thanks. That would be great. Cooking's not my strong suit."

She wondered what he'd be doing if he were out here searching as a wolf instead of as a man. Better not to think about that. But she still believed she should have more information about this hidden community of werewolves. She'd ask him again over dinner.

He swept an arm toward the trail. "After you."

"Maybe you'd rather lead."

"Nope. You know the area. I'll follow you."

"Okay." She suspected he was also letting her lead because then she could set the pace. Although she appreciated the chivalrous gesture, it only emphasized how her presence was hampering him.

As she started up the trail, she battled her conscience. He'd be so much better off out here without her. But then she pictured going back to Grandpa Earl and explaining that she had abandoned the Bigfoot search to Roarke.

While her grandfather would be happy to hear of a positive sighting from Roarke, it wouldn't be the same as if Abby saw the Bigfoot pair. She was Grandpa Earl's eyes and ears on this trip.

That meant she had to maintain a brisk pace even if it killed her. As the trail wound upward, she took a deep breath and walked faster.

Roarke tried to keep his mind off sex as he followed Abby up the trail, but his constant view of her cute little tush wasn't helping. The navy material stretched temptingly across her backside as she trudged doggedly up the incline. He figured she was pushing herself to keep from holding him back, which was endearing but could make her a basket case by tonight.

That wasn't the only problem with having Abby out in front. They were heading into a slight breeze, which neatly blew her intoxicating aroma smack into his face. Not only did that add to his lusty thoughts, but the sensory overload from Abby might prevent him from picking up the scent of the Sasquatch.

He paused. "Hold up a minute."

She stopped and turned, her breathing labored. "Is something wrong?"

"I want to lead, after all. Your scent is interfering with my ability to track the Sasquatch pair."

"Oh! That's not good." Her cheeks grew pink. "Sorry about that. I used deodorant this morning, but I suppose with all the physical exertion I might—"

"Abby, it's not that you smell bad." He smiled at her assumption, which showed how truly human she was. "If anything, you smell way too good."

"I'm sure that's not true. I'm starting to work up a

sweat, and if we end up camping near running water, I'll take a sponge bath. That should help."

"I don't think you understand. Your natural scent is . . . very attractive to me."

She stared at him in obvious disbelief.

"I told you both my sight and sense of smell are better, even when I'm in human form, than the average man's."

"Then you should be more easily grossed out."

"Oh, I can be, especially if a woman wears a lot of heavy perfume."

She grimaced. "Or has been on the hiking trail a little too long."

"No, that only makes your scent more arousing."

"Roarke, that's crazy."

"No, it's your first lesson in the Idiot's Guide to Werewolves. When we first met, I'd recorded your scent and found it pleasing long before I paid attention to how you looked. The stronger your natural aroma, the more I like it."

"You're kidding, right?"

"Nope." And if he didn't get moving *right now* he'd have to do something about the lust boiling through his veins. "Follow me. I'll take it easy."

Without waiting for her reply, he stepped around her and started up the trail. Another second of standing there and he would have reached for her. Once he did that, he was liable to forget about everything else, and he had a job to do.

Chapter 8

Roarke forced himself to go slow for Abby's sake. The snail's pace frustrated him, but he wasn't about to make her more miserable than she already was. She was determined and brave, sexy and smart.

In fact, she had just about every quality he admired in a human being. He could do without her stubborn streak; but then, he wasn't exactly perfect himself. He liked her way too much.

God, what a mess he'd made for himself. Finding the Sasquatch pair would be a challenge under these conditions. Keeping his hands off Abby, who was quickly turning into ideal-mate material, might be impossible.

How Aidan would laugh if he could see his younger brother now. Aidan would say it served him right for being so critical of Aidan's infatuation with the lovely Emma. Karma was a bitch.

Even though he was walking in front of Abby, he couldn't let himself get too far ahead of her because that would be her signal to speed up. So he could still smell her—and he still wanted her with the heat of a thousand suns. When he'd agreed to this hike, he'd neglected to factor in the added allure of a sweaty Abby.

He doubted that she believed him, even after his explanation. Modern-day humans were so conditioned to rid themselves of their natural scent that most of them didn't understand what an aphrodisiac it could be. But he was constructed differently, to say the least, and he should have remembered this would be a side effect of the hike.

Because he was so involved with thoughts of Abby, he nearly missed the faint trace of Sasquatch scent that came to him on the gentle breeze. Naturally it crossed the path, which meant if Abby and Roarke intended to follow it, they'd have to leave the trail.

He'd been afraid of that. The Sasquatch pair wouldn't bother with trails. They'd go cross-country, but he'd hoped for Abby's sake that the trail would bring them into the general vicinity. He paused to sniff again. Yep, faint, but there and off to the right, through what looked like pretty rugged terrain. *Shit.*

At least the rain had stopped for now. That would make things slightly easier, although he realized it could start up again at any moment. For now, though, the sky was overcast but no longer dripping on them.

Turning back to Abby, he was confronted with a pitiful sight. She was limping. Noticeably. Of course she hadn't said anything, stubborn and foolish woman that she was.

Now what? Leaving the trail would have been a challenge for her before, but now he couldn't ask her to attempt it.

She glanced up, as if just noticing that he'd stopped.

He took off his pack and set it beside the trail. "You're limping."

"No big deal. Why did you take off your pack?"

"Because it is a big deal, and I want to help." He closed the distance between them. "Did you trip?"

"No. I have a charley horse in my right calf. I'm walking it out." She backed away from him and made a shooing motion with both hands. "Go get your backpack and we can continue on."

"Stand still for a minute, Abby."

"Look, I'm perfectly capable of—" She cried out a protest as he scooped her up in his arms, pack and all. "Stop this! I'm too big for you to carry!"

"You're not if you'll stop struggling." He was amazed at how right she felt in his arms, even wearing the damned backpack. "My plan is to carry you over to that rock and work on your leg."

"Damn it, no! That's wasting valuable time. Put me down, Roarke. I'm fine!"

"I beg to differ." He tightened his grip, but she stubbornly continued to wiggle and protest as he crossed to a rock about the size of a coffee table. As he started to lower her onto it, she pinched his earlobe.

"Let me go! We need to move on!"

Making an impatient sound low in his throat, he did what he'd been longing to do ever since he'd met her. He kissed her full on the mouth. She went perfectly still, which had been part of his goal. The other part involved taking that brief, almost chaste kiss she'd given him yesterday and turning it into something that wasn't even slightly chaste.

Because he'd surprised her, he'd caught her with her mouth partly open, and he took advantage of that to mount an invasion with his tongue. She trembled on the knife edge between surrender and resistance. Then she lost that delicate balancing act and tumbled into a surrender that took his breath away.

Clutching his shoulder with one hand, she used the other to cup the back of his head and urge him deeper. With a moan of triumph he changed the angle of the kiss and claimed her with a boldness that left no doubt of his ultimate intentions. She welcomed him with such passion that he was afraid he'd drop her. Not cool.

Summoning what little reasoning power he had left, he settled her on the rock, but he didn't end the kiss. He wasn't sure he ever wanted to. She tasted like rain, but she also tasted like licorice, which she must have been sucking on while she battled her gimpy leg.

Arousal made swift work of any remaining composure on his part. He was hard and aching, and he'd decided licorice was his favorite flavor. Sinking to his knees on a cushion of wet pine needles, he cradled her head in both hands as he continued to plunder her mouth. As he combed eager fingers through her silky hair, her ponytail came undone.

Freeing her hair gave him a jolt of desire, as if he'd started taking off her clothes. Now there was an idea. Except she still had a heavy backpack anchored to her shoulders, and his original purpose had been to relieve a pain in her calf.

With immense regret, he ended the kiss, although he couldn't seem to stop running his fingers through her hair. He looked into her blue eyes, smoky with desire. "I knew this would happen," he murmured.

"So did I." She ran her tongue over her lips. "And just so you know, I liked it a lot."

"So did I."

"But if I don't take off this backpack, my shoulders are going to fall off."

"Damn." Cursing himself for being a moron, he eased the pack from her shoulders and set it beside the rock. "You're finished carrying that."

"But—"

He placed a finger against her warm, moist lips. "Yes, you are. I'm very strong, Abby."

"I admit you're stronger than I thought. I'm not a small person, yet you carried me as if I were a little kid."

"Exactly. I can easily transport everything in my pack plus everything in yours. So let me do it."

She kissed his finger and moved it aside. "You may be able to do it, but carrying extra weight has to slow you down. And you can't maneuver as well, in case we come upon the Sasquatch pair. I have to insist that you let me haul what I'm supposed to."

He gazed at her, appreciating the grit that she was showing yet wanting to make sure she didn't hurt herself any more than she already had. "Let me see about your leg, and then we'll discuss who carries what."

"It's a charley horse. Everyone gets them."

He didn't, but he chose not to mention that. "They can be painful, though." Leaning down, he began rolling up her right pant leg. "Are you drinking enough water?"

"Probably not. I get so focused on hiking that I forget. I'll do better. I promise not to be the weak link, Roarke."

As he rolled her pant leg up to her knee, he was feeling like the weak link around here. Her skin was like silk as his fingers brushed her calf, and he caught the scent of lotion, soap, and the unmistakable musk of arousal.

"Tell me if this hurts." He began kneading her calf muscles, taking care not to push too hard or deep. She drew in a quick breath and he stopped. "Too much?"

"No. It . . . helps."

"Good." The scent of arousal grew stronger as he applied gentle, rhythmic pressure. His massage became a caress and he leaned forward, placing soft kisses from ankle to knee. He touched the back of her knee, rubbing in tiny circles, and her breathing grew shallow.

Slowly he raised his head and met her gaze. "Better?"

"Yes." Her voice sounded rusty.

Looking into her eyes, he carefully rolled her pant leg down. "From now on, you need to tell me when you have a problem."

She drew in a shaky breath. "Any problem?"

"Yes."

"Okay, then. Roarke, I have a problem."

He rested his hands on her knees, as if it were a casual, friendly touch. It was anything but that. "What is it?"

"I want to make love with you."

His groin tightened. "Why is that a problem?" He brushed lazy circles over her knees when what he really wanted was to rip off her pants and take her.

"You know why!" She sounded impatient. "For starters, it's not on the agenda. We have a job to do. And it's obvious you're attracted to me, but you don't want to be—I guess because I'm a human, although I don't quite get that, because it's not like I'm asking for a commitment or anything, but—"

"Past history." He stroked her thighs through the Lycra and felt her tremble. Heat danced in his veins. "Not long ago my brother got involved with a woman, thinking they'd just have sex, but the attraction was much stronger than that, and now they're mated."

"You mean married?"

"That, too, although it was just a formality." He continued a slow massage of her thigh muscles. He told himself he was making sure she'd be ready to hike in a few minutes. Yeah, right.

"My brother and Emma had a church ceremony to please her mother and friends, but only for the sake of appearances. The Were bond is more basic and physical than a walk down the aisle and an exchange of rings."

Abby's eyes widened. "You mean she had to become a werewolf, too?"

"No. There's no way a human can become a Were. As I mentioned before, you have to be born that way."

"Will your brother and his . . . his *mate* have children?"

"I just found out yesterday that Emma's pregnant. My parents are excited, but with a mixed mating situation, there's no telling whether the kids will be Were or not, which is—"

Abby gasped. "She could actually give birth to a *werewolf*?"

Her horrified expression was exactly why he'd prefer to mate with his own kind. Humans could never truly understand or appreciate what being a Were was all about. Roarke wouldn't change his status for anything, but a human could easily view him as a freak.

"I'm sorry," Abby said. "That reaction was rude."

He shrugged. "At least you're being honest. And it's not quite what you're picturing. Even if she has a Were baby, the kid will look and act human until puberty."

"Oh."

"At that point he or she will develop the ability to shift if they're Were. If they're not . . . well, they won't." And pity that poor kid, born into a tradition they couldn't be part of. If Emma and Aidan had more than one child, they could end up with one who was Were and one who wasn't. Sibling rivalry would be taken to new heights.

"So what about Emma's mother? Does she know her daughter married a werewolf?"

"God, no. That's the other major problem. Emma's not allowed to tell anyone, not her friends or her family.

As far as her mother knows, Emma married the son of a wealthy financier. End of story."

"That would be a tough secret to keep from your family."

"I'm sure it is tough."

"And what if her baby turns out to be Were?"

"One grandma will be thrilled and the other one will never know her grandchild can shift."

"What a weird dynamic that would be."

"It's the price Emma pays. A steep price." The more Roarke talked about his brother and Emma, the more he realized he was courting danger by even kissing Abby, knowing how she affected him.

He didn't want a human mate, and not because Aidan would never let him live it down. He could handle Aidan's comments. But he couldn't handle knowing what he'd done to a woman's life. To Abby's life.

Apparently Emma had made the choice willingly and was very happy with her decision. But Abby had just registered shock at the idea of producing a werewolf child and keeping secrets from her family. Abby wasn't Emma.

And he wasn't Aidan, either. A werewolf's life was complicated enough without adding in the human mate element. Weres belonged with Weres, and humans belonged with humans. Mating a human with a werewolf put a terrible burden on everyone.

Beneath his palms Abby's warmth called to him, and making love to her right now, on this conveniently flat rock, would be so sweet. But he had to resist or they could both suffer serious consequences. She might think she could walk away from him, but she didn't realize how strong the mating instinct was between them. Humans often didn't pick up on that kind of thing.

Breaking the contact, he rose to his feet. "Yep, weird

dynamics for all concerned. So you can see that it would be risky for us to get involved when it could become intense." He gazed at her. "I'm afraid it would," he said softly.

She gave him a lopsided smile. "I don't know why. I'm a scrawny specimen who can't even make it three hours on the trail without getting crippled up. I can't imagine what you see in me."

If she only knew how sexy she looked right now in her rumpled hiking clothes with her glorious hair curling around her shoulders and her eyes bright as a summer sky. He wanted to kiss every freckle on her nose and then find all the rest that were under wraps so he could kiss those, too.

But he decided not to say any of those things, which would only take them down the very road he'd decided to abandon. "You wouldn't understand," he said. "It's a werewolf thing."

"Meaning you like the way I smell."

"That's a big part of it."

She shook her head. "You're right—I don't understand that part of the attraction."

"Which is exactly my point. We're very different. We're two different species, to be exact." He paused and glanced at his watch. It was getting late.

"We need to get going, don't we?"

"Are you up to it?"

"Of course."

"You'd better test your leg and see if you can walk without limping."

"I'm sure I can." She slid slowly from the rock and stood. Then she walked a few feet, turned, and walked back. "Way better. Thank you, Roarke. You have magic in your fingers."

"I'm not going to touch that line with a ten-foot pole."

She smiled at him. "Believe it or not, I do understand why you think it would be a mistake for us to have sex. After listening to your brother's story, I agree. I could easily fall for you, and then we'd have all those mixed-species problems you just outlined."

"I'm glad you agree with me." He should be over-joyed, in fact. So why the sudden letdown because she was giving up the concept of having sex with him? Surely he hadn't hoped she'd wear him down so he could claim that he'd been tempted beyond all endurance.

"But it's a shame, in a way," she continued. "We could have been good together." She ran her fingers through her hair and lifted it off the back of her neck. "My hair seems to have come undone."

"I think the tie thing came off while . . . while we were kissing." The memory of that flooded him with lust all over again. "Do you want me to help you—"

"That's okay. I know what I'm looking for." She crossed to the rock and leaned over to search for her hair ribbon.

He had to turn away. If he stood there watching her bending over that rock, no telling what he'd do. Or rather, he knew exactly what he was liable to do, and that would be the end of his resolve not to have sex with her.

So he walked over to his backpack and crouched down to rearrange the contents so he could take on some of her stuff. As he did, he caught another faint whiff of the Sasquatch pair. That might mean they'd stopped to rest somewhere instead of moving on.

"I found it."

He turned and discovered she was tying up her hair in a ponytail. The motion lifted her breasts, and his fevered brain imagined how much he'd enjoy seeing that same motion if she were standing naked in the forest. Then he could walk over, lean down, and—

"I never told you the other reason we can't have sex," she said.

He cleared his throat. "What's that?"

"No condoms. At least I didn't bring any. Did you?"

"No."

"There you go. A built-in guarantee that we will concentrate on the task at hand."

He started to tell her that it wasn't a guarantee at all. Whether in human form or wolf form, he wouldn't be able to procreate until he'd found his mate and completed the binding process. Besides that, he was immune to STDs. He wore condoms only because women expected him to use them.

Fortunately, he caught himself before he blurted out all that info. Letting her believe that a lack of condoms was a legitimate barrier to having sex would be a good thing. Besides, she might not believe him if he told her the truth.

"Obviously that subject caught you flat-footed." She sounded amused. "You didn't even think about the fact we don't have condoms, did you?"

"No, can't say that I did."

"You could have picked some up at the store before we left. Grandpa Earl sells them on a top shelf, away from the kids."

"I noticed that."

She arched a brow. "You noticed it, but you didn't act on that knowledge? I guess you really didn't think we'd get horizontal, then."

"I knew it would be a bad idea."

"But you kissed me, anyway."

He grinned. "You wouldn't be still." Then his grin faded. "But it won't happen again."

"You've got that right. Trust me. I don't fool around

with unplanned pregnancies. And that goes double for interspecies sex. You're totally safe from me, Roarke."

He wondered if she was totally safe from him. He'd do his damnedest to keep away from her, but he couldn't pretend it would be easy.

Chapter 9

When Abby learned they'd have to leave the trail and plow through the forest, she finally gave in and let Roarke carry everything but her toiletries and extra clothes. None of that weighed much, and asking him to take those things seemed wrong. But under the circumstances, transferring the bulk of her stuff made logical sense even if it did hurt her pride a bit.

Roarke led the way and was, she supposed, following his nose. Although it wasn't raining, that made no difference to the wetness factor as she brushed against wet bushes and walked under dripping trees. The constant exercise and the nice view of Roarke's backside kept her warm enough, but once they stopped moving and darkness arrived, she knew the chill would set in.

Even though they'd left the trail, she had a fair idea of where they were. As a teenager living out her Indiana Jones fantasies, she'd camped out overnight many times with her brother. Once they'd learned to make cairns to mark their travels, they'd done that incessantly.

Apparently many of them were still there, because she'd already noticed a few. Judging from the cairns, she and Roarke weren't far from a cave Abby and her brother had discovered. A cave sounded like a nice choice for the night provided it wasn't occupied by some critter.

Whether they slept in a cave or out in the open, she wouldn't complain. She'd be the epitome of the happy camper, because thanks to Roarke's much-discussed sense of smell, they were successfully tracking the Bigfoot pair. Roarke said he'd picked up their scent and she trusted him to know what he was talking about.

According to Roarke, the creatures had a substantial lead on them and the chances of overtaking them today were slim. Abby vowed not to feel guilty about that. She'd been doing her best to keep up when Roarke had turned around and noticed her limping.

And kissed her. Lordy, that werewolf could kiss. Then, as he'd worked the charley horse out of her calf, she'd nearly melted into a puddle on that rock.

He liked to go on about how wonderful she smelled, and she had to admit his scent was an aphrodisiac to her, too. If he used cologne, she wasn't familiar with the brand. Whatever it was, it made her think of lying on a bed of moss under a fragrant evergreen.

To be more specific, his scent made her think of lying naked on a bed of moss underneath the hot body of one Roarke Wallace. She wasn't sure if that was due to cologne or pheromones. Maybe it was a combination of both, but the effect was powerful.

She liked to think she wouldn't have had sex with him since neither of them had brought condoms. She liked to think that, but she wasn't sure, and that was scary. She *always* thought of condoms. She wasn't the sort of girl to get swept away and realize later that she'd had an *oops* moment.

But Roarke was one lusty guy. He was also a wolf

sometimes, and maybe that was part of her fascination. Hey, who was she kidding? Roarke was a larger-than-life fairy-tale hero, the kind she used to dream about when she was a little girl. Of course she wanted him desperately.

And of course she would resist such an insane fantasy. Her parents would love to see her settle down with a nice guy and pop out a couple of kids they could spoil rotten. Abby liked that scenario herself. She definitely didn't plan to present them with grandchildren who sometimes turned into wolves.

Good thing she and Roarke had gone over that material as part of his Idiot's Guide to Werewolves course. She couldn't imagine what life was like for Roarke's sister-in-law, Emma. All the important aspects of her life had to remain hidden from her friends and family. That would suck. She must really love Roarke's brother.

Roarke paused again to sniff the air.

"Still smell them?"

"Yep. We're keeping pace with them, but we haven't gained any."

"Then go faster."

He glanced back at her. "Don't worry. We'll catch them."

"When, sometime next year?"

He rolled his eyes. "Abby, we're doing fine. They'll probably stop for the night soon, and then we can make up a little of the distance before we stop."

"Or we could hike all night and catch them."

"*No*, we're not doing that." He sniffed again. "Let's go."

She couldn't smell a thing, which meant the Sasquatch pair was quite a distance away. Her grandfather maintained there was nothing worse than the smell of a Sasquatch. But for all Abby knew, Roarke liked it. He was strange that way.

As she trudged through the forest after him, trying to ignore the ache in her legs, her back—pretty much all over—she decided to ask the question and take her mind off her pain-racked body. "So do you like the way a Sasquatch smells?"

"Hell, no. It's a terrible stench, just like your grandfather said."

"Why do you think that is?"

Roarke laughed. "Poor hygiene?"

"Maybe. Then again, it might be a way for them to identify each other. Maybe a Sasquatch smells just great to another Sasquatch."

"Now you're thinking like an anthropologist."

That comment pleased her. And talking definitely helped her forget she was a walking mass of misery. "What do you like about your job?"

"The people I meet. Some of the populations my team and I study are dirt poor but have a richness of tradition that more affluent cultures would envy."

"That sounds cool."

"It is. Dancing, singing, feasts—all of which promote loyalty to the community. Obviously, as a Were I come from a background that encourages community loyalty. That's how we've survived through the ages. But the people I study often have an even deeper understanding of the meaning of community. I learn a lot from them."

"And then you teach that to your students at NYU."

"I hope so." He held back a branch to give her room to pass.

"I'll bet you do. Especially if you remember to wear the corduroy jacket and plaid vest."

"Oh, yeah. My professor costume." He let the branch go and it *whoosh*ed into place, showering both of them with a fine mist. He didn't seem to notice as he paused to gaze at her. "Do you think the clothes are too over-the-top?"

He asked the question so earnestly that she had to smile. "It's definitely over-the-top, but if you're asking me whether you should modify it, my vote is to leave well enough alone."

"So you think it makes me look dignified and scholarly, then."

"No, I think it makes you look like a geek."

"Damn. I was going for dignified and scholarly."

"Personally, Roarke, I think the geeky look works for you. You should keep it."

"Why?"

"You honestly don't know?"

"If I knew I wouldn't be asking you about this. I loved the Indiana Jones movies as a kid, and so I decided to model myself after him. I wasn't willing to give up my Ferrari, and I still love a good game of touch football, but I wanted people at NYU to take me seriously. So I decided it would help if I looked more like a professor than a rich playboy."

She folded her arms and studied the man in front of her. His dark blond hair was rumpled from wind and rain, and he was sporting a five-o'clock shadow on his extremely square jaw. His shoulders filled out the tan windbreaker, and carrying that huge backpack made him look like some sort of Superman figure.

"If you walked into a classroom looking like this, then—"

"I would never do that."

"That's fortunate, because if you did, all the women in the class would swoon, after which they'd spend the entire class period with their chins propped on their fists, gazing at you."

His cheeks reddened. "No, they wouldn't."

"Yes, they would. You're a hunk, Dr. Wallace. You may want to be admired for your brains, but your body is to die for. Take it from someone who's been jonesing for you ever since we met at the Rotary luncheon."

"When I was wearing my professor uniform."

"I'm old enough to be able to look past that, but the clothes help disguise your hotness from an eighteen-year-old college freshman."

"Ah, it wouldn't matter. To those girls, I'm an old guy. They're interested in the football player sitting next to them in the lecture hall."

Abby shrugged. "So don't take my word for it. Try ditching the vest and wearing a white shirt open at the collar. See what happens. I predict the female population of your class won't take a single note. They'll be too busy staring at you."

Roarke massaged the back of his neck. "I'm not sure you're right, but that would be bad. Anthropology's a fascinating subject and I want them to learn all they can while they're in my class."

"Then take my advice and stick with the plaid vest."

"All right, I will." He glanced at his watch again. "We still have another hour of daylight, and I think the scent is getting stronger. Are you okay to push on?"

"You bet."

"Okay, but let me know when you're ready to stop for the day."

"Sure." Like she would admit to being tired. She'd hike till she dropped. Then she'd drag herself to her feet and hike some more.

But he'd given her another topic of conversation as she followed him through the woods. "You drive a Ferrari?"

"I have a weakness for fast cars. I toyed with the idea of becoming a race car driver, but I don't think that kind of high-profile work is a good idea for my kind."

She smiled to herself. "You'd only be high-profile if you won a lot of races."

"Which I would."

"Obviously self-confidence wouldn't be a problem."

"I just know what I'm good at. Driving is one of those things. Flying is another one."

"You can *fly?*"

"Sure. Why not?"

"Well, I'm no engineer, but I would think the aerodynamics of that would be tricky. I know Pegasus is supposed to be able to fly, too, but somehow a flying wolf just doesn't—"

"In an airplane, Abby."

"Oh."

"I grow fur, not wings and feathers."

"*Whew.* Thanks for straightening that out for me. I was picturing a squadron of werewolves. It was rather frightening."

His shoulders shook, and eventually she figured out he was laughing.

"Oh, man." He turned back to her, still chuckling. "I didn't realize educating a human about werewolves could be so entertaining."

"Does that mean you're having fun?"

"Yeah, I guess I am."

"Makes sense. You're a teacher, and this is a subject you happen to have down cold."

"And you're smart and eager to learn, so that's always a bonus." He gazed at her. "But I'll bet you're not having fun. You look like hell."

"Gee, thanks."

"Sorry, but you look like someone pulled you through a knothole backward."

She was too exhausted to take offense. "At least I should smell yummy—to you, anyway."

"That's a given, but you need to rest. We'll find a place and make camp. There was a clearing back a ways. We can head for that." He started to move around her, obviously ready to lead the way as they retraced their steps.

"No, wait. You wanted to keep going after the Sasquatch pair stopped, so we could make up some distance." But she didn't put much energy into the protest because camping sounded like heaven.

"I did, but if doing that pushes you until you collapse, I'll have to give up the chase and carry you back to Earl."

She managed a weak smile. "Nah, just leave me beside the trail like they do in war movies."

"The heroes in war movies *never* left anyone beside the trail."

"And you're a hero."

"Let's put it this way—I'm not the villain who leaves a friend behind."

"So we're friends?" If they were, she liked that. She'd never had a werewolf for a friend before.

"I thought we were."

"Yeah, I suppose we are. That kiss took us past the acquaintance stage, but we can't be lovers for a whole bunch of reasons."

He glanced away and his jaw tightened, as if he'd rather she hadn't reminded him. "Right."

"So that leaves us with being friends. And friends don't let friends camp out in the open if there's a cave nearby."

He brightened. "There is?"

"I think so. When we crossed over that little stream where we refilled our water bottles, I recognized the area. I marked the way to the cave with a few cairns, if they're still there."

"How far back is the cave?"

"You could make it in ten minutes. I'll probably need more like fifteen."

As if on cue, rain began to fall.

Roarke glanced up at the gray sky visible through the tree branches. "I've never been a fan of setting up a tent in the rain. The cave sounds great. Lead on, hiker girl."

She turned around and started back. Although they were going in the opposite direction from the Sasquatch pair, they wouldn't lose too much time, and moving forward in the rain didn't sound like a great idea.

"I'm glad you know about the cave," Roarke said. "The rain's coming down harder and we'd be miserable out in the open."

"The cave could be occupied by a wild animal, of course."

"I know. I'll check it out." He said it so nonchalantly, as if he wasn't the least bit worried about what he'd encounter in the cave.

And he wouldn't be, she realized. No matter how human he looked right now, he was capable of becoming a wild animal himself. The blond wolf she'd seen wouldn't be intimidated by anything that might live in this forest.

Come to think of it, she hadn't seen many animals on this hike. A couple of squirrels, a rabbit, and several birds, but that was about it. True, the larger animals had mostly left the area as Portland had grown. Grandpa Earl said he hadn't found bear tracks in years. But Abby usually spotted a deer or two when she went hiking.

She'd never gone hiking with a werewolf, though. Maybe Roarke had something to do with the lack of critters romping around. Maybe they could sense him. Maybe they could even smell him.

Now she was curious. "Roarke, do you smell like a wolf?"

He laughed. "No. Why?"

"I usually see deer when I'm out on Grandpa Earl's land. I haven't seen any today."

"You're on the right track. I don't smell like a wolf, but I smell like a werewolf."

"There's a difference?"

"Yep. But deer don't stick around when they smell a werewolf, either. Ever since we left the trail, the wind's been at our back, carrying my scent to whatever's ahead of us."

"Like the Sasquatch?"

"They don't have a good sense of smell."

"Aha! That's why they stink so bad. If they didn't, they'd never be able to pick up each other's scent."

"You could be right about that." He was silent for a moment. "Abby . . ."

"What?"

"Do you find my scent . . . unpleasant?"

"No, I love it." *Whoops.* Better dial back the enthusiasm. "I mean, it's nice."

"I liked your first answer." His voice carried a suggestively husky overtone.

She decided to ignore it. "So, do you wear some kind of cologne or aftershave? Because if I knew the brand, I could buy some for my brother for Christmas."

"Sorry. I don't wear any."

"Then it must be the soap you use that has a woodsy fragrance."

"I use unscented soap."

"Oh." Then it was just Roarke. She'd never thought much about how a guy smelled before, and most of the men she'd dated used cologne or aftershave. "So you don't like fragrances?"

"Just the real ones. Anything artificial drives me nuts. Perfumes of any kind irritate my nose and interfere with my ability to catch important scents."

Like mine. Apparently she and Roarke had an olfactory match going on. There was something primitive and exciting about that—a little *too* primitive and exciting. The more they discussed this, the more she tuned in and turned on.

Too bad about that. They'd decided to forego the pleasure, and even if they hadn't, they were condomless. She could just cool her jets and forget about being naked on a bed of moss with sweet-smelling Roarke hovering over her. It wasn't going to happen.

Chapter 10

A few minutes later, Roarke stood at the mouth of the cave. He pulled back the branches of a bush growing at the entrance to reveal an opening about five feet high and six or seven feet wide.

"Do you think anything's in there?" Abby leaned down to peer into the murky depths.

"Nothing very big, or these branches would be broken."

"Some small things can still bite."

"I know. I'll take a look." He set his pack down and pulled a flashlight out of a side pocket. Flicking it on, he crouched down and edged into the cave. This reconnaissance would have been so much easier in wolf form.

But he didn't want to shift in front of Abby. His reluctance made no sense whatsoever, but he couldn't seem to talk himself into doing it. She'd seen him shift, so he shouldn't care if she saw him do it again. Yet he did.

Shifting was a private event, even among Weres. For one thing, the Were had to get naked first, which set up a certain vulnerability. During the shift, a Were was extremely vulnerable. There was no protection from an outside threat in that state between human and were-wolf.

Roarke didn't consider Abby a threat, but he wasn't ready to put himself completely at her mercy, either. He'd rather exercise some control over their time together. Besides, once he shifted, they wouldn't be able to communicate, at least not the way they could when he was in human form.

So he suffered the handicap of being a biped as he duck-walked into the cave. Using his flashlight, he verified that no animal big or small, warm-blooded or cold-blooded, was curled up in a corner somewhere. The cave smelled musty, but he couldn't pick up any evidence that a creature had lived here recently.

The ceiling rose to almost seven feet toward the back of the cave and he was able to stand. The floor was dry and plenty big enough for a couple of sleeping bags and the camp stove. They wouldn't need to set up the tents, although he immediately understood that would eliminate one of the barriers between them.

The thought of such an intimate sleeping arrangement went straight to his groin. Maybe he'd be better off out in the rain. Damn it, that was stupid. They could cohabit in this cave without having sex. She was appealing, but not so appealing that he'd lose control.

Before he left, he swept his flashlight beam over the gray walls. Something low on the wall caused him to squat down and study it more closely. He grinned. Somebody had been in here playing Hangman with a piece of chalk. They'd gone through a ton of games, too.

He wondered if Abby and her brother were responsible for the faint chalk lines on the cave wall. He had chalk in his pack. A tournament might be the perfect distraction from more dangerous games.

Making his way back outside, he discovered the rain was beating down even harder. "Nothing's in there."

"Good."

"But I found some graffiti."

She looked outraged. "Spray paint?"

"Nope. Chalk. Hangman."

"It's still there? Cool! Can I borrow your flashlight?"

He handed it to her and she slipped past the branches and into the cave. Hoisting his backpack, he followed her. Question answered. She'd been one of the people with the chalk.

But somebody else had been in the cave playing that game with her, and he had the unsettling thought that it might not have been her brother. It could have been a boyfriend. They might have spent the night in this cave playing Hangman and having sex. He didn't like that, and he didn't like not liking it. Her romantic past had nothing to do with him.

He found her kneeling in front of the row of Hangman games.

"We had such fun that night," she said. "I'll have to tell him it's all still here."

"By all means."

She glanced over her shoulder. "Who polished off your porridge, Mr. Grouchy-pants?"

"What did I say? I didn't say anything." He leaned his backpack against the cave wall and started pulling out supplies. First he turned on a small battery-operated lantern so they could see what they were doing.

"It wasn't *what* you said, but the stuffy way you said it."

"Maybe I have more important things to think about than some kids' game you played with your boyfriend." He slammed pots and pans on the stone floor of the cave.

"My boy–" She sucked in a breath. "Roarke Wallace, you're jealous!"

"Why would I be jealous? I have no claim on you." He fumbled with the camp stove. "We need to get this going so we can eat."

"You're ridiculous."

"Thanks. Good to know how you feel."

"You have no idea how I feel." Switching off the flashlight, she stood and walked over to where he was crouched as he assembled the camp stove. "But I'm beginning to get an inkling of how you feel."

"Hungry. I feel hungry. You said you'd handle dinner."

"What are you hungry for, Roarke?"

You. But he'd bite his tongue off before he'd say that. She was in this cave soaking up memories of another man, another night. He'd leave her to that.

He put the stove together and reached for one of the fuel canisters. "Once I get this together, you can start working on the food."

"I'm not in the habit of cooking for a surly man."

"I'm not surly. I'm just—"

"You most certainly are surly. And by the way, I'd consider it a great favor if you'd stand up and face me while we're arguing."

"We're not arguing. We're discussing dinner."

"The hell we are! I'm not cooking a damned thing until you stand up and admit that something's bothering you."

He felt like an ass, because he had no right to behave this way. So she'd had another man in this cave with her. So what? So what if they'd stripped naked in here and screwed all night long? What was that to him? He needed to lose the attitude, and fast.

She stood before him, tapping the toe of her hiking boot.

Reluctantly he rose to his feet and gazed at her. He

owed her an apology. "I'm sorry. Your relationships with other men are none of my business. If you were in here playing Hangman or playing Hide the Salami, it's all the same to me."

She began to laugh. "Hide the Salami? Did you really say that? Tell me you didn't say that."

"Abby, I'm trying to tell you that my reaction to knowing that you had another man in this cave is—"

"I was thirteen."

"*Thirteen?* You were out here alone with a guy at thirteen? Isn't that a little young to be having sex?"

"I wasn't having sex. I was camping out with my big brother, Pete, who was fifteen. We used to go on overnight camping trips during summer vacations. I can't say for sure if Pete got into the whole fantasy angle, but I'd pretend we were on an archeological expedition like Indiana Jones."

"You were here with your brother."

"*Uh-huh.* He was a lot more fun back then, but he's all serious now that he's an accountant. I'm going to take a few pictures of the Hangman games, to remind him of those days. I love that they're still here."

Roarke blew out a breath. He wasn't sure how he'd dig himself out of this hole. He'd made it pretty deep.

"So you thought I'd spent the night in this cave with a boyfriend." She continued to study him with a speculative gleam in her eyes.

"I made a mistake and jumped to the wrong conclusion."

"So you did. But that's not the part that fascinates me."

He groaned. "Could we forget about it? I don't know what came over me that made me act like that."

"Don't you?"

He looked into her eyes, shadowy in the light from the lantern. "If I do, I don't want to admit it."

"Now we're getting somewhere."

"There's nowhere to get. Whatever this . . . *feeling* is between us, we need to ignore it."

"I was trying to do that, Roarke, and then you went ballistic because you thought I'd spent the night in this cave with another man." She gazed at him. "You're becoming possessive of me. What does that mean?"

"It means I have to stop being possessive."

"But what if it's something you can't help? What if it ties into your werewolf nature?"

He looked away, not happy with the insight that she'd neatly handed him. He was the werewolf in this equation, and yet she, the human in the equation, had come embarrassingly close to the truth. He was naturally territorial, and somehow he'd made her part of his territory, which she most certainly wasn't. Would never be.

"Although you have no justification for feeling possessive, I think it's kind of sweet."

He glanced back at her. "I think it's amazingly stupid. I have a brain, a pretty good one, in fact. I don't have to be ruled by my instincts."

"But nobody's brain works as well if they're tired and hungry. And wet. And sore—speaking for myself on that one."

"I'm sure you are." He hesitated. "And I'd like to give you a massage, which would help a lot, but I'm afraid that will lead to exactly what we're trying to avoid."

"Here's the thing." She placed a hand on his chest. "I don't know if it's possible to avoid it."

Warmth from her hand seeped through his damp clothes and made its way to his skin, where it radiated outward. A portion of those warm tendrils went north, and a little bit went east and west, but the majority went straight south. His brain hadn't been working very well before she touched him. Now it was totally MIA.

Still, he owed it to both of them to question her statement. He cleared his throat, because his vocal cords weren't working too well, either. "Anything's possible. We just have to exercise some willpower."

She rubbed her hand over his chest. "We'll need willpower for what I have in mind, because we don't have condoms. But I'd like to propose a compromise between total abstinence and total indulgence."

His brain cells must have retained a little bit of juice, because he quickly imagined what that suggestion would look like, and he was immediately on board with it.

"In other words, I'd still get my massage and some relief from sexual frustration." She slowly unzipped his jacket. "If you don't need the massage, I can skip that step and go straight for the main event."

Oh, yeah.

"I understand all the reasons why we don't want to get too involved, but this is more like fooling around in the backseat, minus the car. We're simply letting off some steam before we become so preoccupied with sex that we can't accomplish anything."

He couldn't argue with her conclusions. He'd been ready to duel with some imaginary lover who'd shared this cave with her. He was strung so tight that the slightest thing could cause him to let fly with arrows of anger and frustration.

Slowly she stepped away from him and unzipped her own jacket. "I'd like to get out of these damp clothes, but once I take them off, I'll need to find a way to get warm." In a move perfected by women over hundreds of years, she glanced up at him through her lashes. "Would you be willing to help with that?"

The move was still effective. His cock surged to full arousal mode. He couldn't agree fast enough. "I'll lay out the sleeping bags." Now would be the time to tell her that they didn't need to worry about condoms and could take it all the way if they wanted to.

But he decided against saying that. Maybe her method would allow him to satisfy his body—and hers—on a superficial, purely sexual level. Maybe he wouldn't totally lose himself in the experience and forget that they were completely wrong for each other.

"I thought you might be willing to consider my compromise." She peeled off the jacket to reveal a white spandex tank top. Her taut nipples pushed against the stretchy material.

Lust roared through him, and he wondered if he'd be able to keep this encounter superficial, after all. She wasn't even naked yet, and already he was shaking.

"Sleeping bags," she said gently.

He swallowed. "Right." Somehow he managed to turn away from her and head for his backpack. His hands trembled as he pulled out both sleeping bags. He could hear her taking off her clothes, but he dared not look or he'd never get the makeshift bed prepared.

Still, her movements stirred the air and brought him her tantalizing scent. In this cave there was no escape from the temptation of Abby. If he'd imagined he could sleep here all night and not go to her, he'd been delusional.

He wasn't usually clumsy, but he had a hell of a time opening up the sleeping bags and laying one on top of the other. He could still feel the stone underneath and wished they'd brought air mattresses, but it was a little late for that now.

"Are you ready for me?"

She had no idea how ready he was. He felt as if he had a rolling pin tucked between his thighs. He gave the top sleeping bag another quick tug and turned, still crouched down next to the makeshift bed.

Whoa, what an angle. His glance traveled from her bare feet, complete with toenails painted mint green, up her slender calves to her creamy thighs, and . . . his brain stalled. He'd assumed she was a natural redhead, but now he knew for sure.

That russet triangle covered all the secrets he longed to know about Abby. He allowed his attention to linger there. To his great joy, he discovered that the apex of that downy triangle was a slightly darker red, obviously moistened by the same desire that seared him with its heat.

Heart beating fast, he lifted his gaze higher, sliding it over her flat belly and upward. The plump underside of her breasts beckoned him to touch, to fondle, and finally to capture each dusky nipple in his mouth.

"You're . . . beautiful," he said. In fact, no woman had ever looked more beautiful to him, and that should have set off alarms in his head. But his natural caution seemed to have left the building—or in this case, the cave.

Pink tinged her cheeks, and as he noticed that, he also saw that she'd let her hair down. It settled over her shoulders, and even in the dim light from the electric lantern, it provided a glorious blaze of color.

Reaching up, he offered his hand to guide her down to the only bed he could provide. If he'd had silks and goose down at his disposal, he would have lavished them on her.

Instead he had two sleeping bags that were known for their ease of transport and their thermal capabilities. He smiled at that last part. He had a feeling neither of them would have to worry about being cold tonight.

Placing her hand in his, she winced as she dropped to her knees on the sleeping bags spread on the floor of the cave.

"I wish they were softer," he murmured.

"It's not the bed. It's my poor muscles. They're wrecked."

How could he have forgotten? Apparently the wonders of her naked body had distracted him from the pain in that beautiful body. She needed his help to ease her suffering, and then ... then he could ease her more primitive ache.

With great effort he tamed the lust seething in his veins. "Lie on your stomach," he said. "Let me see what I can do."

"Thank you. Here's some lotion I brought in my pack." She handed him a slender tube before stretching out on the sleeping bags and pillowing her head on her arms.

"Don't thank me yet. I'm not trained in this." He unscrewed the cap on the lotion and squirted some into his hand.

"Just imagine I'm a glob of Play-Doh."

"A glob of *what?*"

"Play-Doh. Don't tell me you never had any as a kid."

"Nope." He straddled her hips and rubbed the lotion into both hands before leaning down to work on her back muscles.

"Then you were deprived." She moaned softly as he began to knead the muscles beneath her shoulder blades.

The moan prodded his chained libido to break free. He wanted to make her moan for a different reason. "I take it Play-Doh is some sort of modeling clay for kids."

"Exactly. Ah, that feels good, Roarke. Right there. Deeper ... *mmm.*"

"If you want me to finish this, you'll have to curtail the commentary. It sounds like a woman responding to sex."

"Right. So if you didn't have Play-Doh, what did you have?"

"Marble."

"Marbles? That's not the same kind of thing. Oh, God, you hit the right spot. That feels so . . . *whoops*. Sorry. No commentary. Sorry."

"Much appreciated." He battled his urges as he worked his way down her spine to the small of her back, which brought him close to the cutest fanny he'd ever had the privilege of touching. "Are your glutes sore?"

"Not especially."

"Too bad. I wanted to massage them."

Her body shook as she laughed. "Maybe later. Tell me about playing with marbles."

"Not marbles. Marble, singular. My brother and I were allowed to sculpt in marble when we were kids."

"Oh." She sighed in apparent contentment as he started massaging her thighs. "That's a step up from sculpting in Play-Doh."

"I wasn't very good at it. I ruined a lot of marble." He kneaded the backs of her thighs and tried to ignore the way her body quivered in response. Her scent called to him, but he'd promised to give her a massage, and he would by damn go all the way to her toes.

"They should have given you Play-Doh instead." Abby sighed again. "But maybe you didn't need it. You're very good at this."

"You think so?" Without quite realizing how it had happened, he'd begun stroking her inner thighs.

She must have liked having him do that, because she parted them just enough to give him greater access. But he wasn't absolutely sure what she wanted. She'd asked for a massage, and he wasn't finished with that. He hadn't massaged her calves yet, or her feet.

Still, that fragrant place kept calling to him, and he began to explore, sliding his fingers between her silky thighs. Ah, there, right there. She was wet and ready for him, whether she wanted to admit that or not. And if he went a little farther . . .

She groaned.

"Abby." He teased her with feathery strokes. "Tell me what you want."

"Please, Roarke." She lifted her hips just enough to give him all the room he needed. "Please."

He didn't have to be asked twice. Pushing deep with his two middle fingers, he stroked her clit with his forefinger. She pushed back against the pressure of his hand, her breath coming in quick little gasps.

As he stroked her, she moved in time with his rhythm. He could sense her reaching for what she needed, and he increased the pace. She came very quickly, her cries echoing in the small cave as moisture spilled over his fingers.

He kept them deep inside, absorbing her spasms, continuing to stroke her, making the sensation last. And when she finally sank down onto the sleeping bags, quivering and sighing, he slowly withdrew his hand.

Bracing himself on his forearms and his knees, he stretched out and settled lightly over her, giving her cover and protection. He kissed the back of her neck and her bare shoulder, but he resisted the urge to nip her soft skin.

He was flirting with disaster lying with her like this. If she rose to her hands and knees and he did the same, they would be one unzipped fly away from a werewolf binding. But he wouldn't allow that to happen.

He would not lose his head over this woman, even

though her scent filled him with longing. He would enjoy her, yes. Total denial had proved to be impossible.

Slowly he raised his hand to his mouth and tasted her sweetness as visions of thrusting into her made his cock throb and his balls ache. He would have to be very, very careful.

Chapter 11

So good. Abby lay in a dazed and boneless heap, congratulating herself on a most excellent idea. Endorphins surged through her body and muted the pain from the day's hike. Roarke had given her pleasure and now he was keeping her relaxed muscles warm by resting lightly against her.

He must be supporting himself on his knees and forearms, because his full weight would be too much for her to handle, but this was nice, more than nice. She felt cared for, especially when he combed her hair aside to kiss the nape of her neck and the curve of her shoulder. When he began to gently nibble, she became aware of several things.

First of all, she wasn't quite as satisfied as she'd thought. She'd be more than happy to go another round, although that wouldn't be very sporting of her. Technically it was Roarke's turn.

That brought her to the second item demanding her attention. Roarke's package rested lightly, but temptingly, between her thighs. As she knew from the blackmail pictures she'd taken in the woods, he was possessed of a very large package.

She'd promised to unwrap it for him, which she was more than willing to do. But now that his solid length was nestled against her, she'd become greedy. She wanted the full experience that package could provide, and she couldn't have it.

Why, oh why, hadn't she tossed some condoms in her backpack? They wouldn't have weighed much. In fact, ounce-for-ounce, they'd have delivered far more pleasure than the energy bar she'd tucked in a side pocket.

Roarke settled more firmly between her thighs as he nuzzled a spot behind her ear.

Instinctively, she shifted her weight to her knees and lifted her hips to accommodate him.

Drawing in a sharp breath, he slowly fit himself tight against her, but the soft denim of his jeans kept her from the connection she really wanted. Then he rocked forward, nudging the spot that was already wet and ready for him. She moaned in frustration.

His breathing quickened. Swearing softly, he nipped her earlobe. Then he pushed forward again, more insistently this time, and the crease of his fly rubbed in an erotic rhythm that made her gasp with pleasure.

Bracing herself on her forearms, she answered his rhythm as heat pulsed in her veins. "Roarke . . . I want . . ."

"I know." Sliding a hand beneath her, he tunneled his fingers through her damp curls.

No, he didn't know. She wanted more than an orgasm. She wanted him to remove the denim barrier to ecstasy and connect with her the way a man and woman were designed to do. But that was irresponsible and crazy, so she'd take what she could get.

Stroking her with a sure touch, he rocked against her,

his jeans-clad thighs brushing her backside. "You're killing me, Abby," he said in a low, lust-roughened voice.

She was too far gone to respond. Instead she uttered a soft cry as the first wave of her climax rolled through her. Then her world erupted in an orgasmic flow of light and heat that left her breathless with its power.

If he could give her this much pleasure with a mere touch, maybe she wouldn't survive a full dose of Roarke's loving. But she'd like to try. As she trembled in his strong grip, she longed for what she could not have.

Gradually her breathing steadied, but Roarke's had not. She vowed to make good on her promise and give him some relief from what had to be incredible frustration after providing her with two climaxes.

She took a shaky breath. "Roarke, I—"

"It's okay." Slowly he released her and the air stirred as he moved away. "I need to . . . I need to leave for a little bit."

"Leave?" She rolled to her back and sat up. "But it's pouring out there."

"Doesn't matter." He stood on the far side of the cave, his back to her as he pulled off his hiking boots. Next he removed his jacket, and then his shirt. He was stripping down.

Her chest grew tight. Sometimes she forgot who and what he was, but it appeared she was about to get a vivid reminder. "Are you going to shift?"

"Not here."

Her immediate tension eased a little. Capturing it on film was one thing. Watching from a few feet away was a whole other deal.

She swallowed. "But why? I thought that you would want me to . . ." She wasn't sure how to put it into words without embarrassing herself. In some ways they knew each other very well, but in others, not at all.

He kept his back to her as he shoved his jeans and briefs down. "I did. I still do. But it wouldn't be wise right now. I'm thinking with my dick."

"Oh." Now that he'd mentioned it, she wouldn't mind a glimpse of that part of his anatomy. She calculated the chances of that and decided they were pretty good considering he'd have to turn in her direction in order to walk out of the cave.

"A quick run in the rain will cool me down." He turned.

"Stay." It was the only word that her lust-crazed brain could come up with once she'd seen what she'd be missing if he left. The camera hadn't done him justice. The light from the electric lantern revealed a magnificently erect penis surrounded by dark blond hair, and his balls, swollen and tight with excitement, begged for her touch.

He glanced at her, regret in his green eyes. His powerful chest, sprinkled with the same shade of dark blond hair surrounding his cock, heaved in a tortured sigh. "It would be a mistake." Then he took his gorgeous body out of the circle of light from the lantern.

"No, it wouldn't!" she called after him, but he didn't answer. The bush covering the cave entrance rustled, indicating he'd stepped outside. Grabbing up a sleeping bag, Abby wrapped herself in it as she hurried after him. "Roarke, this is silly! Come back!"

But he was gone, using the cold rain, she supposed, as a natural version of a cold shower. She could use one, too, after getting a good look at Roarke's equipment, which she wouldn't be touching anytime soon.

Tossing down the sleeping bag, she shoved past wet branches and gasped as the cold rain struck her heated skin. "Roarke?" She pushed her hair out of her face and peered into the darkness.

Still no answer. She tried to listen for him as rain

pelted her head and streamed in rivulets down her body. She shivered in the cold. Something rustled to her left, and she turned in that direction.

A shadowy form rose from the forest floor about twenty feet away. Her throat constricted and her heart thundered as she stared at the shadow. Was it man or beast? When it wheeled and loped away through the trees, she knew.

She stood there a moment longer in hopes the cold rain would drum some sense into her. What in the name of heaven was she thinking, getting sexually involved, on any level, with a creature that could be a man one minute and a wolf the next? Sure, he had a helluva johnson, but she was a sensible adult woman who could look beyond that kind of eye candy.

Her mission in coming out here had nothing to do with sex, and she needed to remember that. She was here because she wanted to confirm Grandpa Earl's Bigfoot sighting. Period. End of story. Werewolf sex hadn't been part of the bargain.

She'd allowed Roarke's personal magnetism to cloud her judgment, but she wouldn't let that happen again. Yes, she'd been treated to a couple of really nice orgasms without returning the favor, but that was his problem. He'd left. And turned into a wolf.

If he preferred running around on all fours in the rain to sitting in a cozy cave with her, that was his choice, but she had other plans. Food sounded good right now, along with a rubdown with her camp towel and putting on dry clothes. Moving the branches covering the entrance, she ducked back inside.

Roarke kept watch until Abby went back inside the cave. Although he didn't sense any danger nearby, he wasn't about to run off and leave her standing naked and vulnerable in the rain. Naked and beautiful, too.

No wonder he'd nearly forgotten himself back in the cave. He'd gazed with longing as rain had slipped lovingly over her shoulders, her taut nipples, and her supple thighs. Raindrops traced paths he longed to follow with his tongue. He didn't dare, not now that he understood the power of this attraction to ruin both their lives.

He'd been close to unzipping his jeans and taking her. Too damned close. Realizing that had scared him enough to push him out of the cave before he acted on that impulse. He'd bought into her concept that they each needed to blow off some sexual steam, and maybe that had worked for her.

It wouldn't work for him. She would have been more than willing to provide him with a release in a similar way, but it wouldn't be enough, and now he knew that. Better to stay away from sex completely.

Once Abby was safely in the cave, Roarke took off at a run. How he loved the feel of his wolf muscles stretching and contracting! His large paws sent pine needles flying and filled the air with the sharp tang of evergreens.

The run would calm his unruly libido, but that's about all he'd accomplish loping around the forest. They were too far from the Bigfoot pair to make that journey. He'd have to leave Abby alone for a good part of the night, and he wasn't willing to do that.

She would probably be fine, but he couldn't guarantee that, and besides, he'd promised to be back soon. So he traveled in a circle, always staying within a ten-minute radius of the cave entrance.

The rain drenching his coat kept the other creatures inside nests and burrows for the night, although a werewolf in the forest tended to make that happen, too. That meant the only sounds were those of his paws hitting the forest floor and the steady pounding of the rain against the leaves.

Then he heard a noise that had nothing to do with the forest, and everything to do with humans. Someone had started playing "Oh! Susanna" on a harmonica. And not well, either.

Roarke paused and faced the direction of the sound, wincing at more than one sour note. He was upwind of the harmonica player, which was why he hadn't caught the scent of another human in the area. Damn. As if he didn't have enough problems.

He'd have to check this out and then notify Abby that they weren't alone. With luck it was a hiker and not a Bigfoot enthusiast. Either way, Roarke would have to be more vigilant and make sure he and Abby weren't followed.

Moving silently through the trees toward the sound of the harmonica, Roarke decided that a bad harmonica player was better than someone who made no noise and could go undetected, especially if they were downwind. Roarke didn't like to be taken by surprise.

Finally he could see the tent sitting in a small clearing. Dome-shaped and glowing from a lantern inside, it looked like a giant stoplight, except for the peace sign created with duct tape that decorated the back panel. Whoever owned the tent wasn't going for camouflage.

Then Roarke remembered reading a gonzo article claiming that Bigfoot was naturally curious and liked bright colors and shiny things, sort of a Bigfoot-as-packrat theory. It wasn't true, but a few Bigfoot hunters had latched on to the idea because it gave them another technique for making contact.

Roarke wanted to be wrong in the worst way, but he was afraid he'd just found someone from the Bigfoot fringe element. Keeping well hidden by the trees, he circled around to the front of the tent. The front flap was propped up to serve as a canopy, and the harmonica player sat cross-legged in the doorway.

He smelled musty, as if he might still believe in storing his clothes in mothballs. Roarke took note of that so that if the guy popped up on his sensory radar again, Roarke would know who he was dealing with.

Next he made a visual check. The camper looked to be about Roarke's age, but there the resemblance stopped. Well, there was zero resemblance in Roarke's current state, but as a human Roarke was taller, in better shape, and had better eyesight. This guy obviously needed his black-framed glasses or he wouldn't have them on out here in the woods.

Roarke wondered if his outfit was designed to attract Bigfoot, too. The florescent orange sweat suit made him look like a traffic cone and clashed in a spectacular fashion with the red tent. Good thing Bigfoot was colorblind. Roarke wished he could be, at least for the next five minutes.

The guy deserved props for nerve, though. Not everyone would hike into the woods alone and deliberately try to attract a creature reputed to be nearly ten feet tall and weigh close to five hundred pounds. Roarke wondered what the harmonica player planned to do if he actually attracted a Sasquatch into his camp.

He wouldn't, of course. The creatures were terminally shy besides being colorblind. If Roarke were looking for a good match in the world of nature, he'd compare the Sasquatch to a tarantula—big, hairy, and scary, but with poor eyesight and a tendency to flee rather than fight.

As Roarke watched from the shadows, the guy tapped his harmonica on his sleeve and brought it back to his mouth. When he launched into a godawful rendition of "Amazing Grace," Roarke stifled an urge to howl in protest.

Enough. He'd ID'd the interloper and recorded his

scent. If Roarke and Abby were unlucky enough to cross paths with him, Roarke would know what he was up against and find a way to send the guy off in a different direction. Melting into the shadows, Roarke headed for the cave.

Partway there, he caught the scent of food warming. Abby must have decided to fix dinner. Good. They could occupy themselves with eating and cleaning up. He'd tell her about the harmonica player, and then they could both go to bed. Separately.

But the closer he came to the cave, the less he believed in that scenario. Food wasn't the only thing he could smell. Apparently Abby's special aroma had become firmly seated in the pleasure center of his brain. One whiff and he was a moth to flame.

By the time he reached the spot where he'd shifted earlier, he'd started to rationalize. He'd been hiking all day and now he'd just had a good run, so logically he'd be tired tonight. If he had sex with Abby, no doubt he'd conk out immediately afterward. No special significance, no big deal, just good hot sex.

But he needed the full program to be completely satisfied. He'd have to explain to her why they could do that without a condom, but that might not be difficult. So they'd have sex once and both fall asleep right after. It sounded like a reasonable plan as he lay on the wet ground and moved through his shift.

Moments later he stood and brushed away the pine needles clinging to his skin. The rain continued to come down, and it washed away streaks of mud on his arms and legs. He scrubbed his hands through his wet hair, working out any leaves tangled there.

As he plucked a leaf from his pubic hair, he was forced to acknowledge that his interest in having sex with Abby was already evident. But fortunately he wouldn't walk in quite as aroused as when he'd walked out. The run had worked temporarily.

Her scent drifted out to him from the cave, and his penis twitched in response. He decided at that moment that dinner could wait a while. Sex first, then food. After that, they'd be sated from both activities and they'd fall asleep immediately. It sounded like the perfect ending to the evening.

His goal clearly in mind, he held back the branches of the bush covering the opening and called out to her. "Abby, I'm back."

"Good. Don't fall over your clothes. I found some dry ones in your pack and put them right by the entrance for you."

"Thanks." That didn't fit in with his plan, but he could carry them into the cave and put them on later before they ate dinner.

"Be sure to get dressed before you come in here, Roarke."

"Why?" He picked up the bundle of clothes he found neatly stacked and waiting for him.

"Because we're both staying dressed from now on. Having sex is a complication neither of us needs, and you obviously realized it earlier."

"No, I just wanted to dial it back some." He continued walking into the cave.

She glanced up from the pot she was stirring and frowned at him. "I've decided to dial it back completely. So put those on, please."

She'd braided her wet hair into a single strand hanging down her back, which made her look prim and almost virginal. He took that as a challenge.

"I mean it, Roarke." She tapped the spoon on the side of the pot and laid it on a metal plate beside the camp stove.

"I'm sure you do." He studied her outfit—green knit shirt revealing the unmistakable outline of a bra, black Lycra pants, probably with panties underneath. At least her feet were bare, but he had some undressing to do before he could institute his plan of action.

She stood and folded her arms. "I realize that in a sense, I owe you a . . ."

He smiled. "In a sense, I suppose you do."

She glanced at his thickening penis and looked away again, her cheeks flushed. "But we're very different, Roarke."

"I should hope so. That's why things fit so beautifully."

"You know what I mean. We're from completely different worlds. Better to leave well enough alone."

"You're the one who blackmailed me into bringing you along on this trip, Abby."

She focused on the cave wall rather than look at him. "For Grandpa Earl's sake."

"Then how about the fact you're also the one who suggested not so long ago that we could fool around and release some of our pent-up sexual energy?"

She blew out a breath and gazed up at the ceiling of the cave. "I made a mistake, okay? I now realize that there's too much temptation to throw caution to the wind. Without any condoms, we're taking a huge chance that we'll get carried away and I know neither of us wants to deal with that consequence."

"What if there was no consequence?"

Her startled blue gaze met his. "You found a box of condoms in the woods?"

That made him laugh. "No." He dropped the clothes to the floor of the cave. "There's something I didn't explain about werewolves. We can't impregnate anyone until we find our mate and pledge ourselves for life. It's a great system."

She rolled her eyes. "Oh, please. That story's even worse than the old standby of having mumps as a kid. I know guys will go to great lengths to get out of wearing a little raincoat, but I thought you'd be different, considering the stakes."

"You don't believe me." He'd hoped after all they'd shared, she would. "Look, I can understand your skepticism, but I'm telling you the truth."

"Sorry, Professor Wallace, but if what you say is true, you would have told me when I first brought up the issue of condoms. You neglected to do that, so ipso facto, you're making this up as you go along."

"I am not! I thought we needed to have some sort of braking system on our relationship, and that was a good one to use."

She regarded him with narrowed eyes. "So you normally go around having condom-free sex, do you?"

He had a feeling he'd said the wrong thing. "Only with other werewolves when we're both in human form. Obviously I can't explain this to a woman without revealing I'm a werewolf, so I use a condom with humans. You would be an exception to that rule because you know I'm Were."

She stepped back and held up both hands. "Spare me from being the one exception! Condoms serve another purpose besides birth control. If you've had lots of free love with your werewolf girlfriends, bully for you, but I'd rather not participate in that boinkfest, thank you very much."

"I haven't had *lots*." He was getting testy from sexual frustration combined with a need for food. "And werewolves are resistant to disease, if that's what you're worried about."

"How convenient to be disease-resistant as you put notches in your belt."

"Notches in my— Damn it, Abby, I'm not that kind of guy!"

"Then you would have leveled with me in the beginning, wouldn't you? Look, you might as well get dressed, because I don't buy your story and we're not having sex. You'll have to settle for reconstituted beef stew."

"Whatever happened to the concept of me teaching you about werewolves?"

"Let's just say that you have a credibility problem. When you're dressed, I'll dish the stew."

He stared at her. The set of her jaw and the glint in her eyes told him that she'd dug in her heels and wasn't going to budge. He wasn't giving up, but he might as well back off for the time being. So they could have dinner, and then sex. That could work, too.

Chapter 12

While Roarke pulled on his clothes, Abby ladled stew into two tin bowls. Thank God that hikers were always famished when they finally ate a meal, because there was no way a reconstituted stew could compare to something simmered on the stove for hours and served straight from the pot it was cooked in. At this point she would have eaten crackers and peanut butter if that's all they had.

But thanks to Roarke hauling the packages of dried food, they had something more interesting than crackers and peanut butter. She reminded herself of his willingness to carry most of their supplies and gave him a larger portion of the stew. Although she didn't believe a word of his werewolves-don't-need-condoms story, he was still the lynchpin in the Sasquatch operation and she needed him energized and healthy.

She just wished he hadn't insulted her intelligence with that ridiculous story. He might be willing to play Russian roulette with his future, but she'd worked too hard to establish herself as a responsible adult who was a credit to her family and her community. Becoming pregnant by accident would be bad enough. Becoming pregnant with a werewolf's baby had repercussions that extended far beyond the average problem scenario, and she had no intention of going there.

Decently attired in a black T-shirt and gray sweats, Roarke approached the camp stove. "Need any help?"

She glanced at him and revised her opinion of *decently attired.* He was clothed, but the T-shirt was a little snug and the soft material of the sweats emphasized the generosity of his endowments. "Thanks, but everything's under control."

"I'll bet."

"Count on it." She handed him a tin bowl full of hot stew and a spoon. No randy werewolf was going to screw up her life. "I would offer you a glass of the house red to go with this, but the wine cellar seems to be empty."

"Damn shame." He raised the bowl and took an appreciative sniff. "A good red would be the finishing touch."

A good red would finish her off, that was for sure. She didn't believe his story concerning werewolf safe sex, but she wanted to. The more he moved gracefully around the cave, the more she fantasized about what sex would be like with a man so powerfully athletic.

Picking up her own bowl, she lowered herself into a cross-legged position on the stone floor of the cave. The cool surface helped soothe the heat building inside her, despite her vow to remain celibate from this moment on.

Roarke sat across from her in one fluid movement that made her mouth go dry. Why did he have to be so damned sexy? Why did he have to sit cross-legged like that, which caused the fleece of his sweats to outline the very part of him she was trying to ignore?

He took a spoonful of his stew and closed his eyes. *"Mmm."*

She had to look away. His open appreciation of the food reminded her of the way he'd openly appreciated her response when he'd stroked her to a shattering climax. Twice. Now he'd come up with a story about sperm that knew when to swim upstream and when to stay in the tank.

He rested his spoon against the side of the bowl. "Ever read Margaret Mead's studies of the Trobriand Islanders?"

She glanced at him. "Can't say that I have."

"Turns out those people have something in common with werewolves." He took another mouthful of stew.

"Is that so?" She started eating her stew and fought against the potent combination of virility and intelligence that was Roarke Wallace. If he couldn't seduce her with the first quality, he wasn't shy about employing the second.

"The society doesn't curtail sexual behavior among young people, but they don't use any physical method of birth control. From the time they hit puberty, they're allowed as much sexual exploration as they want."

She put down her spoon. "Let me guess. Nobody gets pregnant."

"That's exactly right." He pointed his spoon at her. "Can you guess why?"

"They're all werewolves?"

"Not to my knowledge, but I should probably check into that to be sure. According to Margaret Mead, the girls don't get pregnant because it would be socially unacceptable to do that until they're married. They can control conception mentally."

Abby laughed. "Your justification gets stranger every minute. Now you're telling me that you have some kind of mind control over your sperm?"

"Yes."

"How does that work, exactly? Do you call a meeting prior to a sexual event and remind them to hold tight?"

"Abby, it's far more sophisticated than—"

"And I suppose you must have to hold another meeting when you want to turn those little suckers loose. Shoot off a starting gun, maybe, so they'll know the race to the egg is officially on."

"Go ahead and make fun of it, but no werewolf in history has ever dealt with a paternity issue."

She almost choked on her stew. "Now *there's* a statement that I can fact-check. The minute I get in range, I'm going to fire up my BlackBerry and Google *werewolf paternity cases.* I'm going to take a wild guess that I won't find any, which, amazingly, happens to support your case."

"What reason would I have to lie about this?"

She scooped up the last of her stew and paused before putting the spoon in her mouth. "Oh, gee, let me think. Because you neglected to bring condoms on this trip and you belatedly realized you'd like to get in my pants?"

"Okay, don't believe me." He shrugged. "You're probably right that we shouldn't have sex."

"I am right."

"Besides, it could turn out to be bad sex, and how awkward would that be? We'd still have to finish this Sasquatch project and hang out with each other while knowing we'd had bad sex. Better to have no sex than bad sex, don't you think?"

She should know better than to debate anything with a man who obviously had an IQ that was off the charts. "I'll make this one comment, and then I'll suggest a new topic of conversation."

"Okay." He gazed at her with obvious amusement.

"Damn it, we wouldn't have bad sex, Roarke, and you

know it. You're just trying to get a rise out of me and make me want to prove that sex between us would be exceptional. Which it would be."

His green eyes gleamed with triumph. "You think so?"

"I know so."

"Yet you're willing to give it up because you doubt what I've told you. You once admitted that you know nothing about werewolves and want to learn, but now when I tell you something significant, you refuse to believe it's true."

Electricity hummed through her body and she had the urge to lean toward him. She imagined that if she did, she'd hear the buzzing sound of connections made and the snap of sparks generated. He was part magician, and she was in danger of falling under his spell.

"As promised, I'm introducing a new topic," she said. "How was your run through the woods?"

"You really don't want to talk about sex anymore?"

"No."

He gazed into her eyes. "Abby, you're right. You and I couldn't have bad sex. It would be very, very good. Let's try it."

"No!" She put her hands over her ears. "Women are ruined every day by sweet-talking men. You may be a werewolf some of the time, but mostly you're a guy blessed with the kind of body that makes women weep with longing. And I'm not going to fall victim to—"

"Weep with longing? Really?" He looked quite pleased about that comment. "Do you?"

"Not so you'd notice. I have my pride."

"But if we were Trobriand Islanders . . ."

"All right, Roarke. If we were Trobriand Islanders, you could screw my brains out. Happy, now?"

"No, because we're in a cave outside of Portland, which leaves me with nothing to do."

"Not quite." She grinned at him. "We could play Hangman."

After five games, Roarke was down three-two and had a growing respect for Abby's word skills. His only excuse for losing involved his preoccupation with Abby's breasts. And her mouth, and the nape of her neck, and her cute butt. And always, always, her special scent.

At times he'd catch her looking at him with undisguised lust in her eyes, and he'd imagine that he was wearing her down. She might deny that she wanted him, but the aroma of arousal swirled in the air, giving her away.

Then, just as he'd begin to think he had a chance, her jaw would firm and her eyes would flash, and he'd despair that she'd never get naked with him again. Sadly, she had nothing to fear, but he hadn't told her that in the beginning, and now she thought he was playing her for a fool.

He wouldn't ever do that. And he wanted her so desperately that he could taste it, and he could certainly smell it. Finally he decided to play dirty and make her think about sex whether she cared to or not. She wouldn't want to guess the word *orgasm*, but unless she did, she'd lose the next game.

When she guessed the *a*, he had a feeling she knew what he'd chosen. The *o* pretty much clinched it.

She sent him a reproachful glance. "No fair."

"All's fair in sex and war."

"You're misquoting. It's 'All's fair in love and war.'"

"Yeah, I know. I was trying to be cute."

She faced him, her blue eyes accusing. "That's the thing about you, Roarke. You twist things around to suit you, and then you expect me to trust what you tell me just because you say so."

So much for being cute. He had an uphill battle and he wasn't doing himself any favors, apparently. He decided on a more direct approach.

"Abby, if I made you pregnant, our baby might inherit my ability to shift. Because of that possibility, not to mention my duties as the father of our child, we'd be tied together for years even though we'd made no commitment to each other. Pregnancy without commitment violates Were law and it's the very reason casual sex with a Were can't result in pregnancy. It's a survival mechanism."

She took a deep breath. "Let's finish this round." She proceeded to guess the other letters and won the round. The word chalked on the wall in front of them blazed with unrealized potential.

Roarke took a chance and ran a finger lightly up and down her arm. It was the first time he'd touched her since coming back into the cave after his run. "I'm telling you the truth, Abby."

She continued to face the wall where they'd been creating their Hangman games, but a slight tremble revealed that his touch had affected her. "You're a complicated man, Roarke. Or I should say, a complicated *being*." She turned to him. "You're not exactly a man, are you?"

"I am at this moment. I'm a man who desperately wants to make love with you."

Heat flashed in her blue eyes. "I'm not exactly immune to you, either, as you well know. But you came into town prepared to destroy my grandfather's confidence in his sighting, even though you knew it was legitimate. You cherry-pick the information you give me about werewolves. The fact is, you don't completely trust me, so why should I trust you?"

He sighed. "That's a fair question." He continued

softly stroking her arm, unwilling to break that fragile connection. "Werewolves don't trust easily. We're taught to be suspicious of humans, and loyalty to the pack supersedes every consideration. Because we rise and fall together, that applies to any pack."

"Including the Gentrys." She said the name with distaste.

"Yes. The Dooleys' presence has threatened the Gentrys with discovery from day one. There's the overlook that provides an excellent view of their property, and then there's been the preoccupation with Bigfoot. Earl's sighting had the potential to destroy all hope of privacy for the Gentry pack and put them in grave danger of being exposed as werewolves."

"I have a hard time working up any sympathy for them. They have money. They could move."

"True, but once a werewolf family settles on a property, they truly take possession of it in the deepest sense. Uprooting a pack causes great distress. That's why they've put their efforts into obtaining Dooley land."

"By making Grandpa Earl out to be a doddering old fool."

Roarke cleared his throat. "Sorry, but yes. And although I may disagree with their methods, I'm pledged to help as best I can. If the Gentrys are exposed, there will be a domino effect throughout the packs in North America, and eventually throughout the world."

"So my grandfather, who's never in his life intended to harm anyone or anything, unknowingly put every werewolf at risk?"

Roarke brushed her cheek with his thumb. "That pretty much sums it up."

"Let me ask you again: Is he in any danger?"

"And let me say it again. He's not in danger because

he has no idea werewolves exist. In this case, there's safety in ignorance."

"But I know they exist."

He held her gaze. "As I've mentioned before, I will protect you with my life."

"And as I've said before, that's impossible."

He smiled and dared to cup her face in both hands. "You really don't believe a thing I say, do you?"

Her voice softened. "I want to, Roarke."

Hope stirred within him. "You do?"

"Why wouldn't I? Believing you would mean I could feel safe."

"That's all you want? A feeling of safety?"

"Well, not *all.*"

Excitement thrummed in his veins. She was yielding. "Then believe me, Abby. Believe *in* me. Know that I would never cause you harm."

She smiled, and her eyes spoke of surrender. "You're a very persuasive guy, Professor Wallace."

Slowly he drew nearer until his lips were almost touching hers. "Welcome to the Trobriand Islands," he murmured. Then he kissed her.

She caught fire instantly, grasping his head in both hands and deepening the kiss. He wound both arms around her and hauled her into his lap. Wasting no time, she positioned her knees on either side of his hips and neatly aligned all her significant parts with his.

He groaned as she wiggled closer and rubbed against his cock. In response, it strained to be released from bondage. No doubt they could both come without removing a stitch of clothing. Rocking against each other would do the trick. But he wasn't about to settle for that, especially when so little material separated them.

Foreplay had its place, but this wasn't it. She welcomed the thrust of his tongue with a whimper that told him exactly what she wanted from him. And he was only too happy to comply.

When he began peeling down her stretchy Lycra pants and her underwear, she stretched out her leg and helped him with the process. After he'd worked one leg free, he didn't worry about the rest of the undressing routine. He had what he needed—direct access.

Sliding his arm under her bottom, he urged her to lift up so he could shove down the elastic waist of both his sweats and his briefs. His erect cock stood at attention, ready to seek her heat.

Cupping her bottom in both hands, he guided her into position and then ... *ahh*. Heavenly contact. Grasping her hips, he kept the descent gradual so he could savor her slick, tight welcome, the scent of her arousal filling his nostrils, and her low moan of pleasure filling his ears. A moment so long anticipated shouldn't be rushed.

And she felt so damned right to him. He should be worried about that, because she wasn't right for him at all. But this glorious sensation of sliding toward her womb was too wonderful for him to be worried about anything. His heart beat joyously, flooding him with a sense of homecoming. Unwarranted, obviously, but he would enjoy now and question later.

When her thighs rested on his and she'd taken all of him, when they were as intimately joined as any two creatures could be, he lifted his lips from hers and drew back to look into her eyes. He knew what he wanted to see there, but he might be asking for too much.

She gazed back at him, her eyes dark with sexual excitement. He'd expected that, but his heart filled with joy when he saw more than excitement in those blue depths. He saw trust.

If that trust had been missing, they still would have had sex. He wasn't that noble. But if he'd won her on sexual magnetism alone, he would have felt more like a seducer than a lover.

Her soft breath caressed his face, and he closed his eyes to better enjoy being surrounded by her body and her scent.

"You look happy," she murmured.

He opened his eyes. "I can't imagine being happier."

"Oh, I can." Rising up a fraction, she settled back down while holding his gaze. Then she tightened around him.

The easy friction and brief squeeze sent shock waves through his system. "I stand corrected." He stroked her hips and thighs. "You can do that again if you want."

"Oh, I want." Bracing her hands on his shoulders, she initiated a slow rhythm, all the while keeping her attention on his face. "Do you like that?"

"You have no idea how much." His hands loosely bracketed her hips because he loved feeling her move beneath his fingertips, but he didn't want to control those movements. He wanted her to direct the action. He suspected when she was finished with this directing job, he'd want to give her an Oscar for it.

"How about this?" Instead of pumping up and down, she rotated her pelvis.

It was a wonder his eyes didn't roll back in his head. They might have except he was concentrating on watching her eyes, which had become heavy-lidded with banked passion. Under her shirt, her breasts quivered with her rapid breathing.

He wanted to see. "Lift up your arms." When she complied, he pulled her shirt over her head and tossed it away. One flick of his fingers unhooked the back fastening of her bra, and that was quickly gone, too.

"Your turn."

He put his arms up and she yanked off his T-shirt. Then she flattened her palms against his chest. He realized at that moment that although he'd touched her quite a bit, she hadn't spent much time touching him. And he liked the way she touched him.

Continuing to gently rotate her hips, she massaged his pecs, and the combination was more erotic than he ever would have believed. When she paused to pinch his nipples, he clenched his jaw against the sudden urge to come.

"My turn." His voice sounded strained, not at all resembling the smooth talker that he liked to think he was, especially in situations like this.

"Be my guest." Clutching his shoulders, she went back to the easy pumping action that made her breasts quiver.

He cradled one in each large hand and gripped firmly enough to hold them still while he brushed his thumbs over her tight nipples.

"Mmm." Easing down so that she took him in right up to the hilt, she closed her eyes and let her head roll back. Then she tightened her pelvic muscles again, squeezing his cock in a delicious, repetitive motion.

He groaned. "That's going to make me come."

"I know." She lifted her head to gaze at him. Her lips were parted and her breathing was ragged. "Me, too. But before I do, I'm ready for some speed."

His heartbeat thumped in his ears and his chest tightened in anticipation. "Go for it."

Her eyes blazed hot as she began to move faster, and faster yet, until her thighs slapped against his and the hoarse sounds of their breathing filled the cave. He struggled to hold back his climax, but she was riding him with wicked intent, massaging his aching cock from one end to the other, until . . . oh, God . . . he was losing the fight.

Coming . . . he was coming, and miracle of miracles, so was she. With a shout of triumph, she dug her fingers into his shoulders and milked him with her contractions.

They held on to each other and gasped for breath. He was convinced that leaning against her was the only thing holding him up, and vice versa. His mind spun in crazy circles of delight and he wondered if his body was shooting off sparks. He wouldn't be surprised.

He'd thought they'd be good together, but he'd underestimated. They were spectacular together. After all his pushing to get to this point, she'd taken the lead and given him the best climax of his life. Sexually, they were perfectly matched.

And he wanted more. He'd foolishly thought that once would be enough. It should have been enough, considering how tired they both were. Maybe it was enough for her.

If so, he should be a gentleman and let her go to sleep. He should be grateful for what he'd enjoyed and not expect more. He should— *She was nibbling his ear.*

That didn't seem like the action of a woman who was ready to pack it in. Then again, he didn't know how she reacted after mutual sexual satisfaction. Maybe ear-nibbling was her way of winding down.

"Roarke?" Her breath warmed the damp spot on his ear.

"Yes, Abby?"

"Could I talk you into doing this again?"

He smiled, and right on cue, his cock began to thicken. "You know, I think you might be able to."

Chapter 13

Abby credited adrenaline for her new burst of energy, but she also credited amazing sex with a man-slash-werewolf who was built like a brick house. She usually subscribed to the theory that it wasn't what a guy had but what he did with it that counted. Well, no, sometimes it was what a guy had. And Roarke, bless his heart, had it.

And bonus—apparently he didn't have to cover what he had with latex. For years Abby had tried to tell herself that condoms could be sexy. They weren't. They were necessary evils, but there wasn't a single sexy thing about them.

Discovering the delights of a bare penis, Abby felt as if she'd found a new toy and she couldn't wait to play with it again. And she would, right after she went along with Roarke's idea that they rinse off in the rain. She had to admit they were both a little sticky.

Anyway, sex with a werewolf seemed to have brought out the nature girl in her. Stepping out of the cave and into the rain where Roarke stood naked in the downpour had a primitive feel to it that matched her erotic mood. She would have appreciated a full moon with which to admire her muscular lover, but as her eyes adjusted, she managed a fairly detailed inventory of the wonders of Roarke, including his semi-erect cock nestled in hair beaded with rainwater.

When he held out his hand, she walked across the damp leaves and pine needles to join him. His palm was warm and slick with rain. His body would be, too.

He lifted his face to the pelting drops. "Isn't this great?"

"S-sure." She hadn't meant to let her teeth chatter. She'd been going for the image of a wild woman at home in the elements.

"Come here. I'll warm you up." He pulled her into his arms and their wet bodies slipped against each other as if they'd been oiled. He made a soft sound of approval and shimmied against her. "Nice."

"Sexy."

He slid both hands down her back and over her bottom in a liquid caress. "Ever been naked in the rain before?"

"No, but you have."

"Granted, but I've never been naked in the rain with a naked woman in my arms." He spread his fingers over her hip bone and then moved his hand up to the curve of her breast.

As he caressed that slippery slope and teased her nipple, she felt moisture gathering that had nothing to do with the rain. Judging from the hard ridge of his penis pressed against her belly, this rinsing-off exercise was having an effect on him, as well.

Two could play the game. Reaching down, she circled his impressive piece of equipment with her wet fingers and began to explore.

His breathing changed. "Have something in mind for that?"

"I might." She ran her thumb up and down the ridge along the sensitive underside of his cock. When she reached the tip, he sucked in a breath.

She smiled, anticipating what would come next. She was about to play with her new toy. "Any requests?"

"Just . . ." He gasped again when she rubbed her thumb across the rounded top. "Use your . . ." He swallowed. "Your imagination."

"All right. I'll see if I can lick you dry." Sinking to her knees on the wet, leaf-strewn ground, she began using her tongue like a cat would, swiping at the rain on his rock-hard penis. She worked bottom to top, all the while marveling at the length and breadth of him.

A woman lucky enough to enjoy Roarke's attentions would discover her G-spot with no problem. She might find a whole alphabet of spots, in fact. As she licked, she cupped his weighty balls and felt her womb contract with that elemental need of a woman in the presence of extreme virility.

She reminded herself that he was on temporary loan, hers to ravish for now, not to keep forever. She could make him tremble with desire, but she couldn't have more than this forest interlude. So she would make the most of it.

Taking him into her mouth at last, she ramped up her assault and wondered if she could make him lose control. His big hands cradled the back of her head, gently at first. As she sucked harder, his fingers tightened on her scalp. She tasted salt, knew he was close.

With a muttered oath he pulled away, his chest heaving as he sank to his knees in front of her. Then his mouth found hers, and before she quite knew how she got there, she was on her back in the wet leaves.

She'd thought she was ravishing him, but he'd neatly

turned the tables. His cock thrust deep with unerring accuracy, pinning her to the forest floor with a soft squishing sound. When he drew back and drove forward again, her wet body slid on the slick leaves and patches of mud beneath.

With a soft growl, he braced one hand on the ground and gripped her shoulder with the other, anchoring her in place as he pumped into her, his breath coming in quick gasps, his large body looming over her and partly blocking the rain.

But he didn't block all the rain, and she tasted it on her mouth and felt the cold drops pattering against her arms and legs as the center of her body became an inferno. She lifted her hips to join in the rhythmic dance as he pumped relentlessly, creating a friction that threatened to make her mindless with pleasure.

Her cries grew in volume as her climax bore down on her. The rain was no longer cold. The leaves and mud beneath her writhing body grew warm and welcoming. She melded into the forest floor below and Roarke's body above. When she came, her wild cry was filled with triumphant joy.

Roarke's bellow of male satisfaction was followed with one last powerful thrust before his big body shuddered and was still. Mud oozed up through the leaves and caressed Abby's hot skin. She urged Roarke down, wanting his weight pressing her deeper, connecting her to the earth in a way she'd never felt before.

It was magic, and she knew that. She also knew that without Roarke, she might never find it again.

When the red haze began to clear from Roarke's passion-soaked brain, he groaned. Lifting his weight from Abby, he gazed down at her. "I'm so sorry."

She blinked. "Sorry?"

"That was inexcusable, throwing you to the ground and taking you like that. I—"

"But I loved it."

He stared at her. "But you're a mess! You have mud and leaves and pine needles everywhere, and if there were any rocks under the leaves, no telling how many bruises you might have."

To his total amazement, she began to laugh, sounding giddy as a teenager. "I doubt there was a single rock, and even if I end up being black and blue, I owe you more than you'll ever know for giving me an experience I might never have had otherwise."

"You can't be serious."

"You're probably right about that. I may not ever be serious again." She reached up and grabbed his face in both hands. "Roarke, thank you for ravishing me like that. All I've ever known about sex pales in comparison with what just happened."

He could feel the mud on her hands being transferred to his face, but he didn't care. Her reaction was at once both wonderful and unsettling. "You're not upset with me? You don't think I'm some kind of brute?"

"Not in the least." She caressed his cheeks, smearing the mud. "But I suppose we could both use a little cleanup. I just got mud all over your face."

"I know. I could feel it." He was having trouble categorizing this experience. It should have put her off, and instead she'd reacted in a way that was almost Were in nature. Humans weren't supposed to like lying in the muck while having sex.

"You look like a Scotsman about to go off to battle," she said.

"Doesn't matter. You're the one I'm concerned about." If she'd express some dismay at his behavior, he could get his bearings. He stood and helped her up. Then he turned her so he could see her back. "Good Lord. Abby, I didn't mean for—"

"You could help wash me off."

"Absolutely." He wasn't sure where to start. She had mud and leaves in her braid, which was nearly undone, and plastered on her back, her bottom, and the backs of her thighs. She'd be within her rights to ream him a new one, and yet . . . she seemed to have enjoyed every bit of his rutting behavior.

As she stood there, the rain had some effect on her condition, but not enough. He needed containers of water he could pour over her hair and her back. If he brought out their two cooking pots, he could collect the water and do a better job. And he could use his camp towel, too.

"Wait right here. I'll get some stuff."

"Okay."

He grabbed everything as quickly as possible, stopping long enough to grab a small plastic bottle of shampoo he saw sticking out of her backpack. Then he rushed back out. She would be fine out there on her own for a minute or two, but he was becoming more protective now that they'd made love. *No, they'd had sex*, he told himself sternly. It was great, but it was still just sex.

Or it had been until he'd lost his mind and taken her right there on the ground, in the pouring rain, sliding on wet leaves, squishing in the mud. It had been . . . monumentally good. He might as well admit that to himself, even if he curbed his reaction when discussing it with her.

He dashed back out of the cave and came to a screeching halt at the sight that greeted him. Abby stood in the rain, arms outstretched, hair loose, face lifted to the rain. Because she was still decorated with leaves and pine needles, she looked like a wood nymph giving thanks for the bounty spilling from the heavens.

She looked like . . . a woman he could love. Was this what his brother, Aidan, had encountered in Emma? A woman who was right in every way but one?

Damn it. Roarke didn't need this problem, nor did his family and his unborn children. Abby didn't deserve to deal with it, either. But he was making one big assumption—that she was developing feelings for him, too.

If she wasn't, then he didn't have anything to worry about. She hadn't said anything along those lines. Obviously she had a thing for his johnson, but that wasn't the same as wanting him, Roarke Wallace, PhD, second son of Howard Wallace, werewolf pack alpha.

He'd be wise to dial back the sexual involvement with her, because good sex could sometimes lead to emotional attachment. Maybe that's all he was feeling. But he had a tough time convincing himself of that.

Sex with Abby had been beyond great, no doubt about it. But he hadn't felt that tug on his heart until he'd walked out here and caught her worshipping the rain. Something in her spoke to something in him, although he could work to tune out that frequency.

He would do exactly that, starting now. Walking toward her, he set the pots on the ground so they'd fill with rain. He'd help clean her up and then suggest they climb into their sleeping bags for the night.

At the pinging noise of the rain in the metal pots, she turned, looking for all the world like a startled creature of the forest.

He shoved that thought out of his mind. "I thought having containers of rainwater would help," he said as he approached her. "We'll start with your hair. I brought your shampoo." He handed her the small bottle.

"Thank you!"

He kept his tone businesslike as he picked up one of the pots. "Tip your head back and I'll pour a little water through it. Then you can soap up."

"All right." She leaned back and let her hair flow downward.

"It'll be chilly."

"That's okay. I'm used to it now."

She was far too adaptable. He hadn't counted on that. Most women would have been protesting the minute he started pouring cold water on their head.

Abby said nothing. Instead she kept her head back as she squirted shampoo into her hand. Then she handed him the bottle. "Can you hold this for a sec?"

"Sure." He watched her massage the shampoo into her hair, which was a mistake on his part. Earlier today he'd wished for a chance to watch her put her hair in a ponytail while naked. This was way more provocative.

She arched her back to keep the soap from going in her eyes as she reached up and worked the shampoo in. Naturally her breasts lifted and quivered with every motion. Two steps, and he'd be in position to lean down and take one of those dancing nipples in his mouth.

Thinking about that had a predictable effect on his cock. If he'd hoped that two hot sessions with Abby would have tamed that bad boy, the hope died as his penis began to throb. He stared at the ground and willed it to behave.

"Ready to rinse?" she asked.

He glanced up to find her still leaning back, but she'd stopped soaping her hair.

"Or I can do it." She reached out her hand. "Just give me the container. You don't have to wait on me."

"I'm happy to." He probably shouldn't have said that, but the truth popped out before he could censor himself.

"Thanks, Roarke. You're a true gentleman."

He didn't deserve that label when all he could think about was stroking her soft skin until he made her want him again. She was susceptible to him, and he was more than ready to take advantage of that. He was no gentleman. He was a werewolf who couldn't seem to control his sexual appetite.

Picking up the second pot, he slowly poured water over her soapy hair and followed the streams with his fingers, working the suds out. He'd never washed a woman's hair before, but he liked doing it. Or maybe he only liked washing Abby's hair.

She murmured something, and he stopped pouring to lean closer. "What did you say?"

"I said it feels nice."

"The water?"

"No, your fingers in my hair. I like it."

He heaved a sigh and gave another lecture to his cock. This could get out of control so fast. "I think most of the soap's gone."

She stood up straight and looked at him. "Are you angry with me, Roarke?"

"No, of course not."

"You sound angry. Or abrupt."

He gazed at her and decided she deserved nothing but the truth from him. "You're far too appealing, Abby. You may have no feelings for me other than sexual ones, but I'm worried that I might start caring too much for you. That would be a mistake."

"So you really are still scared you'll fall for me."

He hesitated. "Yes."

"After the way things turned out for your brother, I don't blame you for being concerned. Do you think we should stop having sex? Would that help?"

His body rebelled against the concept, but his brain

had already decided abstinence was the right move. "I'm sure it would."

She continued to gaze at him. "I'm sorry if I've caused more problems. I kidded myself that you were this iron-willed being with his path mapped out and I'd only be a slight detour along the way."

"That's the way it should be, but . . ."

"It's not. I can see that, and I'm honored that I've touched you that much. I don't want to mess up your plans, or mine, either, for that matter. I can't imagine living a dual life. Not that you've even suggested such a thing," she added quickly. "Chances are you want to get away from me quickly and put yourself back on the werewolf track."

He couldn't help smiling at her terminology. "Something like that."

"Then by all means go back in the cave, put on some clothes, and climb into your sleeping bag. Shampooing my hair washed off most of the leaves and mud, so I should be finished up in no time."

"There's no way you can wash your back." He picked up the other pot of water and dipped a section of the camp towel into it. "Turn around and let me do that."

"I'm not sure that's a good idea."

"It'll be fine." He made a circling motion with his finger. "Go."

"But you see, Roarke, I have a very appealing back."

Even in the dim light he caught the glint of mischief in her eyes. "It's not your back that gets to me." He walked around her since she'd refused to turn for him. "It's your cute little butt." Unable to resist, he gave her a playful pinch on one creamy cheek.

"Hey!" She spun around to retaliate, but he dodged away from her, laughing.

She gave chase, but she was no match for an agile

werewolf. He teased her by letting her get close and then feinting to one side, neatly avoiding her. He shouldn't have started this game, but God, it felt great to run through the rain with Abby.

A moment later he faked her out and grabbed her around the waist. The rain and the romp had dislodged almost all the mud and leaves from her body, and he was left with a squirming, damp, extremely desirable woman.

"Let me go." She struggled to get loose. "Before you do something you'll regret."

"Too late." He caught her chin in one hand and held her still. "Way too late." Lowering his mouth to hers, he decided he would definitely put some space between himself and Abby . . . tomorrow.

Chapter 14

Abby had tried to do the noble thing and save Roarke from himself, but if he insisted on kissing her like that, what was a woman to do? When he picked her up and carried her into the cave, she surrendered to the concept that they'd have more amazing sex. A girl had only so much willpower.

One good thing, she thought as he pulled her down to the sleeping bag and rolled to his back so she could climb aboard, was all this sex was sending blood to every part of her body and working muscles that would have been stiff as hell tomorrow if she hadn't spent the evening getting naked and having orgasms with Roarke.

A more intimate part of her anatomy might be sore, though. As she took his considerable length deep inside and leaned forward so he could draw her aching nipple into his mouth, she acknowledged that his supersized equipment would leave her with a few twinges to remember him by. A steady diet of Roarke would have taken care of that as her body stretched to accommodate him, but she couldn't look forward to that kind of adjustment period.

She'd have to take comfort in knowing that he found her *way too appealing* and that he'd tried and failed to keep his hands off of her. Those were gratifying truths to remember. They wouldn't make up for that awful moment sometime in the near future when they'd have to tell each other good-bye, but they both knew that would have to happen eventually. They'd survive.

Together they reached another shattering mutual climax and slept wrapped in each other's arms. Abby thought that would be the end of their night of passion, but Roarke kissed her awake sometime during the night and moved between her thighs once again. This time his lovemaking was slow and sweet, at least until the last, when they both were captured by the frenzy that seemed to claim them whenever they set each other on fire.

Afterward, he propped himself on his forearms and gazed down at her as his breathing gradually returned to normal. "Wow." He drew in a shaky breath. "Thank you, Abby. You're . . . someone I never expected to find."

Her body still humming from her orgasm, she touched his cheek. "That goes double for me. Triple for me."

He chuckled softly. "I suppose so. Having sex with a werewolf isn't all that common."

"Just so you know, I won't ever reveal you. Never, Roarke."

"I know that." He kissed her gently. "You said I didn't trust you, and you were right. I didn't at first. But now I'd trust you with my life."

Her heart warmed. "Same here, Roarke. Same here."

"Good." Easing away from her, he lay on his side and tucked her in close, spoon-fashion. "Sleep, Abby. Sleep, my . . . friend."

She didn't think they were friends. Any fool could tell that they were lovers. But it wouldn't do either of them any good to label themselves that way. Nestling in the curve of his body, she slept.

When she woke, she was alone in the cave and wondered if he'd shifted into werewolf form to scout around. Daylight filtered through the leaves of the bush hiding the cave entrance and she couldn't hear any rain. Only voices.

Voices! Dear God, who could it be? She lay very still and listened. One voice was definitely Roarke's. She'd developed an ear for that timbre, that cadence. She didn't recognize the other man's.

She should probably get dressed and at least peek through the branches to see who was out there. She didn't know if Roarke would want them to know about her or not, but she could find out if it was anybody she knew.

Like Cameron Gentry. Now there was a scary thought. Yeah, she'd better be quiet as a mouse until she found out who she was dealing with. But as she started to get up, she yelped.

She clapped a hand over her mouth and clenched her jaw against a moan as she sank back to the sleeping bag. Damn, she hurt all over. But she should still get dressed.

Every muscle in her body announced its displeasure as she rose to all fours and scanned the cave searching for the clothes Roarke had pulled off her the night before. She was sore in places she hadn't known she had. Ouch and double ouch.

Remembering the small bottle of ibuprofen in her backpack, she crawled over and rummaged around until she located it. The water bottle was too far away considering the suffering involved in fetching it, so she swallowed a couple of tablets dry and sat on the cool stone floor waiting for them to kick in.

Nature girl had morphed into couch-potato girl, but

alas, she had no couch on which to spend the day. Her gaze fell on the cave wall where she'd played Hangman with Roarke the night before. There it was, the word that had launched their spectacular boinkfest.

She was sore down there, too, but she didn't mind that. She hadn't had such great sex in . . . actually, she'd never had sex like that. The sex had probably kept her from stiffening up even worse.

Or not. Didn't matter. She didn't regret a second of the time she'd spent getting horizontal, vertical, and sideways with Professor Wallace. Maybe, if the ibuprofen kicked in and he could get rid of their visitor . . .

Oh, what was she thinking? They had a couple of big hairy creatures to find, and they needed to get on that program, pronto. Also, Roarke had mentioned last night that he was becoming attached to her and wanted to avoid that. She hated to admit that she was becoming attached to him, too.

Considering the whole werewolf situation, which presented quite the big obstacle to a continued relationship, she should probably cool her jets. She wanted to be dry-eyed when they said good-bye. No drama for this chick, other than the obvious dramatic point that she'd met and shagged a werewolf. No one would ever know that but her, though.

Keeping his secret wouldn't be tough. She could just imagine trying to tell a friend or family member over coffee. Two minutes into the story, they'd be speed-dialing the local booby hatch. Of course she had pictures, pictures that had worked to get her on this trip, but she wasn't sure anyone would believe the pictures were legit, either.

She gazed at the word *orgasm* that she'd filled in for the last round of Hangman. She'd have to scrub that out. No telling whether little kids might someday find this cave and she wasn't into shocking innocents.

No time like the present, before she became involved in the day and forgot. Roarke's camp towel lay near enough that she wouldn't have to work very hard to reach it. On all fours, she got the towel and began rubbing the cave wall to erase the last game of Hangman.

"My God."

Hearing Roarke's startled voice behind her, she spun around and clasped the towel to her breasts as she plopped her bare butt on the cave floor and covered her crotch with her other hand. When she saw he was alone, she sagged in relief and dropped the towel. "I was afraid that you'd brought that guy you were talking to in here."

He looked hurt. "I wouldn't have done that without warning you."

"Of course you wouldn't, but I was concentrating on what I was doing, and when I heard the shock in your voice, I reacted." She gazed at him. "Why *did* you sound so shocked, by the way? It's not as if you haven't seen me naked before."

"It wasn't shock you heard."

She took a closer look at him, all of him, and noticed the bulge behind the fly of his jeans. "Oh."

"Male werewolves have a special . . . fondness for that position."

She had to stop and think what he meant. When she realized he'd come into the cave and found her on all fours mooning him, she flushed. She'd presented an open invitation to do it doggie-style, and apparently he had a weakness for that.

The longer he stood there staring at her, his morning scruff making him look slightly dangerous and his arousal making him look sexy as hell, the more turned on she became. "If that's true, why didn't you suggest it last night? I would have been game." She would have

been willing to try it standing on her head last night, before the reality of muscle pain had set in.

He shook his head. "That's the mating position."

"You mean the until-death-do-us-part routine?"

"Yes. Taking a female that way, either as a human or
a Were, initiates the binding process."

That shouldn't make her hot. She had no interest in
that binding stuff or the possibility of creating little
shape-shifters in the process. But thinking of Roarke
wanting her like that and picturing him following through
on that lusty urge made her *very* hot.

She squirmed against the cave floor and decided to
change the subject. "I was just erasing the *orgasm.*"
Which didn't change the subject at all.

He gave her a lopsided smile. "If only I could do the
same. Although I have to say, even if we'd kept our relationship strictly platonic up to now, seeing you crouched
on the floor of the cave was guaranteed to jack me up."

"If we'd kept it platonic, I wouldn't have been crouch-
ing naked on the cave floor."

"Which might have helped . . . some." He sighed. "I
was probably doomed from the minute I agreed to bring
you out here."

"*Doomed* is such a negative word. Can't we both be
happy for what we've shared and move on?" That was
her hope, although it seemed to be fading into the distance. He was under her skin and in her blood, and she
knew it.

"I'm working on that." He massaged the back of his
neck. "If you'd consider getting dressed, that would help."

"I was headed in that direction." And now that the
ibuprofen had hit her system, she might be able to do
that without hobbling around like a cripple. She managed to stand upright with only one tiny gasp. She was
proud of that.

"You're sore." Roarke took a step toward her. "I wondered how you were doing, but when I heard someone outside the cave I got out there as soon as I could to keep them from potentially coming in."

"And I appreciate that. Who is it?"

"His name's Donald Smurtz and he's looking for Bigfoot."

"Is he still out there?" She eyed her panties, which lay on the stone floor halfway between her and Roarke. Walking to the spot wouldn't be so bad, but then she'd have to bend down and get them, and that kind of effort would hurt.

"Yes. I invited him to join us."

"You *what?*" She forgot all about her panties. "Are you insane?"

"Often, especially when you're standing there without a stitch on."

"Sorry about that." She started for her panties. "I'm moving a little slower this morning."

"Then let me help." He reached the panties before she did and scooped them off the floor. Then he closed his eyes. "Oh, man. Maybe I won't help, after all." He looked directly at her.

The intensity in his green eyes made her breath catch. Right on cue her body grew moist and ready for the kind of pleasure only her werewolf lover could provide. "I thought you said this Donald person was still out there."

Roarke stepped closer. "Yeah, but I told him we were honeymooners."

"Cute." She backed away. "But I'm still not having sex with you while some stranger can listen in. Go be kinky with someone else."

Roarke kept advancing. "He won't hear us. We'll be quiet."

"Says you." Her back met the cave wall. She was out of real estate.

Roarke unzipped his fly as he closed the gap. "He's not standing by the entrance. He's relaxing on a rock a good fifty feet away eating fruit leather and checking his GPS." He propped both hands on the cave wall, effectively caging her in as he leaned forward to kiss her. "Good morning, Abby."

What little resistance she had vanished the moment his lips touched hers. She kissed him back, and he absorbed her soft moan as he slipped a hand between her thighs.

He lifted his mouth a fraction from hers as he caressed her. "Are you sore here?"

"Not anymore." Funny how the prospect of climax could make a girl forget those pesky little aches and pains.

His hand stilled and he drew back to look into her eyes. "What do you mean, *not anymore*? If you're the least bit sore, then maybe we shouldn't."

"For your information, I took ibuprofen, and if you don't do me after getting me all worked up, Roarke Wallace, I'm going to march out of this cave and tell Ronald—"

"Donald." His eyes narrowed. "Just what are you threatening to tell Donald?"

"That you're—"

"Careful, Abby." His words vibrated with warning. "Don't mess with me on this subject."

"Gay."

He snorted. "Allow me to neutralize that threat right now." Grasping her hips, he lifted her against the cave wall and thrust home.

She gasped, simultaneously wrapping her legs around his waist and clutching his shoulders to make sure she didn't fall. She needn't have worried. His steel grip held her perfectly in place. She wasn't going anywhere.

He stood there, his massive chest heaving and his cock buried to the hilt. "What was that again?"

God, he was virile. She might be able to come just looking at him. "I retract my threat."

"I should hope so, but just in case . . ." Both his grip and his gaze were steady as he began to pump. "This should take care of any doubts."

"Go for it, Professor." She returned his steady gaze, but the rest of her spiraled quickly out of control. Each time he pushed deep, the friction sent waves of reaction through her quivering body. At first she felt the brush of denim along her thighs, but soon the furnace of her needs burned away every sensation except the rapid slide of his penis. As he stroked faster, she began to pant.

"I love making you come." He shifted the angle slightly and increased the tempo as his own breathing grew ragged.

Ah, there. Right *there.* "And you . . . do it . . . so well."

"Your pupils are huge."

"Because I'm . . . oh, Roarke . . ." Her climax swept over her, wringing cries of delirious pleasure from her lips, cries that she was powerless to hold back.

Roarke's laugh of triumph changed to a groan of satisfaction as he drove forward once more and came in a hot, pulsing rush.

Leaning his forehead against hers, he swore softly and breathlessly. "Too damn good," he murmured. "Too effing good, Abby." Slowly he lifted his head and looked into her eyes. "And I'm not sure what we're going to do about that."

She struggled for air and sanity. "Doesn't look like . . . Ronald will be much of a . . . deterrent."

"Donald."

"Donald won't be much of a deterrent."

Roarke sucked in air. "Apparently not."

"Did you think he would be?" Her breathing grew more even. "Is that why you invited him to tag along?"

"Partly that." He cleared his throat. "But mostly because he has some high-tech listening device that might track Bigfoot's movements even better than I could. I was afraid he'd get there first, and we can't allow that."

"How do you know he hasn't taken off already?"

"Because he's lonesome and seemed thrilled to hook up with somebody, even if it turned out to be two honeymooners who would be shagging every chance they got." Roarke leaned back and glanced at the spot where they were still joined. "Look at us. You're soaked and I'll have to change out of these jeans."

"And no rain to wash off in."

"No. It's cleared up some." His gaze returned to her face. "I didn't count on this."

"Clear skies?"

"Smart-ass. You know what I'm talking about. Sex so good I can't stop."

She stroked a finger along his prickly jaw. "So don't."

"Obviously I'm not making any effort in that direction."

She took a deep breath. "The way I look at it, we both know the parameters. You don't want to hook up with a human, and I don't want to hook up with a wolf. But for now, while we're thrown together, we either give in to the chemistry, or . . ."

"Or what?"

"Go crazy."

He nodded. "Yep, that's about how I had it figured, too." He eased her slowly back to a standing position. "You okay?"

"Wet but happy."

He pulled a handkerchief from the back pocket of his jeans and handed it to her. "You can use this, seeing as

how we don't have any rain. We do need to get back out
there so I can introduce you to Donald."

"And who am I supposed to be, other than your
bride?"

"You can be Abby."

"Then I'll be Abby Winchell."

He gave her an assessing look. "You're not into taking your husband's surname?"

"No, as a matter of fact."

"Not even if we're only pretending to be married?"

"Not if we're pretending and not if we'd done it for
real. Not that we ever would," she added immediately.
She could feel tension in the air, both hers and his, and
yet they were only talking hypothetically. Strange.

"All right." He didn't sound pleased.

"I'm guessing in your world that's frowned upon."

"In my world you would become a member of the
Wallace pack, and you'd be expected to take that name
to designate your affiliation."

"And if you had a sister? Would her husband become
a member of the Wallace pack and take her name?"

He paused as if considering that possibility. Finally he
shook his head. "If I had a sister, she'd be strong like my
mother, which means she'd need a dominant alpha by
her side, someone who'd never settle for a subservient
position in the Wallace pack. She'd join his pack and
take his name."

"Well, seeing as how I'm not joining your pack, I'll
just be Abby Winchell, feminist bride."

He shrugged. "If you insist."

"I do."

"But it's probably better if you don't mention your
connection to Earl."

"That goes without saying. That could lead to all sorts
of problems. So does this Donald person have a tent?"

Roarke seemed happy to leave the subject of surnames and family connections as he took off his shoes and began shucking his jeans. "Does he ever. And he's also the worst harmonica player in the world."

"How do you know that?" Abby wiped her thighs with Roarke's extremely soft handkerchief. She glanced at the corner and saw that it was monogrammed. His middle name began with an A, and she made a mental note to ask about that later on.

"I came upon the guy's camp last night when I was out roaming the forest. I meant to tell you about him, but he soon became less important than ... other things." He sent her a heated glance.

"Speaking of those other things, what should I do with this?" She held up his damp handkerchief.

"I'll take it. Carrying that in my pocket all day will keep your scent with me. I like that idea."

She shook her head in bewilderment. "I suppose it's a werewolf thing."

"Yep. We're all about enjoying the earthy scents."

"Seems to me the less we're reminded of sex today the more likely we'll get to the business at hand." She began collecting her clothes from the floor of the cave.

"You're right, but if I have to put up with Donald, I'll need to inject a little joy into my life. Especially if he pulls out that harmonica. *A-yi-yi*."

"So you heard him play last night?"

"Yes, if you define the word *play* very loosely." Roarke pulled on the sweats he'd worn the night before. "He has a tin ear, but he's convinced the sound of a harmonica will bring Bigfoot running, or rather his mate if she's pregnant. He read somewhere that her hormones make her crave harmonica music."

"Is that true?"

"Not that I know of. There are tons of crackpot theories out there, and this is one of them. I don't think his damned harmonica will do anything except annoy the hell out of you and me."

"Then again, maybe his harmonica playing will effectively block out the sound of two people having sex."

Roarke gazed at her and slowly began to smile. "On second thought, I love that stupid harmonica."

Chapter 15

Roarke got dressed faster than Abby did, so he quickly hauled out his safety razor and managed a quick shave. He'd worried about scratching her this morning, but he was also thinking of the future. He still had much to explore when it came to Abby.

He'd promised himself to kiss all her freckles, and he hadn't done that yet. She also had hidden riches to taste. He'd hate to irritate her sensitive thighs while he was savoring those riches.

By the time he'd finished with his shave, Abby had her clothes on and was putting her hair in a ponytail. The gesture reminded him of last night in the rain, when she'd worked shampoo into her hair and caused her breasts to quiver with the motion.

He'd be wise not to spend too much time thinking about last night, or the hot wetness of her this morning, when she'd insisted she wasn't willing to have sex with him. She'd been more than willing, and he'd known it. She couldn't fool him when his excellent sense of smell gave him all the information he'd ever need about her readiness.

To think he'd expected Donald's presence to slow them down. Hell, he'd very quickly realized he wanted to make Abby cry out during sex so that Donald would have no doubt Roarke was the alpha male around here. Even someone as geeky as Donald brought out Roarke's need to mark his territory.

But he hadn't gone into the cave with sex on his mind. He'd only meant to see if Abby was awake so he could let her know his plans regarding Donald. Then he'd walked in on a werewolf's fantasy—a naked, voluptuous woman on her hands and knees, facing away from him on the stone floor of a dimly lit cave.

On top of that, her scrubbing action had made for some interesting hip movement, almost as if she were taunting him with her availability. Of course she hadn't been. She didn't understand the sexual subtleties of a werewolf's mind, and probably wouldn't have time enough to explore them.

But thinking about Abby on the cave floor still got him hot, even though he'd just had sex with her. She had no idea what a temptation she'd unwittingly presented this morning. He deserved credit for not taking her on the spot.

Sure, that action would have had serious consequences for both of them, but unexpectedly discovering her on all fours had awakened powerful instincts that he had trouble taming. He was already half in love with her, and that combined with lust could easily have trumped logic.

Somehow he'd controlled himself. But when she'd continued to stand there in all her naked glory, he'd decided to claim his consolation prize. As consolation prizes went, it was a pretty good one, and certainly a safer route than the action that had instantly flashed into his head when he'd first glimpsed her bare and very provocative backside.

"All righty." Abby walked over as he was stowing his razor in his backpack. "I'm ready to meet The Donald."

"Trust me, this guy is just Donald, not The Donald."

She gave him a curious glance. "It just occurred to me that you, owner of a very pricey watch, might know The Donald."

"I don't, but my father does."

She slowly nodded. "Out here in the woods it's easy for me to forget that you come from a very wealthy family."

"Does it matter?"

She gazed at him. "When two people are living for the moment, nothing like that matters, I guess."

"Not really." But it made him a little sad that she'd never meet his family. They'd like her . . . as a family friend, of course. They'd accepted Emma, but they wouldn't be happy if both their sons went off the deep end and chose human mates.

He felt the need for a change in subject. "I'm thinking after we get the introductions out of the way, the next step is coffee and breakfast."

She smiled at him. "Worked up an appetite, did you?"

"You could say that."

"You shaved." She touched his jaw. "Was that on my account?"

"As a matter of fact." He cradled her face in both hands and tipped it up so he could examine her freckled skin. "I irritated your skin a little when I kissed you this morning. I feel bad about that."

"No worries. I think you look kind of dashing with stubble."

"Thanks, but stubble gets in the way of certain activities."

"Like kissing?"

Leaning down, he brushed his mouth over hers. "Like that. And . . . other fun stuff."

"I can't imagine what you're talking about."

"Then imagine this." He put his mouth close to her ear and told her in graphic detail what he had in mind for the next time they were alone and naked.

"Roarke!" She pulled away from him and pretended to look shocked, but her eyes grew dark and sparkly. "You, sir, are no gentleman."

"I never claimed to be. I'm a werewolf, Abby. We have voracious sexual appetites."

"That's an understatement." She fanned her pink cheeks. "If I didn't know better, I'd suspect you of deliberately planting that idea in my head so I'd think about it all day."

"Me?"

"Uh-huh."

"Will you think about it all day, Abby?"

"Probably."

"Good."

Abby stepped out of the cave into the pearl-colored light of an overcast morning. Mt. Hood, the most dominant feature of the area on a clear day, was still covered. But no moisture fell from the sky. She almost missed being pelted by raindrops. From now on, a rainy day would remind her of being here in the woods with Roarke.

"Ah, there you are!" A pudgy guy in a bright orange sweat suit jumped down from the rock he'd been sitting on and walked toward her. His fluorescent green ball cap carried the slogan *Bigfoot Lives!* across the crown.

She stepped forward and offered her hand. "I'm Abby Winchell. And you must be Donald Smurtz."

"You've heard of me?" He pumped her hand enthusiastically. Behind thick lenses his eyes were a pale gray with surprisingly beautiful dark lashes.

"From Roarke."

"Oh. I thought maybe you'd read some of my articles in *Cryptozoology Today*. I'm multipublished in that journal."

"Sorry." She extricated her hand from his grip. "I'm new to the study of Bigfoot. So you came up here all by yourself?"

"I did." He puffed out his chest. "I thought of taking along my peeps on this quest, but then I told myself, *Donald, my boy, strike out on your own.*"

"Self-reliance is a good thing." Abby glanced over at Roarke, who was standing to one side, arms folded, as he watched Donald's performance.

The performance obviously wasn't over. Donald lifted one finger toward the sky. "I said to myself, *Be your own person, Donald Smurtz! Take that equipment you invented and prove that you're an engineering phenom. Follow your heart!*" Punching his fist into his chest, he promptly doubled over in a coughing fit.

Abby moved toward him. "Are you all right?"

"Sure. Probably got some fruit leather caught in my throat."

"Let me help." Abby moved into position and whacked him between the shoulder blades, but nothing popped out of his mouth. She pretended not to notice. "Better?"

"Much." Donald took a deep breath. "That fruit leather can be wicked stuff if you get a piece crosswise in your windpipe."

"I'm sure."

Donald straightened and adjusted his ball cap. "I understand congratulations are in order."

"For what?"

"Hel-*lo*. Marriage? Holy matrimony? The tie that binds?"

Roarke stepped forward and put his arm around Abby. "You'll have to forgive my bride. She's still not accustomed to thinking of herself as a married woman, probably because the rings I ordered never arrived. So no engagement ring for Abby and no wedding rings for either of us."

She took note of how easily he created that story to explain the absence of rings. He was a smooth one, this Roarke Wallace. His story about not needing condoms better not have been just another smooth lie. If she turned up pregnant with shape-shifters, there would be hell to pay.

For the time being, though, the arrangement was pure heaven. For the first time in her life, she could enjoy spontaneous sex. She thought about what had happened recently in the cave and wondered if Donald had heard any of it.

He pulled the hem of his orange sweatshirt down over his rounded hips. "I just want to say, for the record, that I appreciate you two inviting me along on what was obviously intended as a private journey to find Bigfoot. I wouldn't have dreamed of intruding, except Roarke insisted."

"Donald has amazing equipment," Roarke said.

Abby couldn't resist. "So do you, dear."

Roarke stared at her and actually blushed.

"Pardon us, Donald." Abby smiled up at Roarke, who was definitely giving her the evil eye. "A little honeymoon humor."

"Oh, sure, sure. Don't mind me."

Roarke cleared his throat. "Anyway, Donald, my brother's an expert in surveillance, but I think he could learn a thing or two from you."

Donald preened. "Have him give me a call. I'm always willing to share my techniques. Is your brother a Bigfoot aficionado, as well?"

"He dabbles," Roarke said.

"Ah." Donald rocked back on his heels. "I'm well acquainted with the weekend Bigfoot hobbyist, but they're not like you and me, are they?"

"No." Roarke gave Abby's shoulder a squeeze. "We're hard-core."

"You and I are the kind of guys who will come up with the goods, get the confirming evidence, enlighten the unenlightened. After this, we might get some talk-show gigs, Roarke. I'm thinking Letterman."

"You know what?" Abby stepped away from Roarke. "I think I'll go grab the camp stove and some supplies so we can start the coffee. Roarke, would you like to help me with that?"

"Sure thing, Abby."

She marched back to the cave and shoved her way through the bush guarding the entrance. Instead of holding it for him, she let it snap back and was pretty sure he got a shower. He mumbled something, but she didn't try to figure out what it was.

She waited until they were both able to stand before whirling to face him. Although she was fuming, she kept her voice low so Donald wouldn't hear. "He's a total nutcase! What were you thinking, inviting him along?"

"He has equipment. You should see the dish he has. It's small, but extremely powerful. Battery operated. He's an engineer, so he very well could have built it himself. The guy's probably some sort of genius."

"I don't care if he's Albert Einstein! He's the kind of guy who will find Bigfoot and broadcast his findings to the world. Did you hear him? He wants to get on Letterman!"

"I suppose he'd like to, but—"

"Exactly! After what you've told me, that should be the last thing you want for these fragile beings. I don't get this at all!"

Roarke glanced at the cave's entrance, as if to make sure Donald wasn't coming through to check on them. "He'll never see Bigfoot. I'll make sure of that."

"How? You describe these amazing listening devices, which he could be using right this minute to hear what we're saying. You do realize that."

Roarke pulled a wire out of his pocket. "I asked him to show me how it works, and while I was examining it, I unhooked this. I'll put it back at some point, but I can always pretend I was fooling with it and didn't realize this was an important part. Don't worry. I'll make up whatever I need to in order to protect us."

She wished he wasn't quite so good at doing that, but she'd deal with that issue later. "Okay, so if we need his equipment to help us track Bigfoot and his mate, how can you utilize his equipment and keep him from seeing those creatures?"

"You're going to help me."

She stared at him. "I assume that means you have a plan."

"I'm working on one. Trust me, Abby."

Folding her arms, she looked down at the floor beneath their feet. "I just listened to you come up with a lie to explain why we were honeymooners with no rings on our fingers. Then you show me the wire you filched from his listening device. You do these things so easily, and it made me wonder . . ." She glanced up at him. "Would you have created a similar story to make me think I would see Bigfoot, too? Or worse yet, would you have lied about not needing to wear condoms to get the sex you wanted?"

He groaned. "God, no. Yes, I made up that story about the rings, and I certainly swiped a critical wire from Donald, but I'm not making up the things I tell you." He sent her a pleading glance. "What can I do to convince you of that?"

"I don't know. When all is said and done, what do I really mean to you, beyond a few rounds of good sex?"

"You mean a lot more. That's what I was trying to say when I mentioned getting attached."

"But you won't allow yourself to do that. Not really. You have your werewolf future and I won't be part of that."

"You hold my future in the palm of your hand."

"Do I really, Roarke? Let's say I tried to convince people that I'd been hanging out with a werewolf, and that werewolves were everywhere, especially in high society. Who would believe me?"

He gazed at her for a long time. "I don't know, but it doesn't matter, because you're not the type to do something like that and risk harming others."

He had her pegged, all right. He was safe from her, but was she safe from him? As she looked into his green eyes, she wanted to believe that he shared that same reluctance to harm others. "It's just that you can be so glib."

"I have a quick mind. I was born that way. But consider this, Abby. As a werewolf, I have to be constantly on the alert to protect myself and others of my kind from detection. In order to function in your world, yet maintain my other life, I need to be glib or risk exposure."

She could see some truth in that. "But can you choose when to lie and when not to? Or do lies jump to your mind automatically?"

"I can choose. And with you, I choose to tell the truth."

"Once I forced your hand with those pictures, you had no choice."

He inclined his head in acknowledgment of that. "True. But as you now realize, the more you know, the greater your personal danger. If I could have lied my way out of that lunchtime confrontation with you, I would have."

"To protect yourself."

"And to protect you."

She regarded him silently for several seconds. Finally she sighed. "I want to believe that. All right, Roarke—I *will* believe that. I've trusted you with my body, and there's no turning back on that score. My family's known for its fertility, so if you've misled me, we'll have a bouncing baby . . . *something* in nine months."

"That isn't going to happen."

She didn't want a pregnancy, either, and yet he'd just underscored the finite nature of their relationship. Someday he would have a child with another werewolf, and Abby would be a distant memory. She pretty much hated that.

She drew a calming breath. "Are you planning to allow me to see the Bigfoot pair?"

"Yes."

"All right." She'd have to trust him on that, too. "Then what about this Donald character?"

"Once we get close enough that I can cover the distance in about an hour as a wolf, we'll create a distraction that keeps Donald in camp with you."

"Like what?"

"I don't know that yet. Be thinking about it, okay?"

Despite herself, Abby began to get into the spirit of the game. "I can do that."

"I know you can. You're very smart. So, with you distracting him, I'll shift, make contact with the Bigfoot pair, and set up the procedure for relocation before re- turning to camp and shifting back."

"Then what?" She noticed there was no provision for getting her to the Bigfoot camp or for spiriting Donald away from it.

"I don't know that yet, either. I'm hoping it will come to me."

"But you *will* let me see those creatures, right?"

"You have my word. We're in this together, Abby."

She half expected him to pull her into his arms and try to convince her of his sincerity with a soulful kiss. When he didn't do that, she realized he wasn't trying to manipulate her into believing him.

"Okay, Roarke. I'll help you as much as I possibly can."

"Thank you." His response was low and quiet, and he didn't grace her with one of his oh-so-charming smiles.

Maybe she could trust him, after all. Either that or he was a lot slicker than she thought—and she already be- lieved that he was a very, very clever werewolf.

"Well, that's that." She glanced around the cave. "We'd better gather up the stuff for breakfast and head outside before Donald thinks we're in here boinking again."

"Now there's an idea."

"Hey!"

He backed away, palms extended. "Just kidding. Be- lieve it or not, I do think of other things now and then."

She laughed. "Then that would make one of us."

Chapter 16

Three hours later, as Roarke followed Donald and Abby through the forest, he could have cheerfully hoisted Donald up by his orange sweat suit and left him dangling from the nearest tree branch. The guy hadn't stopped talking to Abby since they'd left camp. Apparently he was head of a product development team for Sony, and his endless stories of life at work gave the impression that the corporation would fold if Donald Smurtz left.

He might be wearing a primo listening device around his neck, but Roarke wondered how the guy could hear a thing through his earphones with all the noise coming out of his mouth. Roarke had never been tempted to shift into wolf form just to shut somebody up, but he was sorely tempted now.

He wouldn't do it, but he amused himself by imagining the expression on Donald's round face if he turned and discovered a supersized wolf walking quietly behind him. That would be one sweet moment.

Speaking of sweet moments, Roarke decided to pull out his handkerchief, ostensibly to mop his forehead.

Pale sunlight filtered through the trees, but it wasn't nearly hot enough to work up a sweat, especially at the snail's pace Donald was setting. Still, Roarke could pretend he needed to wipe his weary brow.

Ah, yes. The musk of Abby's aroused body improved his mood considerably. He hated to put the handkerchief away again. Then he had an inspiration. It was a generously sized handkerchief, and by stretching the opposing corners and rolling it up, he could create a sweatband.

He'd just tied the ends behind his head when Donald raised his hand like a traffic cop, as if he were Dr. freaking Livingston on safari. This was a guy who deserved to have crackers dumped in his sleeping bag, but Roarke wouldn't do that, either. With his sweatband on, he could be mellow.

Halfway through a small meadow, Donald made a dramatic turn toward Abby and Roarke and spoke in measured tones. "My friends, the Sasquatch pair has changed course. They're coming in our direction."

"They're coming toward us?" Abby spun around. "Roarke, what do you—" At that moment she must have noticed his sweatband, because her eyes widened. Then they crinkled at the corners and she slapped her hand over her mouth. She was laughing.

Roarke deadpanned her, which only made her laugh harder. He pretended to ignore her and addressed Donald. "That's excellent news, Donald. Can you calculate how fast they're moving?"

"Not fast at all. The sound of their progress was a steady tone as they moved in the same direction as we did, but now it's getting louder."

Roarke took off his new sweatband with great reluctance and tucked it in his back pocket. He needed to focus on the Sasquatch scent, and he didn't want any olfactory distractions. Okay, now he could recognize that the faint scent was growing imperceptibly stronger.

He didn't like admitting that Donald had been of any use when he was also a royal pain in the ass, but he had been the first one to notice that the Sasquatch pair had changed direction and were circling back. Now that Roarke agreed with Donald's assessment, it was time to put some plans into place.

To prepare the way for those plans, Roarke would have to kiss some ass. He'd love for it to be Abby's— literally—but sadly, it would have to be Donald's— metaphorically.

"I'm really impressed with the efficiency of your equipment, Donald," he said. "If you don't have a patent on that thing, you should get one the minute you get back."

"Don't worry." Donald looked extremely pleased with himself. "I wanted to field test it first, but this baby is going to make me a bundle." He smacked the listening device vigorously and then winced and took out the earbuds. "Forgot it was on. Powerful little thing."

"Indeed." Roarke fought to keep a straight face. Donald was a real piece of work. "I'd say it's just saved us a whole lot of hiking."

"Don't you think we should just keep going? Unless they stop, we might sight them before dark."

"But we don't know what the terrain will be when that happens. Here we have a nice open meadow."

Donald nodded approvingly. "Good thinking, Wallace. So we set ourselves up to wait, with our cameras ready, so we're not taken by surprise. I knew you'd be a valuable asset to this operation."

"Thanks. I also have to admit I'd like a break from hiking. You're probably still fresh, but—"

"Oh, yeah. I could go all day."

"Well, I can't, and I'll bet Abby would like to rest, too."

"I'd be very grateful," Abby said right on cue. "I haven't wanted to say anything, but I scraped my thigh on a jagged branch back there, and I'm afraid to look at it. It feels as if blood's dribbling all the way down my leg."

"Uh-oh." Roarke's stomach twisted as he hurried toward her. "You should have said something, Abby. Let me take a look."

Donald turned pale. *"Uh,* I'll step away, if you don't mind. I'm not so good with blood."

"Thanks, Donald," Abby said. "You'll help preserve my modesty that way, too, because I'll have to pull my pants down to show Roarke."

Something in her tone, something that was almost a giggle, clued him in that she might be faking. God, he hoped so. He'd asked her to start thinking, and maybe this was what she'd come up with. The thought of her bleeding profusely was simply not acceptable.

Donald wandered up the trail. "You guys let me know when you're finished there. Sorry about being so squeamish, but I've been like that all my life."

Roarke knelt in front of Abby and reached for the waistband of her Lycra pants. "Are you really hurt?" he asked in a low voice.

She leaned down. "No."

He sighed in relief as he worked her pants down. "Good."

"Sorry if I worried you, but I wanted your reaction to look authentic."

"Believe me, it was authentic. The thought that you'd ripped open this soft skin . . ." He caressed the inside of her right thigh and shuddered. She shuddered, too, which stroked his ego.

"No funny business, Roarke."

"Not even a little funny business?"

"Not now. Maybe later. Here's what I came up with. I have a bad gash. You'll bind it with gauze and keep checking on it the rest of the day."

He pulled her pants down to her knees. "I like that part. God, you smell good. Which leg?"

"I don't care."

"Your right, then." He raised his voice. "Damn, Abby, you should have said something! You're a mess!" Taking off his pack, he located his first aid kit and took out the roll of gauze.

She leaned closer. "Whenever you're ready to intercept the Sasquatch pair, you'll check my bandage and decide my wound's infected and you're leaving Donald in charge while you head back to civilization to pick up some antibiotics."

"But nobody would prescribe—"

"Just say you have a doctor friend who will. And I have ibuprofen gel caps that should look close enough."

"Abby Winchell, you're brilliant."

"Thank you."

"Now spread your legs a little."

"Roarke, I told you not to—"

"As much as I'd love to fool around with your warm and sexy body, I agree that now is not the time. I just need room to wind this gauze around your thigh. Do you want it closer to your crotch or your knee?"

"Closer to my crotch."

He glanced up to find her grinning at him. "Somehow I knew you'd say that. You love to torture me, don't you?"

"Who says you're not torturing me?"

"I sincerely hope so." He breathed in her special aroma as he wound the gauze around her thigh about two inches from the entrance to all things wonderful. "I'm going to recommend you rest in your tent for the rest of the day."

"What if I get lonely?"

"I'll check on you often." His groin tightened at the prospect of all the times he'd have to play doctor with her today.

"I think you like my plan."

"I'm crazy about your plan." He reached up and pinched her butt.

"Ouch!"

"I'm so sorry, Abby!" he called out loud enough for Donald to hear. "I didn't mean to hurt you, but it's a really deep cut."

"Smart aleck," she murmured. "You could have warned me you were going to do that."

"I wanted it to be authentic."

"And I suppose you just had to pinch me *there*."

"I've wanted to do that again ever since last night. It's one of my favorite parts of you." He finished winding the gauze and tied it off. "I suppose we didn't even have to do this part. He'll never see your bandage."

"I never told you to actually bandage me, now, did I?"

He looked up and saw the mischief dancing in her blue eyes. "Then why did you go ahead and let me do it?"

"Why do you think, big boy?"

He caressed the silky skin of her thigh. "To get me hot, I suppose."

"And me."

He ran a knuckle over the crotch of her panties. They were deliciously damp. He stifled a groan. "Time to pitch your tent, little lady."

"Thank you for tending to me, Dr. Wallace."

He pulled her pants up and stood. "Oh, I'll be tending to you a lot more. You're going to need some serious tending." He raised his voice. "All done, Donald! I'm going to help Abby to that rock over there and let her sit down while I pitch her tent. She needs to get off that leg."

Donald walked back in their direction. "Pretty bad, *huh*?"

"Nasty gash." Roarke hooked a shoulder under Abby's right armpit. "If you have a queasy stomach, you don't want to look at it."

"Other side," she muttered.

"Huh?"

She rolled her eyes. "It's the right leg, so you want to support me on the left side so I can hop on my left leg."

"Oh. Right."

"No, left."

He blew out a breath. "That's what I meant. I can already tell you're going to be a difficult patient."

"I think she's a trouper," Donald said. "Don't worry about a thing, Abby. Roarke and I will handle this situation."

"Thank you, Donald. I feel like the weak link."

"Nah," Donald said. "One thing about all this. Neither of you will forget this honeymoon!"

"I'm sure you're right." Roarke eased Abby down onto the rock. He'd never given much thought to his actual honeymoon—where he'd like to go or who he'd be spending it with. Up to now, he hadn't been able to picture anyone in that role.

He didn't have that problem anymore. Instead he had a different one. He couldn't picture going on a honeymoon with anyone but Abby.

Abby lay in her small tent and listened to raindrops patter on the teal-colored nylon while the guys fixed lunch. According to Roarke, Donald's tent had a front flap that could be propped up to provide shelter for things

like making food. Roarke had promised to make sure
Donald's tent was set up a good distance from hers in
the hope that Roarke and Abby could enjoy some alone
time later.

She still wasn't sure how Roarke planned to get her
to see the Sasquatch pair and keep Donald away, but
she'd handed him the first part of the plan and it seemed
as if it would work. Her plan had come to her while listening to Donald's monologue this morning.

Although he was the hero in nearly every story he'd
told her, he'd mentioned an incident in which he'd cut
himself on a sharp staple and his beautiful secretary had
rushed to his aid with ointment, a bandage, and plenty of
sympathy. His hands, it seemed, were critical to his team
at Sony. On a hunch Abby had asked whether there had
been any blood involved in this industrial accident of
mammoth proportions. That's when she'd learned that
Donald had a serious phobia.

"Abby? Ready for some soup?"

"Bring it on, Professor." She sat up and scooted back
in the tent to give him room. They hadn't tried sharing
this space yet, and she was curious about how they'd maneuver. He was very large.

He unzipped the flap and crouched down with a tin
cup in each hand. "Minestrone."

"Sounds great."

"It will be if I can get it in there without dumping it
all over both of us."

"Well, we can't eat outside in the rain. Let me help."
Donald wouldn't be able to see through the opaque material of the tent, so she gave up the pretense of her in-
jury and crawled toward the entrance. "Give me one of
the cups."

He handed it to her, and she crawled backward and
set the cup on a bare spot on the tent floor. Careful not

to kick it, she crawled back. "Now the other one." She repeated the process so that both cups were together on the floor. Then she carefully took a cross-legged position and hoped she'd left enough room for Roarke.

"This is one small tent." He got on all fours, pulled off his hiking boots, and tucked them just inside the entrance before coming in. Closing the short distance to Abby, he kissed her full on the mouth.

She wouldn't exactly say she'd been bored lying alone in the tent, but that kiss made life a whole lot more interesting. Cupping his head, she delved into his mouth with her tongue and made a happy little sound low in her throat.

He drew back with obvious reluctance. "You need to make that sound more like a moan of pain than a moan of ecstasy," he murmured softly. "At least until he starts in with his harmonica."

She kept her voice low. "Is that likely to happen soon?"

"I never thought I'd say this, but I hope so. I told him that playing the harmonica would be a good idea so the Sasquatch couple would be drawn to this very spot."

"Smart man."

"The problem is, he likes his food, and I don't think he'll start playing until after lunch. So maybe, all things considered, we should have our soup before I"—he paused to waggle his eyebrows at her—"take off your bandage."

"Do you think you can sit down?"

"Sort of." He maneuvered into the spot she'd left for him and copied her cross-legged position, except he had to hunch over or his head would have made a dent in the roof. "Whose idea was it to bring these tiny tents, anyway?"

"Yours and Grandpa Earl's, if I remember correctly. I

wasn't involved, and I came out to discover you'd both agreed these would be marvelous." She handed him one of the cups.

"Yeah, well, they're not. And explaining the separate tent thing to Donald was quite a challenge."

"I didn't hear that part." Abby picked up her cup and took a sip. "What did you say?"

"I told him that when we got married, you were a virgin."

Abby choked on her soup.

"Sorry." Reaching over, he rubbed her back until she could breathe again. "I should have led up to that."

"No, really? What makes you think so?" She glared at him, but kept her voice lowered. "That was the best you could do? A virgin?"

He shrugged. "I had to think fast, because he was obviously confused when he saw that we had two separate tents. I told him that you were so shy at first that you didn't want me to see you dress and undress, so you wanted your own tent for that."

"If he heard us in the cave this morning, I'm sure he knows I've recovered from that problem."

"Oh, yeah, he knows. I told him that after a couple of nights with me, you'd turned into a wild woman."

"You didn't!"

"Shh." He placed a hand over her mouth. "No, I didn't. I can't seem to resist teasing you, probably because I'm getting horny as hell and we can't do anything about it until he starts playing his damned harmonica."

"So what did you say about me?"

"That with some gentle persuasion, you'd emerged from your virginal shell and were starting to enjoy the benefits of marriage . . . to a stud."

She whacked him on the arm. "You're incorrigible."

"I told you. I get like this when I'm sexually frustrated."

"So think about something else. Tell me how you see the rest of this playing out. Unless you think he has his listening device pointed this way."

"Nope. It's permanently set up pointing at the Bigfoot pair lumbering in our direction."

Her pulse rate spiked. "That's pretty exciting, Roarke. Aren't you excited?"

"Not about that."

"Why not?"

"I've dealt with these creatures before, so it's not quite the thrill for me that it is for you. Besides, they really do stink. That part won't be any fun at all."

"So how will this work, exactly?"

"I've been thinking about it, and here's my idea." He lowered his voice and leaned closer. "You lie down close to the edge of the tent, and if I lie on my side, I should be able to—"

"The Bigfoot plan, you sex maniac."

"Oh. I assumed you meant how we could enjoy some nooky."

She couldn't help laughing, but she muffled it because she was supposed to be in pain. "You assumed wrong."

He sighed. "Too bad. All right, I've been thinking about the other plan, too."

"That's reassuring."

"Do you want to hear this or shall I just start kissing you again?"

"I do, I do." She gestured for him to continue. "Please."

"Okay, once I make contact, I'll figure out a place the Bigfoot pair can hide for a day or so. A cave would be perfect. I'll tell them they have to be absolutely quiet so they won't show up on Donald's surveillance equipment. I'll set a time when the helicopter will pick them up."

"What about me seeing them?"

He rubbed her knee. "Take it easy. I'm getting to that.

We'll figure out a way for you to watch them board the helicopter."

"And what about Donald?"

"I'm thinking some sort of misdirection. The Sasquatch will have gone silent, so when I come back with some fake antibiotics for you, I can bring news of sightings in a different part of the forest. If this trail has gone dead, I think he'll go."

"We absolutely can't let him near those creatures, Roarke. For all his brains, he's incredibly insecure. He would use them shamelessly if he thought he could make a splash in the media and get his fifteen minutes of fame."

"I know. Don't worry. I'll protect them from him."

"This time. But he's developed that equipment specifically so he can locate them. He's a menace."

Roarke frowned. "You're right. Maybe I need to arrange for a good scare while he's out here, so he'll give up on this idea completely."

"I'd be in favor of that. Something involving blood should work."

"Right." Draining the last of his soup, Roarke set down his cup. "And speaking of squeamish Donald, I sure would appreciate him playing us a little tune."

"Are you sure about this idea? Even if he can't hear anything, I'm afraid we'll look like a couple of cats in a bag."

"You just have no faith in me at all, do you?"

"Yes, I do, but—"

"There's a slight breeze blowing, so I suggested that he face his tent away from it so he can sit in the doorway under the flap to play without getting wet from the rain. Turns out the breeze was very cooperative, and now the front of his tent faces in such a way that he can't even see yours."

She gazed at him admiringly. "I'm impressed."

"You ain't seen nothin' yet. Hark, is that the sound of 'Oh! Susanna' I hear?"

The notes piercing the air threatened to pierce Abby's eardrums, as well. "You weren't kidding. He's terrible."

"Actually, I'm becoming quite fond of his playing. I can't speak for Mrs. Bigfoot, but that harmonica is certainly sending my hormones into overdrive."

Abby laughed. "They were already there."

"True." He held out his hand. "Give me your cup."

She handed it to him, and he put both cups outside the tent and zipped it closed. "And now, my poor injured bride, I need you to take off your pants. Both pairs."

"Do you, now?"

"Absolutely. I'm a doctor."

"Not that kind of doctor."

"Hey, we're out in the wilderness, and you obviously need a doctor. Are you going to be choosy?"

She had no idea how they were going to engineer a sexual experience, but with lust raging through her body, she was more than willing to try. "Yes. And I choose you."

Chapter 17

Roarke might have had sex under more difficult conditions, but he wasn't sure when. Back in the cave he'd promised Abby an experience he might have trouble delivering unless he wanted to open the tent flap and stick his feet out into the rain.

Then again, maybe that wasn't the only alternative. A little creative thinking might be in order. While he'd been trying to figure out the logistics, his extremely cooperative patient had removed not only her outer pants and underpants, but also her bandage, her knit top, and her bra. Lucky him, he was in this tiny space with a naked woman, one he craved beyond all reason.

"Maybe this isn't so bad." He gathered her into his arms. "In such close quarters, you can't get away."

"Neither can you." Sliding her hand under the elastic waist of his sweats, she soon had eliminated the barrier of his briefs and was stroking his rock-hard penis. "My, what a big dick you have."

"Wait. Are you actually doing a riff on *Little Red Riding Hood*?"

"I suppose you're tired of hearing *Little Red Riding Hood* jokes."

"Well, no woman has ever known what I am, so I don't get too much of it."

"Then it's about time you had to deal with *Little Red Riding Hood* jokes." She continued to fondle him. "After all, we are in the middle of a forest, and you are a big bad wolf."

"You are so right. And do you know what big bad wolves do to little red-haired girls like you?"

She laughed. "No."

He grasped her wrist and pulled her hand out of his pants. "They eat them right up." His reflexes had always been excellent, and before she completely understood his intent, he'd reversed direction and had a knee on either side of her shoulders and his head between her thighs.

"Roarke!"

Her startled exclamation told him she hadn't expected him to deliver on his morning promise. But deliver he would. He'd had soup for his main course at lunch, and now he'd enjoy some dessert.

He started by using his tongue, and she tasted better than cherries jubilee and chocolate mousse combined. He vowed to sample this treat more often . . . and then realized that he wouldn't have many more opportunities to nestle between her legs and feast like this. He'd better enjoy it while he could.

From his first contact with her moist treasures, she'd begun to whimper and moan. Thank God for harmonica music, because he wanted to hear more of those sweet sounds of hers. Scooping his hands under her bottom, he lifted her toward his eager mouth and delved deeper.

He was so involved in loving her that at first he didn't

realize that a second event was beginning at her end of the tent. But when her warm fingers wrapped around his cock, which she had freed from his clothes, he stilled.

"Little Red Riding Hood has an appetite, too," she murmured.

If he hadn't been crazy about this woman before, he was now. With a groan of joyful surrender, he lowered his hips and felt her warm tongue and hot mouth rise to meet his throbbing penis.

After that he had a little trouble concentrating, but he was determined not to come until he felt the jolt of her climax roll through her. More than once he thought he might lose that battle because she had a real talent for this erotic game. But then her thighs began to quiver, and her cries became more breathless. He had her.

She came gloriously, and he feasted on the bounty of her orgasm until . . . oh . . . yes . . . *yes*. The urgent pressure of her mouth and tongue destroyed the last of his will-power and he let go. He wanted to yell as she drank him in, but he didn't dare, so he smothered his cries against her slick heat. The vibration of his muted shouts of triumph spurred her to lift her hips in a silent request, and he gladly plundered her moist softness until she shivered against him once again.

He would have given her a third orgasm, but she sank to the floor of the tent and brought her thighs together, shutting him out.

"Abby?" He kissed her wet curls. "Girls don't have a limit like guys. You can have more."

She gulped for air. "Not now. He stopped playing."

"Really?" Apparently his pounding heart had drowned out everything but the beautiful sounds of Abby coming. He'd completely lost track of the harmonica music and whether or not it provided cover for their activities.

"So that means he might hear us," she said.

He traced lazy circles over her still-quivering thighs. "I don't care."

"Yes, you do," she said softly. "We need him to believe I have a bad cut on my leg. The rest of the plan depends on it. If he knows what we're doing in here, he'll doubt that I'm hurt and it all falls apart."

She was right, and it should bother him that she was more intent on the Bigfoot plan than he was. He needed to focus. But how was he supposed to do that, when he'd begun to question everything he'd believed about how his life would go?

Twenty-four hours earlier he'd told himself that he could easily walk away from Abby. That was no longer true. And it wasn't only because of the great sex. That explanation was backward.

He felt completely tuned in to her, as if he could read her mind and she could read his. That was why they had such great sex. He'd never felt so mentally connected in a sexual relationship. The implication of that was huge.

"Wallace?" Donald's voice came from right outside the tent. "Everything okay in there?"

Shit. Roarke lifted his cheek from Abby's damp curls. "Just fine, Donald."

"I thought I heard Abby moan, so I wanted to make sure she's not worse."

"I'm okay, Donald," Abby said. "After we finished our soup, Roarke checked my bandage and it turns out I'd started bleeding again. He had to put some pressure on it to stop it. It was kind of gross, but everything's settled down, now."

"Oh. Well, that's good. I'm glad you can deal with blood, Wallace. I'll just be in my tent, then." His announcement was followed by the sound of his quick retreat through the wet leaves.

Roarke reversed direction again, this time a lot more slowly than the first time. A fantastic orgasm could affect a guy's reflexes, and besides, Abby had shoved his sweats to his knees, which made maneuvering awkward.

Once he got his briefs and sweats back in place, he covered Abby's body lightly with his own and gazed into her eyes. "Nice touch, emphasizing the blood."

"Thanks. I learned all I know about telling glib lies from you."

"I'm not feeling particularly glib right now."

"No?" She combed his hair back from his forehead.

"We're almost done with this project."

"Don't count your chickens, Professor. We still have a lot to accomplish."

"Yes, but it's pretty much laid out, and by this time tomorrow . . ."

"We won't be together."

"Right. And that's depressing the hell out of me."

"Don't think about it." Her eyes told him she was thinking about it, though. And she didn't look any happier about the prospect of saying good-bye, either.

He reminded himself that she'd recoiled at the idea of having children who could turn out to be shapeshifters. She'd hated the thought that Emma couldn't tell her family and friends the true details of her life and had to feed them fancy lies instead. Hell, she'd even made it clear that she wanted to keep her own name when she married.

She ran a finger down his cheek. "You should probably go reassure Donald that all is well with me. I think he stopped playing because he heard me cry out and he was worried."

Roarke nodded. "Yeah, he's not a bad guy. I feel sort of guilty knowing he'll never get to see Bigfoot."

"Yes, but his motives aren't pure. Don't forget that

he's not strong enough to see Bigfoot and then not tell anybody. Even my grandfather wasn't."

"Do you think Earl could be trusted now, though? If you told him what was at stake?"

Her eyes lit up. "Are you saying that maybe he could be with me when I watch them get into the helicopter?"

"I'd like that. It would help make up for the way I've disgraced him in his hometown."

"Roarke, you're a prince." Cradling his face in both hands, she lifted her head and kissed him.

He would have loved to kiss her back. Then he'd begin kissing every inch of her body so he could map all those freckles he'd vowed to find. He longed to stroke her until she writhed against the floor of the tent, until she wanted him again. He would take her in one smooth stroke. She was so easy to love.

Easy to love. God, he was in so much trouble.

Reluctantly he ended the kiss. "Technically I am a prince, but I'm not in line to inherit the throne. That would be my brother, Aidan."

"Literally? You have a throne at your house in New York?"

"No, not an actual throne. Nobody would want to sit on something like that. But there is a hierarchy. It's that way in all werewolf packs."

"So does that make Cameron Gentry the reigning king of their pack?"

"It does." Roarke rolled away very carefully and scooted down to the front of the tent. "Which means Cameron outranks me."

"I don't like that. I don't like *him.*"

He picked up a hiking boot and pulled it on. "Neither do I, but I owe him my respect. And I've given my word that I'll take care of his Sasquatch problem for him."

"And you will. Your plan is going to work."

"*Our* plan."

She scooted to a seated position. "That's nice of you to say, but if you hadn't been saddled with me in the first place and you'd been able to work on your own, you'd probably be done with the whole thing by now."

He gazed at her. "If you think for one second that I regret any of this, then—"

"I know you don't."

"I'm glad you know it. Sharing this time with you has been incredible." He could say a lot more, but he wouldn't. No point in going into detail about how she'd enriched his hours in the past two days. He'd only make things worse.

"Same here, Roarke," she said gently.

He held her gaze. "Good to know."

"I just meant you would have been more efficient without me."

He smiled at her as he pulled on his other boot. "Efficiency is highly overrated." Then he left the tent before he became even less efficient and wrecked the entire plan.

Abby wished she'd brought a book, but she'd never expected to spend this much time alone. Refastening her fake bandage and dressing didn't take much time, and then she was left to lie there and listen to Roarke and Donald talking. She couldn't even amuse herself with that, though, because she couldn't hear what they said.

Predictably, Donald's voice was the one she heard most of the time, and she didn't envy Roarke having to listen to all those self-aggrandizing stories. Still, she would rather listen to Donald's boring conversation than lie here alone with her thoughts, which played in a continuous loop in her mind.

Roarke didn't want their time together to end, and

she didn't want that, either. But end it would. If they didn't live almost a continent apart, they could be lovers a little while longer, but that would only make the inevitable breakup worse.

They'd be wise not to see each other again once this was over. She'd certainly hate to face the prospect of running in to him after he'd chosen his werewolf mate. That would be excruciatingly painful. Thinking of Roarke with someone else sent slivers of glass into her heart, so the reality would be even more horrible.

But she wouldn't run in to him, because he'd go back to his job at NYU, and she'd go back to being a claims adjuster in Phoenix. Now that she knew the truth about the Gentrys, she'd find a way to move Grandpa Earl to Phoenix, too. That project should occupy her for several months and give her time to get over Roarke.

She was whistling in the wind on that estimation, and she damn well knew it. Getting over Roarke would take longer than a few months. It might not happen at all.

The child who had loved fantasy had grown into a woman who had denied that part of herself. But these past days with Roarke had reawakened her love of fantasy and intrigue. After knowing Roarke, how could she ever be happy with anyone else?

Although he'd made it clear that he didn't want a human for a mate, she'd begun thinking of how she might be able to live a double life, after all. If Roarke could do it, why couldn't she? Still, he hadn't ever hinted that he wanted her to try. She'd have to let him go, no matter how much that hurt.

Gradually the patter of the rain on the tent lulled her into a light sleep, but the rasp of her tent zipper brought her instantly awake and her body tightened in anticipation. "Roarke?"

He shoved his big shoulders through the tent opening. "I know you must be going stir-crazy in here, but I can't stay," he said in a low voice. "Donald's suspicious."

"I was afraid of that. Do we have any ketchup?"

Roarke stared at her, and then he began to chuckle. "Good thought, but I didn't bring any."

"Maybe I should prick my—"

"Oh, no, you don't. I won't have you sacrificing any of your precious blood to satisfy Donald. However . . ."

She could see the wheels going around. "Don't you dare cut yourself."

"Why not? You were willing to do it."

"And you couldn't stand the idea. I can't stand the idea of you inflicting pain on yourself, either, so you'd better not, or . . ."

"Or what?" His gaze made it plain he had the upper hand.

And she felt impotent. "I will be really, really mad at you."

His expression softened. "And I wouldn't like that."

"So don't do it, okay?"

Instead of answering, he pulled a magazine from inside his jacket. "I brought you some reading material."

"Thank God. I've been wishing I'd brought a book."

"I wish I had one to give you, but this is what's available." He handed her an issue of *Cryptozoology Today*.

"I'll take it. I'll bet one of Donald's articles is in here."

"Yep, which is the only reason he packed it, in case he met somebody out here he wanted to impress. Enjoy." Then he was gone.

Abby read the slim magazine from cover to cover and learned more than she'd ever wanted to know about cryptids, including Nessie, Sasquatch, Yeti, and a giant anaconda that made her vow never to visit Brazil. Give her a beautiful werewolf any day.

As if she'd summoned him, Roarke unzipped the tent

flap. "I've got stew." He held the same tin cups with spoons sticking out of them.

"Great. Thanks." She moved to all fours and took one of the cups of stew before crawling backward and placing it at the far end of the tent in the same spot where she'd put the soup. "Can you stay awhile?"

"Not long."

She reached for the other cup of stew, but he set it down by the entrance. Instead of taking off his boots, he sat with his feet outside the tent.

She was disappointed that he'd be leaving soon, but he knew best how to handle things with Donald. She sat cross-legged and picked up her stew. "I guess our friend's still suspicious."

"Actually, he's not. I took care of that."

Her eyes narrowed. "And how did you do that, pray tell?"

"You don't want to know."

"Roarke Wallace, if you—"

"It was the logical answer, and I want to thank you for suggesting it."

"I did not!"

"Keep your voice down. You're supposed to be getting sicker and feverish as the infection sets in. In fact, I'm taking back one helping of stew so I can tell him you weren't hungry."

"But what about your dinner?"

"I have some jerky in my pack. I'll be fine."

"I want you to eat mine, then." She shoved it toward him. "I'm just lying here. You're the one who needs energy."

"Abby, you might as well eat the stew, because I'm not going to. And I need to get out of here soon with at least one empty cup."

She glared at him mutinously.

"Don't be stubborn, Red Riding Hood. Eat your stew. If you don't, you'll just be causing more problems for the operation."

Abby didn't like the way this was turning out, but she ate the stew. "So what did you do that convinced Donald this was legit?"

"Just used a razor blade on my calf where he wouldn't be able to see what I'd done. Honestly, it was no big deal. I didn't need much blood because I wiped my hands in it and then made sure I washed them in his line of sight. He assumed I'd just come from your tent. I didn't have to say a word."

She blew out a breath. "I am really, really mad at you."

"I hope you'll forgive me quick, then."

"Why?"

"The Sasquatch pair is traveling faster than I expected. It's time for me to intercept them before they get too close."

She began to tremble and put down the tin cup in hopes he wouldn't notice her shaking. Suddenly the plan seemed filled with danger. He might be a werewolf, but he'd be facing two really huge creatures. "Is it safe for you to confront them alone?"

"Perfectly safe. Weres and Sasquatch get along fine."

"So this is it."

"Yes, this is it. You might want to give me your bottle of ibuprofen now."

"Okay." She reached for the pack she'd been using as a pillow and unzipped one of the pockets. "If you have to show these to Donald when you get back, just hold them so you're covering up the label." She handed him the container.

"I will." He slipped the container into his jacket pocket. "I'm going to tell Donald that you'd rather be left alone, but I can't guarantee he won't come over here and bore you to death."

She managed a smile. "I can handle him."

"I'll be back as soon as I possibly can. I don't know if it's logical for me to put in an appearance before morning, but just know that I'll be around long before that, watching over you."

"As a wolf?"

"Yes."

She crawled over toward him. "I don't want you to go."

"I don't want to, either." He cupped her cheek in one large hand and leaned forward to kiss her gently. He lifted his mouth from hers. "When I come back, we'll have to concentrate on getting out of here, so I can arrange for the Sasquatch transfer."

"So no more nooky."

"No." He kissed her again. Then, with a groan, he kissed her harder, thrusting his tongue in deep. Then he pulled back and gazed into her eyes as his filled with sorrow. "Thanks for everything, Miss Riding Hood."

"You're welcome, Mr. Wolf."

Grabbing the tin cups, he edged out of the tent and zipped it closed.

She sat back on her heels and closed her eyes so she could savor the taste of him that lingered on her mouth. Her lips still tingled from his last forceful kiss, but the rest of her was blissfully numb. She would love to keep it that way, but she knew any minute her brain would send a message to her heart, and then all hell would break loose.

Chapter 18

Roarke didn't have any trouble sounding worried when he hurried over to where Donald sat just inside his tent eating his stew. Leaving Abby to the care of this doofus, even if she wasn't actually injured, went against Roarke's every instinct. But he had no choice if he expected to solve the Bigfoot problem.

"Bad news, Donald." He held the two cups of stew, the one Abby had eaten and the one he hadn't touched. "Her wound's infected and she's running a fever." He held up the full cup of stew. "She couldn't eat."

Behind his thick lenses, Donald's eyes looked huge. "Good God. What are we going to do? The Sasquatch could be here by morning!"

"They could, but they'll probably stop for the night, so it could be midday before they arrive." Roarke was counting on the pair stopping to rest. "I hope to be back before they get here."

Donald's eyes got even bigger and he scrambled to his feet, spilling some stew on his orange sweatshirt. "You're *leaving*?"

"I want you to stay with Abby while I head back to get some antibiotics for her."

"No reputable doctor will give you a prescription without seeing her."

Roarke mentally thanked Abby for giving him the answer to that one. "I have a friend who will, once I describe the situation. Look, I'll travel as fast as I can. Believe me, adrenaline is pumping through my system and I'll make good progress."

"Yes, but—"

"I hope to get back here before the Sasquatch pair arrives, but in case I don't, I'll feel good knowing you're here, getting the evidence and watching over Abby."

"But what should I do about her? Does she need me to sponge her down?"

"No!"

Donald shrank back in alarm.

Roarke toned down his response. "I mean, she would hate that, being so modest and all."

"Well, yeah, but if she has a fever, I've always heard you're supposed to sponge people down."

Roarke hated that idea on so many levels. "You might cause her to start bleeding again if you did that."

"Oh." Donald paled. "Well, then, better not chance it."

"She's not going to die, so don't panic. But I can't expect her to hike back out of here when she has a fever and she needs something to counteract that infection."

"No, no, of course she can't hike out when she's like this."

"Once she has the antibiotics, she'll start to recover. But I need to get them for her now."

"Right, right. It's just that I thought you'd be here when Samson and Delilah showed up."

"Who?"

"The Sasquatch pair."

"They don't have names."

Donald brightened. "They do now! I named them to-day, while you were taking care of Abby. It'll play better with the media if we give them each a name, like every-one uses Nessie for the Loch Ness Monster. Personal-izes the creatures, you know. It would be good if you started referring to them that way, too."

Roarke started to deny that he'd ever refer to the Sasquatch pair by the names Samson and Delilah, but decided not to waste his breath. It wouldn't matter, be-cause Donald would never make contact with them.

"We should name the baby, too."

Roarke patted Donald on the shoulder. "You think about that while I'm gone. Now, if you'll excuse me, I'll throw a few things into my pack and be off." He turned toward his tent.

"I sure wish we got cell reception out here," Donald called after him.

"But we don't," Roarke said over his shoulder. And now he was thrilled about that. "I'm afraid hiking back is my only option." He made a dash for his tent before Donald could hold him up any longer. The Sasquatch odor grew stronger with every passing minute.

Fortunately the rain seemed to be letting up, which would make the forest floor a little less slippery as he loped along. Anticipating this change into wolf form, he'd brought a plastic bag for his backpack and his clothes. He stuffed that in the empty pack along with Abby's ibuprofen. He decided to leave his watch in the tent. Donald wouldn't notice he wasn't wearing it and it was one less thing to leave out in the forest after he shifted.

As a human, he would have needed to take more on this trip. As a wolf, he needed nothing, but he had to leave camp as if he were a man going for a long hike, so he tucked some other clothes in the pack. In the process he came across the handkerchief he'd made into a headband. He allowed himself one long inhale before shoving that into his pack, too.

He was ready. Ducking out of the tent, he zipped it closed and stood. "See you, Donald."

Donald stood watching him, anxiety etched on his round face. "Hurry."

"Don't worry. I will." Then he walked quickly over to Abby's tent. "Bye, Abby," he said softly.

"Bye, Roarke." She sounded a little bit nasal, as if she'd been crying.

"It'll be okay."

"I know."

Shit, she had been crying. And there wasn't a damned thing he could do about that. Anything he said would only make it worse. "Bye," he said again, and walked away before he could hear her response.

In order to fool Donald, he had to walk back the way they'd come, at least until he had enough cover. As the light faded from the sky, he plowed quickly through the trees and underbrush, following the trampled leaves and broken branches from their passage through here earlier.

He walked nearly a mile before he considered it safe to strip down. As he took off his clothes and stuffed everything in the plastic bag he'd brought, he thought of Abby's pictures and wondered what she planned to do with them. If she cared about him the way he cared about her, she'd destroy the flash drive and the prints when she returned to her grandfather's place.

She was in control of that decision, because she hadn't told him where she'd hidden the flash drive, only that her grandfather would look there if for some reason she turned up missing. But she wouldn't turn up missing. She'd be fine in camp until he could go back for her.

Telling himself that and believing it were two different things. As he lay on the cold ground and willed his shift, he realized that being separated from Abby was a condition he didn't care for at all. It felt unnatural, as if he'd left part of himself back at camp.

But he wouldn't want her here, either, to witness his transformation into a wolf. She might have pictures of it, but that was one step removed. Aidan claimed that Emma was used to seeing her husband shift, but Roarke questioned that.

He still believed in the separation of humans and werewolves. It defied the natural order to throw them together. What a cruel joke, that fate had placed Abby in his path.

As he rose from the ground and shook himself from head to tail, he glanced down at his large forepaws. A few hours ago, they'd been human hands capable of caressing Abby. How could he expect her to accept that he could become . . . this? He couldn't.

Nudging the plastic bag under a bush with his nose, he turned, caught the scent of the Sasquatch, and headed back the way he'd come. When he sighted the camp through the trees, he paused, head up. A light was on in Abby's tent, and . . . damn it to hell, that traffic cone of a man was sitting in front of the open flap, probably droning on about his accomplishments at Sony.

Roarke fought the urge to charge in, take him by the throat, and shake him like a rag doll. But that would be stupid. Although Donald wouldn't know the wolf shaking him was Roarke, he'd certainly tell everyone who would listen about his life-threatening encounter with a giant beast, and Weres didn't need stories like that floating around.

Skirting the camp, Roarke picked up the pace. He had a job to do.

Abby pretended to fall asleep during Donald's description of a conference he'd attended as, of course, a featured speaker. Donald didn't seem to care whether she was conscious or not. Abby wondered if he talked to the wall at home. She couldn't imagine Donald *not* talking. For all she knew, he held some sort of world record.

"So then, you'll never guess who came up to me after my speech," Donald said.

Abby faked a soft snore.

"The Terminator himself! Arnie! I pointed a finger at him and said, in his accent, *Hasta la vista, baby,* and he just cracked up. He said I should've been an actor. Which I thought about back in college, but I—" Donald paused. "Did you hear something?"

Abby's eyes snapped open. She couldn't possibly have heard something with Donald droning on, but now that he'd stopped, she did hear a rustling noise. Were those footsteps?

Propping herself on her elbows, she rose so she could see Donald. She'd no sooner done that than he scrambled into the tent with her and zipped the flap. Like that would protect him.

Outside a stick cracked as if someone, or some*thing,* had stepped on it. All the possibilities ran through Abby's head—Bigfoot had given Roarke the slip, a bear had smelled their food and wanted some, a herd of deer had shown up now that the werewolf had left the area. Or it could be a human, although why a human wouldn't call out a greeting made her think whatever was out there wasn't human.

She eased to a sitting position. She wasn't quite ready to give Donald the information that she wasn't hurt, after all. But if push came to shove, she'd rather use her legs than be trampled or eaten or whatever else might happen to her if she kept up the charade of being a maiden in distress.

Donald was shaking and his face had lost all color. "It can't be Samson and Delilah," he murmured. "I checked the equipment an hour ago and their position was static. They've stopped for the night."

"Maybe they changed their plans." Donald had informed her earlier about his decision to name the Sasquatch pair, so she knew who he was talking about. But she was inclined to believe that it wasn't them. For one thing, she couldn't smell them, and both Roarke and Grandpa Earl had assured her she would gag once she did.

"Could be a herd of deer," she said.

Donald stared at her, hope struggling with terror in his eyes. "You think?"

"Bigfoot would smell."

"Oh my God, you're right." His shoulders sagged in relief. But then they hunched up again. "Could be a griz."

Abby smiled and shook her head. "Not around here. Could be a bear, though. I'll grant you that."

He began to shake again and his teeth chattered. "Which means we're supposed to curl up and play dead, right?"

Abby felt sorry for the poor guy. "Why did you come out here by yourself if you're so afraid?"

"My sister double dared me."

"Oh." She made sure not to let a hint of a smile cross her lips.

"I researched the area, and bear sightings are rare."

"That's true." And now Abby had a good idea why. With a pack of werewolves living on the Gentry estate, bears would tend to go elsewhere rather than fight for territory. She had seen deer over the years, but they were used to sensing predators nearby and the foliage was lush and plentiful enough to keep them hanging around, werewolves or no werewolves.

"I thought if I could get a picture of Bigfoot, I could stick it to all those people who think I'm some kind of nut, including my older sister," Donald said.

Abby was tempted to ask him if he worked for Sony at all, or if he was a technician in a second-rate repair facility. But she didn't want to kick a guy when he was down. Roarke was convinced Donald was really smart, but his lack of social skills might have caused him to be underemployed.

Another branch cracked. Whatever was out there hadn't gone away. "I'll bet it's deer," Abby said, more to calm her own jumpy pulse than to reassure Donald. She'd never camped overnight alone. She'd always had her brother along.

"I hope you're right. Deer are cool."

Abby decided to give him a chance to be manly. "Do you want to go out there and make sure?"

"Oh, I think we should leave them alone to do their thing. No use scaring them, right?"

"I guess you have a point, Donald." He was beginning to grow on her. Or maybe it was any port in a storm.

"Think about it, Abby. If I walked out there, they might think I was some big, bad hunter ready to fire away. I saw *Bambi* as a kid. I can relate."

"Okay, then." Abby had to say this for the experience: It was a lot more exciting than listening to Donald bragging about his life as an engineer. She was beginning to suspect most, if not all, of the things he'd told her weren't true.

But all guys couldn't be like Roarke, who had the muscles, the looks, the courage, the brains, the fur . . .

Something sent a rock skittering along the ground very close to the tent and Donald flinched. "They wouldn't stampede or anything, would they?"

"I've never heard of deer stampeding through a camp. You might be thinking of a cattle drive, or maybe even wild buffalo, back in the Old West."

"You're right." His shoulders sagged again. "You know how it is in the dark, when your imagination runs away with—"

"You there, in the tent!"

Abby's wide gaze met Donald's and she couldn't have said who was more scared. She couldn't speak for him, but she almost peed her pants.

Even so, she must have found some courage somewhere, because she piped up immediately with "Who's there?"

No answer. Her skin prickled. "I *said*, who's there?"

Apparently they weren't going to play her game of Knock, Knock, because no one bothered to answer her question.

"Drug dealers," Donald whispered.

She shook her head. "They wouldn't want anything to do with us." She lifted her eyebrows. "Would they?"

He gulped. "I have some grass in my backpack."

"Just so you don't have any crystal meth, I think we're okay."

"God, no, but still, they might think that—"

"Come out of the tent," said a voice cold as the waters of the Columbia. "We don't want to have to wait for you." Then light poured through the nylon tent from what had to be several battery-operated lanterns.

If this had been a movie, Roarke would have arrived just at that moment to save the day and put the intruders, whoever they were, in their place. But Abby didn't think Roarke would show up just now. And she had a very bad feeling about who was outside the tent.

Donald could barely speak, but he leaned toward her. "Do you think it's banditos here to rob, rape, and pillage?"

"No." She would have preferred bandits. At least they had a profit motive.

Donald cleared his throat and clenched his fists. "We have an injured woman in here!" His voice quivered as he said it, but at least he'd tried.

"Thanks, Donald," she said softly. "Don't be a hero. I'll be okay."

"No, you stay here. They might have guns." He looked as if he might pass out at any moment. "I'll see what they want."

"Maybe you should let me go first."

"Nope." Resolution gleamed in his gray eyes. "Wallace told me to watch out for you, and I will." He lifted his round chin as if he figured he was about to meet his death. *"Semper fi."*

"You were a Marine?" She regretted the disbelief in her voice, but if Donald was a former Marine, she was a former Miss Universe.

"No, my sister was." With that he zipped open the flap and crawled out into the glare from the lanterns.

She couldn't let him do that alone. Crawling out after him, she blinked in the bright light. Then she stood and faced—damn it all—Cameron Gentry, king of the Portland werewolves.

Chapter 19

All Roarke had to do at this point was follow his nose. Why anyone would want to track down Bigfoot was beyond him. The creature might be sweet and exotic, but an open sewer couldn't rival the stench.

When he was about two miles from the pair, he started looking for another cave. The one he and Abby had so thoroughly enjoyed wouldn't have been big enough, so he was hoping for something a little larger. There—a shadow in the side of the hill. Bingo.

A family of coyotes had taken up residence, but he convinced them to vacate for the next couple of days. He didn't tell them they'd have to fumigate when they returned, but if they were this close to the Sasquatch pair already, they couldn't be all that particular.

A half-mile away from the Sasquatch, Roarke buried his nose in some wild mint for a few seconds, just so he could go on without barfing. He doubted any creatures had remained this close to the encampment. Roarke hated to move the Sasquatch somewhere else, because he'd only be transferring the noxious odor to another part of the pristine forest. But the creatures had to live somewhere, and they were part of biodiversity, so Roarke was committed to the relocation plan.

Finally he could see their camp, such as it was. Sasquatch weren't known for their domestic skills. A pile of mangled roots and berries lay in the small clearing, and the mated pair lay sprawled against each other near the pile of what was essentially garbage.

Although the common wisdom pegged Sasquatch as omnivores, Roarke had never known them to eat meat. But he'd never figured out why, if they were herbivores, they smelled so bad. Maybe they simply had bad digestion, which might be an inherited trait. A creature that large could give off some serious gas.

Especially when they were asleep after a meal. Jesus. Roarke wondered if he'd be asphyxiated before he completed his mission. But he took a moment to recognize that cryptozoologists the world over would sacrifice their retirement account to be where he was right this minute, gazing at two mythical creatures seldom seen by the human eye.

They weren't being seen by the human eye, now, either. They were being seen by the werewolf eye. But he hoped to lay this spectacle at Abby's feet, and maybe at Earl's as well. That possibility helped him deal with the fetid odor of the Sasquatch camp.

The light was dim, so he couldn't make out the color of their shaggy coats. The scientist in him wondered where they fit along the known spectrum of dark brown to red, but clouds obscured the moonlight that might have revealed that.

Padding silently toward the sleeping pair, he lifted his head and howled, the werewolf version of an alarm clock. They woke up slowly, groggily, as if some of the berries they'd consumed had been fermented. Roarke hoped not, because that wouldn't be good for the little one carried in the female's rounded belly.

The male stood, all nine feet of him, and towered over Roarke. But he was flabby and Roarke was solid muscle. Besides, Sasquatch and Weres had never fought over anything. The huge creatures seemed to recognize a superior intelligence and deferred to it.

Roarke sent the telepathic message he'd mentally constructed as he traveled here. Through images he hoped they would understand, he told them they were not safe here and needed to find another place to have the baby.

There was no response at first. Roarke expected that. The Sasquatch were slow thinkers and needed time to assimilate new facts. The male's protruding brow wrinkled as he struggled with the proposition.

At last the answer came, and it was as he'd expected. The female had been born near here, and she wanted her baby to be born here, too.

Roarke understood that urge. His kind were territorial in that way, too. But he projected the image of werewolves and let the pair know they'd invaded Were territory.

The female rose and shuffled over to join her mate. She stared at him stubbornly, defiantly. Obviously she didn't want to go elsewhere, despite the Weres.

Roarke looked into her dark eyes and absorbed the rest of her message. She was too far along to go a great distance.

Roarke wondered if he'd be able to pull this off, after all. He'd never coaxed a mated pair into a helicopter before and he didn't know if they'd understand the concept. He mentally projected climbing aboard a helicopter, lifting off, and then landing somewhere safe.

If he hadn't been about to gag from the stench, he would have found the scene pretty funny. They turned to each other, their brows wrinkled in an obvious effort to figure out the whole flying concept. Then they literally put their heads together and muttered in a language Roarke hadn't yet studied. Telepathy was much more efficient.

Finally the male turned and puffed out his chest. Then he shook his head and put a protective arm around his mate.

Roarke admired the male's protective stance. If Roarke were in their shoes, he wouldn't trust his mate to some unknown mechanical bird, either. But they had to go.

He decided to try a different approach. He projected an image of humans tracking them down. For good measure, he threw in a scene of them being captured and hauled away.

The male glanced around the clearing as if expecting hunters to rush out of the trees. When nothing happened, he turned back to the female and they muttered some more. Apparently she held equal power in the relationship, and Roarke took note of that so he could add it to the accumulated knowledge about the creatures.

He would have to remember to tell Abby about that. In fact, he needed to remember every detail of this interaction so that he could relate it to her. He imagined how her blue eyes would shine with wonder and all the questions she'd ask.

Once again the male faced Roarke, but he seemed more open, more willing. He wanted to know more about the helicopter.

Roarke did his best. He projected images of safety, but added that there would be noise and wind from the whirling blades. He didn't want them to be unprepared and turn tail at the last minute. They seemed to be concentrating very hard as they tried to understand.

So much depended on that moment when the Sasquatch were expected to climb into a machine that would take them up in the air, something they'd never experienced. They would be terrified. Roarke became so involved in his task that he almost forgot that he was in sensory hell. These creatures might not be particularly intelligent, but they were kind and respectful to each other, and that counted for a lot with Roarke.

Finally he realized what had to happen. He'd meet them at the cave in wolf form, escort them to the waiting helicopter, and ride with them on the way to their new home. He'd show them with his calm demeanor that there was nothing to be afraid of. That meant Earl wouldn't be able to watch the departure, but Abby still could.

Facing the Sasquatch pair, Roarke communicated the plan, and they both brightened considerably. They conferred once more in their muttered language before facing Roarke again.

Interestingly, the female was the one who transmitted their thoughts. Apparently because she was the one having the baby, she had the final say. They would go on the helicopter.

Abby would love hearing that the female had the authority. He could hardly wait to tell her. In the back of his mind lurked the thought that soon he wouldn't have the luxury of being able to tell Abby things, unless he wanted to keep in touch via the Internet.

Yeah, right. They could be Facebook buddies. Not. There was no way in hell he'd be willing to maintain some anemic online contact with a woman with whom he'd shared copious orgasms. It was all or nothing.

But he couldn't think about that now. He had to focus

on finishing this task. Coaxing the pair to follow him to the cave he'd picked out was much easier than convincing them to fly in a helicopter.

He suggested they gather food along the way, enough to get them through a couple of days, until he could come for them. They left quite a trail of destruction on the way to the cave, ripping up entire bushes until both of them had more than they could carry.

After multiple relays, they seemed to think they had enough food to last for the duration. After extracting their promise that they would not leave the cave until Roarke showed up, he started back. He moved quickly, eager to tell Abby that he'd set up the relocation plan.

Abby had seen Cameron Gentry twice in her life, both times in downtown Portland. The first time she'd been about six and had gone into town with her brother, Pete, and her grandparents for an ice cream sundae. Cameron, a teenager, had been in the same ice cream parlor with his parents. Abby distinctly remembered he'd treated the waitress like dirt.

The second time she'd encountered Cameron had been about fifteen years later on a crowded sidewalk when he'd hurried past with some business associates. In his complete self-absorption, he'd nearly knocked her grandmother down and then hadn't bothered to apologize. Grandpa Earl had wanted to challenge him, but Grandma Olive had talked him out of it.

Abby doubted Cameron would remember her from either incident. As she studied him now, she decided he hadn't aged well. The touches of gray at his temples should have made him look distinguished, but the lines of cruelty around his mouth eliminated any attractiveness he might have.

As for his attitude of entitlement, that hadn't improved one damned bit. He obviously still thought the world was his oyster. But he didn't have the brawn to back up that belief, so he'd brought along three burly guys on this mission. Abby was willing to bet all four men could shift into wolves at a moment's notice.

Good thing Donald didn't know that. The poor man acted pathetically grateful to discover their visitors seemed normal and weren't carrying weapons. What Donald didn't know couldn't hurt him. What Abby knew could hurt *her,* though, so she'd play dumb for as long as she could get away with it.

Once Donald had verified that he wasn't in danger of being shot, he'd started to babble. "You guys gave us quite a scare. I bet you're with the forest service or something, *huh*? Want some coffee? I could make some on the camp stove in no time flat. I have cookies, too. Oreos. They pack better than—"

"Where's Wallace?" Cameron looked directly at Abby.

She shouldn't have been surprised that they'd immediately known Roarke had been here. They were werewolves, so they could probably stick their sensitive noses in Roarke's vacant tent and smell that he'd left a few hours ago.

Still, she did her best imitation of a clueless female. "Wallace who?"

"He means Roarke, Abby," Donald said helpfully. "You should probably go back in the tent and let me handle this." He glanced at Cameron. "She's not herself, which is understandable considering that this is her honeymoon and her groom is off getting antibiotics for her infection."

Cameron stared at Donald as if trying to decide whether he was crazy or just stupid. "What the hell are you talking about?"

Donald laughed nervously. "I know it seems weird, that Roarke and Abby would invite me to team up with them on their honeymoon hike, but we found out we have a lot of things in common, so we—"

"Shut up, whoever you are." Cameron turned back to Abby. "I sincerely doubt that Wallace got married in the last two days, let alone to Earl Dooley's granddaughter."

Donald gasped. "You're his *granddaughter*? What a coincidence! He's the one who sighted the mated Bigfoot pair!"

Abby felt sick to her stomach as she looked at Cameron. Dear God, if Cameron had done anything to Grandpa Earl . . . but Roarke had said he was safe because he didn't know about the Weres. She'd hang on to that thought.

She took a deep breath. "How did you find out I'm Earl's granddaughter?"

"Wallace had suddenly become very sympathetic to Earl's situation, and he was acting odd before he left on this hike, so on a hunch I went over to Earl's store this afternoon. He proudly, and somewhat defiantly, I might add, told me you and Wallace had set out together and you were going to bring back evidence that Bigfoot exists."

Donald stared at her. "So are you two married or what?"

"I told you to shut up!" Cameron motioned angrily to one of the three guys standing behind him. "See that he doesn't bother me again."

Donald gasped as two of the men started toward him.

Abby stepped in front of him. "Don't either of you dare lay a hand on this man! If you do, I'll have you arrested for assault."

One of the men picked her up by the waist as if she were a piece of furniture in his way and set her to one side. As she spun around with a cry of protest, they each grabbed one of Donald's arms and propelled him backward, out of the circle of light.

Donald's mouth rounded in terror, but nothing came out.

Abby started toward him, but the third man closed his large hand around her biceps and held her in place. She considered kicking him in the crotch, but she wasn't sure that would be wise, all things considered. If this incident turned physical, she and Donald wouldn't stand a chance against a quartet of Weres.

"All right, Abby Winchell," Cameron said, his voice deceptively soft. "We're not going to play games. What are you to Roarke Wallace?"

Now there was a million-dollar question. "Nothing," she said. "My grandfather wanted to go with him on his search for Bigfoot, but he's not physically up to it, so I volunteered to go instead."

Cameron sighed. "Wallace wasn't on a sightseeing trip and he would have had no logical reason to take you along." He gave Abby the once-over. "Well, I can see one possible reason."

She flushed. But if Cameron wanted to think that Roarke had brought her along to warm his sleeping bag at night, then she'd let him think that.

But Cameron shook his head. "Doesn't make logical sense. He might want you, but not on this trip, where all you'd do is slow him down. He would have accomplished his mission first and had fun with you later."

"That wasn't possible. I'm leaving town. He had to take advantage of the time I'd be here."

"Sorry, that won't wash. Wallace is resourceful when it comes to the ladies. He would have followed you to Phoenix for some R and R if that's what he was really after."

She hated that Cameron obviously had checked up on her before coming out here to find her. He probably knew everything about her entire family. Maybe he'd always known everything, in case it would help him in his quest to get the Dooley property.

"I'm going to assume that Wallace is off doing the business I asked him to do, but that still doesn't explain you."

"Maybe Roarke isn't as dedicated to efficiency as you think," she said. "Maybe he wasn't willing to wait until he could meet me in Phoenix."

"Maybe, but I still can't see him dragging you along on this trip, or hooking up with the geek over there, either. It doesn't add up."

Abby shrugged as if she didn't care what Cameron thought, but her mind was going a mile a minute. If they'd talked to Grandpa Earl this afternoon, they'd arrived at this campsite damned fast. The reason for that chilled her. They'd made the trip as Weres, moving swiftly down the trail like bloodhounds. Yet what about clothes once they arrived?

Each of them wore a small backpack, and then she figured it out. They'd shifted before they'd left and then someone at the mansion had strapped the packs on their backs. In shifting back to human form, they'd simply slipped out of the packs and dressed in the clothes tucked inside.

Knowing how quickly they could traverse the forest as Weres, she understood just how much of a handicap she'd given Roarke by tagging along. No wonder Cameron couldn't believe that Roarke had taken her willingly. She caught the Were studying her and looked away. She didn't want anything in her expression to tip him off about what she knew.

Cameron tapped a finger against his chin. "Something's missing from the equation, and I'll bet you could tell me what it is, Abby Winchell."

"I have no idea what you're talking about."

"I think you do, but maybe we need to continue this discussion somewhere else."

She couldn't imagine what he had in mind, but then she heard the *whomp-whomp-whomp* of rotary blades. There was a helicopter in the area, and she didn't have to guess who owned it. Roarke had said the Sasquatch pair would be airlifted out, so of course the Gentrys would be doing that via private helicopter.

"Kidnapping is a federal offense," she said. "If you take me out of here against my will, that's kidnapping. And I'll press charges, too."

Cameron ignored her as he pulled a walkie-talkie out of his jacket pocket and clicked it on. "You can pick us up now."

For one heady moment Abby tried to tell herself that by *us* he meant the four of them. They'd take the chopper out of here and leave her in the clearing with Donald.

"We'll have two extra passengers."

Her brief hope died. "What about Roarke? He'll come back here and won't know what happened to us."

Cameron gave her an icy smile. "That wouldn't be polite, would it? Thanks for reminding me. I'll leave Wallace a nice note."

Chapter 20

As Roarke loped through the forest, making much better time going back, he heard a helicopter in the distance. He briefly thought about Cameron's chopper, probably because he had that particular one on the brain after working so hard to describe it to the Sasquatch pair. But this helicopter was probably on military maneuvers. Cameron would have no reason to be flying around tonight.

Unless he decided to check up on me. Nah, that was paranoid thinking. Cameron was sitting in his study with a snifter of brandy and one of his favorite Cuban cigars while he glanced through his stock portfolio to assure himself that he was as rich as ever.

Still, Roarke would be glad to get this business with Cameron wrapped up. He shared Abby's dislike of the werewolf. Roarke had to be loyal to the pack, but that didn't mean he had to like every Were he met.

Unfortunately, wrapping things up with Cameron also meant leaving Portland and Abby Winchell. Then again, she'd be leaving soon herself. Thinking about the short time that remained to them, Roarke bounded even faster over the damp forest floor. He was making excellent time, and he might even get back to camp before midnight.

If Donald was a sound sleeper, Roarke could creep into Abby's tent and spend a little quality time with her. That would simplify the situation with the meds he was supposed to be delivering. Abby could say she had them and was taking them as prescribed.

Then they all had to get themselves back to Dooley's General Store without anyone besides Earl knowing that Roarke had not been alone on this trip. That would be tricky, but as he ran, Roarke considered the possibilities.

Donald was the first order of business. Roarke had revised the plan concerning Donald. Instead of mentioning information about a Bigfoot sighting in another part of the forest, Roarke would mention a Bigfoot mauling near Portland. Lots of blood. Suspicion that the Sasquatch were on a rampage. That might spur Donald to get the hell out of the forest, and quickly.

He hoped they would all move more quickly, too, since the packs would be lighter after they'd eaten a lot of the food. If Roarke carried everything of Abby's, they could make it in one long day. Abby would have to stage a miraculous recovery, but if Donald was spooked, maybe he wouldn't question her ability to hike.

Abby might have some other ideas, maybe even some better ideas, which was another good reason to get back before Donald woke up. Abby and Roarke could brainstorm their next plan of action. Yeah, right. As if they'd spend their time together brainstorming.

Still, they could have time to talk after they'd rolled around on Abby's sleeping bag for a while. Roarke put on a burst of speed as he caught Abby's scent on the breeze. Not far, now. He'd have to circle the camp and retrieve his clothes, damn it.

He calculated whether he dared stop short of the clearing, shift, and then crawl naked into her tent. That would save some time, and if he could manage to return to his tent unnoticed by Donald, he could dress in the clothes he'd left there. No, too risky.

All he needed was for Donald to suspect he'd been lied to and the whole program would be jeopardized. Keeping Donald in the dark was . . . Roarke paused as another scent drifted toward him, a scent he would have caught immediately if he hadn't been so focused on Abby. *Were.*

His hackles rose as he crept forward, using the trees for cover as he neared the campsite. The clearing was empty. No tents, no cookstove . . . *no Abby.*

Her scent still clung to the area, but Abby, the producer of that lovely fragrance, was gone. *Gone.* Frantic with worry, he raced around the camp looking for clues as to what had happened, although in his heart he knew.

A stray tent stake showed that the camp had been dismantled in a hurry. The Were scent was stronger by the flattened grass, but the wolves were no longer there, either. Dread clawed at his chest. This had to be Cameron's work.

A breeze ruffled his fur and he caught a movement to his right. A piece of paper fluttered under a rock. Running to it, he nudged the rock away with his nose and placed a paw on the corner of the paper to hold it in place. Something was written on it, but clouds covered the moon, leaving him with very little light. He strained to read the message, pushing it this way and that.

And then the moon broke through the clouds.

My dear Wallace—
I trust you've taken care of the business we agreed upon. However, I'm puzzled by your deci-

sion to bring Abby Winchell on this assignment, and she's unwilling to discuss it. The other member of your party seems to be an accidental addition, but according to Earl himself, you chose to take his granddaughter.

She and I, along with the engineer, have returned to the estate. Perhaps she'll be more talkative there.

Regards,
Cameron

So that *had* been Cameron's helicopter he'd heard. Rending the note into small bits with his teeth, he allowed the scraps to blow away. The contents were burned forever into his brain, anyway.

He had clothes hidden in the woods, but his wolf shape would serve him better than his human form now. Leaving the clearing, he ran, his body stretched out, his belly low to the ground. He'd vowed to protect her, and he would do that with his last breath.

Abby had never been inside the Gentry mansion and she would have been happy to forgo the experience, but Cameron's goons propelled her under the whirling blades of the helicopter and up the steps of a side entrance, into a marble hallway. Cabinets on either side contained all sorts of sporting equipment, from snowshoes to hockey sticks. She supposed this was the wealthy family's version of a mudroom.

Behind her, she could hear Donald's ragged breathing. All during the helicopter ride he'd tried to explain that he was an important personage in the Sony Corporation and they'd better let him go because high-placed executives would be looking for him soon. No one in the helicopter had responded.

"It'll be okay, Donald," she said over her shoulder. She thought it would be for him, once they realized he didn't know anything. But Cameron sensed that she did, and that wasn't going to help her cause any.

After following a maze of deserted hallways, a course that Abby was convinced Cameron had designed to make escape more difficult, her host opened tall double doors and ushered them all into a room lined with bookshelves and dominated by a large ornate wooden desk.

"You can let them go now," Cameron told his henchmen. "I want two of you outside the door at all times."

The men nodded and left, closing the door behind them.

Abby rubbed her arm where the werewolf had been gripping it. She'd have bruises, but that might be the least of her worries.

Cameron gestured toward two leather armchairs in front of the massive desk. "You may each take a seat."

Abby remained standing. "I don't care to sit. I demand that you take me back to my grandfather's place. This is an unconscionable violation of my rights as a citizen of the United States of America."

"And I demand to be set free, as well." Donald's mouth quivered, but he kept his shoulders back and his gaze steady. "I promise you that you'll regret detaining me against my will."

Go, Donald. Abby admired his courage, something she couldn't have predicted when she'd first met him. "I also hope you have good insurance," Abby added, "because I plan to sue you for the bruises I've sustained at the hands of your employees, and I'll tack on a hefty amount for pain and suffering, too."

Cameron walked behind his desk and settled into his burgundy leather desk chair. "Suit yourselves. But you should both know that I'm the wealthiest man in Portland, and I contribute heavily to every civic charity in this fair city, including any and all that support the police department. It's a long-standing Gentry tradition."

Abby folded her arms. "Why don't you call them what they are, Cameron—bribes."

"They certainly are not. They're legitimate donations reported to the IRS. I'm a responsible citizen who loves his native town. Plenty of high-placed officials will step forward to vouch for me, especially when I tell them I caught the two of you breaking and entering."

"Oh, yeah?" Donald moved toward the desk. "No one would believe that."

"Of course they'd believe that." Cameron gazed up at him. "I have a house full of fine art and precious antiques. Everyone knows about the Gentry collection. You're a stranger around here, and Abby's the granddaughter of a Bigfoot nut. Neither of you would have any credibility compared to me."

"I don't get it," Donald said. "Why are you harassing Abby and me and trying to get us in trouble for something we obviously didn't do?"

"I don't intend to explain myself to you."

"Yeah, well, don't expect me to just stand here and take this crap. I've figured out that Abby and Roarke aren't actually married, but why does that matter to you? So they're having sex without the benefit of marriage. Lots of people do that these days. It's not a crime."

Abby glanced at him. "Thanks, Donald. I appreciate that, considering that Roarke and I weren't completely truthful with you."

"Hey, Abby, it's okay. It's your business."

Cameron cleared his throat. "If I may interrupt this lovely display of solidarity, I'd like to interject that I appreciate your candor, Donald. I suspected that Abby and Wallace were sexually involved, but thanks to you, that's a confirmed fact."

Donald looked horrified. "Don't take my word for it! I wasn't exactly there, you know? Maybe they weren't having sex at all! I mean, unless a person actually witnesses the horizontal mambo, they can't be sure that it really took place, now, can they?"

Cameron smiled. "In this case, I think they can."

"Sorry, Abby." Donald hung his head. "But I still don't know why this has anything to do with the price of beans."

"It may not," Cameron said, "but I like to gather all the information I can. I'm convinced you've told me everything you know, Donald, so I'm prepared to offer you a deal."

Donald squared his shoulders. "I don't deal with terrorists."

Cameron, the arrogant bastard, laughed at that. Abby would have loved to punch him in the nose, but the satisfaction of that probably would be short-lived. She thought about the note Cameron had left and knew that once Roarke had read it, he'd come to the rescue.

Exactly how he'd effect a rescue was still hazy in her mind, but until Roarke showed up, she planned to hold the line with Cameron Gentry. Donald was welcome to cave, though. She wouldn't blame him at all for doing that. He had nothing at stake here.

"So you don't want to hear my offer?" Cameron asked him.

"Not particularly."

"Well, I'll make it anyway, because I can see you're a discerning man and I want to present you with all the options."

Abby thought Donald would react well to the flattery, but instead he sniffed in disdain. Her respect for the tubby engineer grew. Depending on how this all worked out, she'd like to keep in touch with Donald Smurtz. He had hidden depths.

"Here's my proposition," Cameron said. "I have no quarrel with you. You stumbled upon Abby and Roarke by accident, so—"

"Or maybe it was fate," Donald said.

"That's for you to decide, but if you'd like to walk out the front door and get on with your life, I have only one request. That you won't speak of this incident to anyone, ever. If you wonder how I'd know if you did, let me assure you that I, too, have contacts in the Sony Corporation."

Donald took several deep breaths.

"You should take that deal," Abby said. "You didn't ask to be part of this craziness. Just put it behind you and move on."

Donald shook his head. "I can't. I promised Roarke I'd watch out for you. So I'm not leaving."

"It's okay!" Abby was desperate to get an innocent bystander out of the line of fire. "Roarke meant for you to watch out for bears and stuff. He didn't mean you should defend me from crazy rich guys." Abby sent a searing glance in Cameron's direction when she said that.

"I know," Donald said. "But I can't help thinking he would want me to stick around."

"Suit yourself." Cameron raised his voice. "Samuel! Colin!"

Two of the men from the helicopter came through the door immediately.

"Show this gentleman to his room. And see that he does not leave it."

"Hey!" Donald tried to resist, but he was no match for those two. "Abby, I wasn't going to leave you! I wanted to stay with you and make sure you'd be okay!"

"I'll be fine." She gave him a reassuring smile as he was practically dragged from the room. "Take care of yourself, Donald!"

Once he was gone, Cameron gestured to the armchairs in front of his desk. "*Now* will you sit down, Miss Winchell?"

"All right." She chose the armchair on the right, because it was closest to the door. She didn't give herself much chance of escaping through that door, but if the opportunity presented itself, she wanted to be ready.

"May I offer you a glass of wine?"

Said the spider to the fly. "No, thank you."

"I'll have some, if you don't mind. It's been a trying few hours."

"Go right ahead." Maybe she could coax him to get drunk. That would have distinct advantages.

He left his desk chair and moved to a sideboard where he uncorked a bottle and poured red liquid into a crystal goblet. "Fortunately my wife and two children are away visiting relatives in San Francisco, so they were spared this nasty business." Returning to his desk, he set the wine on a coaster.

"It doesn't have to be nasty, Cameron." She reconsidered her strategy. "Maybe I will have some of that wine, after all."

"Excellent." He returned to the sideboard and poured a second glass. "I have a cellar full of French wines, but I'm old-fashioned. I prefer the local Willamette Valley wines. Besides, I have investments there."

She didn't doubt it. He was proud of his wealth and his standing in the community. She'd do better if she catered to that instead of fighting him.

"Is this from one of your vineyards, then?"

"Yes, as a matter of fact."

She sipped the wine. "It's very good."

He looked pleased. "Do you come up here often to visit Earl?"

"I did as a child. But as an adult, I haven't spent nearly as much time here. I regret that."

"Have we met?"

"Not officially."

"I didn't think so. I would have remembered you."

No, he wouldn't, but she wasn't about to correct him. "Your family and the Dooleys have been neighbors for a very long time."

"Yes." Draining his glass, he walked over to refill it. "Too long. It's time for your grandfather to sell."

She pretended to sip her wine, but she wasn't about to drink much of it. "Here's the interesting part, Cameron. He might have done that if you'd allowed him his moment of glory with the Sasquatch."

"Excuse me?"

"All he wanted was to go out with a bang. Sighting that mated pair would have allowed him to do that, after a lifetime of searching in vain. And then you brought Roarke in to ruin it. Grandpa Earl dug in his heels."

Cameron rested his forearms on his desk and stared at her. "I'll be damned."

"If you would allow Roarke to confirm that my grandfather saw something out there instead of insisting it was only hikers, I might be able to convince him to sell. Maybe not to you, but—"

"I can create a dummy corporation to buy it. That's not an obstacle. It could all be so simple, except for one thing."

"What's that?"

"You, Abby Winchell."

"I'm nothing, a cog in the wheel, a person trying to make this come out okay for my grandfather."

"Ah, Abby, you are also a person trying to pull the wool over my eyes, and I can't let you do that."

Her heart beat faster. "I don't know what you mean."

"Yes, you do. Now tell me how you convinced Roarke to let you go along to look for the Sasquatch."

"I told you why. He was feeling guilty about Grandpa Earl, so I convinced him to take me in Grandpa Earl's place."

Cameron looked at her over the rim of his crystal goblet. "This was a top-secret operation, and no matter how guilty Roarke felt about discrediting your grandfather, he wouldn't have been eager to take anyone with him unless he had no choice. I want to know what leverage you used to make him agree to take you, Abby."

"I had no special leverage." She wondered how long it would take for Roarke to get there. Yes, they'd hiked for two days, but not steadily, and in wolf form Roarke would move much faster.

Still, she couldn't reasonably expect him anytime soon. Once he arrived, Roarke would corroborate her story because he was as dedicated to keeping Cameron in the dark as she was. Maybe he could convince Cameron, werewolf to werewolf, that she was no threat to the Were community.

"I believe you did have leverage," Cameron said. "And that information happens to be critical to me. I'm afraid I can't let you leave this house until I find out what I need to know."

Abby met his cold gaze as if what he'd said made no difference to her whatsoever, even though her stomach churned. "Surely you'll give me a place to sleep. It's been a long night." Yes, this place looked like a fortress, but left to her own devices, she might figure out a way to escape.

"That would be the hospitable thing to do, but I'm afraid I'm not feeling hospitable right now. You and I are going to sit here until you decide to tell me the truth."

She lifted her chin. "Will you bring out the thumb-screws, then?"

He smiled. "I hardly think that will be necessary. My goodness, you've barely touched your wine."

She leaned forward and set her glass on his desk. With luck it would leave a ring. "You know, it's amazing how quickly a good glass of wine can turn to vinegar."

Chapter 21

By the time Roarke came in sight of the mansion, his paws were bloody and every breath brought a stab of white-hot pain. He disregarded both problems. Unless Gentry had misdirected him, Abby was in there, being held prisoner.

He spotted a sentry in human form at the entrance to the wolf tunnel. The sentry appeared to be unarmed, but Weres seldom openly displayed a weapon, even if they were carrying one.

Roarke wondered if the sentry would try to prevent him from going through that tunnel. If so, Roarke would have to take him out, and he could do that more effectively as a wolf. He trotted closer, mentally preparing to attack if necessary.

Then he noticed a Bluetooth attached to the sentry's ear and heard the man say something to whoever was on the other end of the connection. Obviously the sentry had been posted to sound the alarm, not prevent Roarke from entering. That made sense. Gentry had left a note inviting Roarke to come after Abby, so barring the door would serve no purpose.

Roarke pushed at the revolving tunnel door, leaving a bloody print on the stone as he entered the system of passageways that led to each of the mansion's bedrooms. Exhausted though he was, Roarke traversed every tunnel and climbed every stone stairway, leaving bloody tracks as he went.

At the top of each stairway he paused to sniff at the revolving panel that opened into the bedroom beyond. Outside of one room he caught what seemed to be Smurtz's mothball odor, but he couldn't very well go into the room and confirm it. He checked all the other rooms to no avail. Wherever Gentry was holding her, it wasn't in one of the sleeping rooms.

At last he approached the narrow stairs to the guest room he'd been assigned, and his head lifted in surprise. He knew that scent as well as his own. His brother, Aidan, was in his room.

He didn't know for certain why Aidan was here, but he could guess. Gentry had summoned him to deal with the problem brother. Aidan's presence lowered Roarke's stress level considerably. He couldn't believe Abby was in immediate danger with Aidan on the premises.

Chances were Aidan had taken the corporate jet over, and he hated to fly as much as Roarke loved it. No doubt Aidan had left Emma at home, too, because this wasn't a social call. With the combination of high-altitude flying and no Emma, Aidan would be in a mood. Roarke prepared himself for that as he pushed through the revolving panel into the bedroom.

Obviously Aidan had been stretched out on the king-sized bed, but he sat up immediately. His golden eyes narrowed as he surveyed Roarke. "You made good time, but you look like hell."

Roarke had many things to say to his brother, but although he could understand human speech in wolf form, he couldn't speak himself. And telepathy only worked when both Weres were wolves.

Running his fingers through his dark hair, Aidan swung his long legs off the bed and began putting on his wingtips. "I left clothes in the bathroom for you. We need to get downstairs, pronto."

Roarke didn't have to be told twice.

"Christ, Roarke. You're bleeding all over the Aubusson."

Roarke would have liked to take the time to dance a tango on Gentry's damned antique rug. Instead he gave Aidan a look and padded into the bathroom.

"Yeah, I know." Aidan's feet hit the floor. "He's an asshole, but that rug's gotta be at least a hundred years old and you just reduced its value by several thousand dollars."

Roarke liked the idea of that. Once he was capable of using gardening shears, he might decide to reduce the value of the rug some more. But in the meantime, he had to find out where Gentry had stashed Abby. He told himself that she was okay or Aidan wouldn't have been lying peacefully on Roarke's bed waiting for him.

Once Roarke had shifted, he called out to his brother as he turned on the shower. "Where's Abby?"

"With Gentry in the study. How're your hands and feet?"

"Fine." In actuality they hurt like hell, but at least they weren't bleeding anymore. Fortunately, shifting speeded up the healing process considerably. "Is Abby okay? Have you seen her?"

"No, but when I walked past the study door not long ago, she sounded all right. Feisty as hell."

"Redhead."

"Ah. Anyway, Gentry seems to think she's keeping something from him. Is she, Roarke?"

"Tell you in a minute." Roarke stepped into the shower and gasped as the water hit his abraded hands and feet. He made the shower quick and stepped out to find his brother leaning in the bathroom doorway.

Aidan threw him a towel. "You might want to tell me now."

"Well . . ." Roarke considered what to say as he quickly dried off.

"She knows, doesn't she, hotshot?"

"Don't get all huffy with me, bro. You aren't exactly the poster boy for pack security, either." Roarke reached for the clothes Aidan had left in the bathroom. Roarke would have been fine with sweats and a T-shirt, but he dutifully put on the slacks and white dress shirt Aidan had left there.

Aidan sighed. "So she knows you're Were. How much else?"

"Pretty much everything else." Roarke buttoned the shirt and tucked it into his slacks. "And she has pictures of me shifting."

"You *posed* for her? What kind of an idiot—"

"No, I didn't pose, for God's sake. I didn't know she was there." He glanced around the bathroom. "I need shoes and socks."

"Wear the oxfords." Aidan stepped out of his way as Roarke left the bathroom. "Gentry returned all your camping stuff, by the way. Your watch is on the bedside table, so you might as well wear it."

"I get the idea you want us to walk in like urban professionals."

"It's what Gentry understands. If we show up looking like the heirs to the Wallace fortune, he'll respect that. If you want to get Abby safely out of this situation, you need to play the game. So what's this about pictures?"

Roarke sat in a wingback and put on his shoes and

socks. "She happened to be in the woods when I was shifting and got me with a zoom lens. Then she black-mailed me into taking her along on the Bigfoot hunt."

Aidan groaned. "Shit. I thought you'd fallen for her. But instead she's a scheming—"

"She's not scheming." Roarke stood and finger-combed his damp hair. His camping gear was piled in a corner of the room, but he wouldn't deal with it now.

"Roarke, she *blackmailed* you."

"For a good reason." He grabbed his watch from the bedside table and put it on. "Let's go."

"I don't care what her reason was." Aidan followed Roarke out of the bedroom and fell into step beside him as they walked down the hall. "If she's capable of black-mail, then we're in big trouble. At least with Emma I knew her heart was in the right place."

"Abby's heart is in the right place, damn it. You don't have to worry about her."

"I assume she knows the Wallaces have money."

"She knows."

"So what's to stop her from using what she knows to blackmail us for money?"

Roarke shook his head. "She would never do that."

"Why not? If she blackmailed you for a good reason, then why not blackmail the family for more good rea-sons? There are any number of causes she could decide to support with money she extracted from us. She could—"

"Hold on, bro." Roarke grabbed Aidan by the arm and pulled him to a halt. "We're not going down there until I straighten you out on this score. I won't have you dissing Abby like that. She's a good person who doesn't deserve the crap that's been thrown at her."

Aidan's eyebrows rose. "You're the one who said she blackmailed you. I'm only following the information to its logical conclusion."

"And you're dead wrong. Abby saw me as the enemy who was destroying her grandfather's reputation, which I was. She caught me in the act of shifting and called me hypocritical, which was also true. I hated giving lectures debunking Bigfoot and making Earl Dooley look like a fool."

"You were doing it for the good of the Gentry pack," Aidan said quietly. "They couldn't be overrun with humans looking for Bigfoot, and you're the expert on cryptids, so you were the logical one to handle this. If you hadn't, this pack would have been in danger of exposure."

"Yeah, but making fun of Earl Dooley's legitimate sighting was a nasty business, Aidan. You wouldn't have liked it any better than I did."

Aidan held Roarke's gaze. "So you have fallen for Abby."

"I didn't say that."

"You didn't have to. You've defended her the way I would have defended Emma."

Roarke's chest grew tight. "Look, it may be working for you and Emma, and I'm happy for both of you, but that doesn't mean I'm in favor of a Were mating with a human."

"Tell that to your heart, Roarke." Aidan clapped him on the shoulder. "Come on. We need to go down there and break up whatever happy little party Gentry has going on."

Abby couldn't remember ever being so tired. Cameron kept grilling her, and she'd managed to avoid saying anything incriminating, but she wasn't sure how much longer she'd hold up. Cameron had switched to coffee, but he didn't offer her any. He wanted her groggy and confused, and she was fast getting there.

Cameron's study had a fireplace, but it wasn't lit, which figured. Everything about the bastard was cold, including his hearth. Leaving her chair for another walk around the study to stay awake, Abby glanced at the mantle clock. After four in the morning.

She turned to Cameron. "I vote we call it a night. You can keep asking your questions, and I'll keep giving you the same answers."

"Maybe. And maybe I'll outlast you. I'm an insomniac, anyway, so late hours are no hardship for me. However, if you'd like to go relax on a nice pillow-top with thousand-thread-count sheets, tell me the truth about your arrangement with Wallace, and someone will escort you to a guest room."

Abby's composure snapped and she whirled to face him. "My arrangement with Roarke is exactly what you implied back at the camp. We're one hot combo. We can't get enough of each other. He decided to combine business with pleasure, and we screwed like bun—" She gasped as the study door opened and Roarke, one of the bunnies in question, walked in, followed by a man with a similar build to Roarke's but with darker coloring.

Abby instantly pegged him as Roarke's older brother, Aidan, and just as instantly wished she could melt into the floor. She *would* have to lose her temper right then and make a very bad first impression on Roarke's brother.

Roarke crossed to her and took her by the shoulders as he gazed into her eyes. "You okay?"

"Other than terminally embarrassed, you mean?"

"Don't worry. It's just my brother."

"I know." She loved having Roarke's hands resting on her shoulders, but under the circumstances, she decided to scoot out from under his touch. She glanced over at Aidan. "Nice to meet you, Roarke's brother."

"It's Aidan."

"I knew that. I was just being cute. I'm Abby Winchell."

"I knew that."

She couldn't read anything in his expression. Well, at least she wasn't tired anymore. That little episode, coupled with having Roarke back, had given her a shot of adrenaline. It wouldn't last, but for now, she was wide awake.

"So, Aidan." Cameron rose from behind his desk and walked toward the dark-haired man, hand outstretched. "It was good of you to fly out on short notice."

"No problem." Aidan exchanged a brief handshake with Cameron before turning back to Abby. "I understand you're visiting from Phoenix."

"That's right." So Aidan had been doing his research, too. "The rest of my family is down there," she said. "Grandpa Earl is the only one still living in the Portland area."

Cameron walked over to join the group. "Abby's a claims adjuster in Phoenix, but I wonder if they shouldn't switch her to sales, with her gift of persuasion."

"I don't like sales," Abby said.

"But you're so good at it. You managed to talk Roarke, here, into taking you out on the trail with him, even though he knew full well that was a really bad idea. Either you're the best little saleswoman around, or you had something to hold over Roarke's head."

Abby took a deep breath. "Sex. That's all we're talking about here, gentlemen. I used sex to convince Roarke to take me on his Bigfoot hunt. I was determined to validate my grandfather's claim, and seducing Roarke seemed like the way to go." Her cheeks felt hotter than the desert summer sun, but she'd decided this was her best defense and she'd stick to it.

Roarke shrugged. "What can I say? It worked. Abby may not like sales, but she can be extremely persuasive."

Aidan shook his head and let out a long, despairing sigh. "I can't say I'm surprised that my little brother succumbed. He's always had a weakness for the ladies, and now that I've met Abby, I completely understand what happened, Cameron."

Cameron balanced on the balls of his feet, as if he wouldn't mind being a few inches taller when he stood next to the Wallace brothers. "You know, I could almost buy that explanation. Almost. Except that two people who head into the forest with sex on their minds would want one big tent, not two single-person tents."

"Grandpa Earl outfitted us for the trip," Abby said. "And a girl doesn't want her grandfather to know what she has in mind."

"I didn't relish the idea of Earl knowing, either," Roarke said. "I didn't want him coming after me with a shotgun. Two single tents seemed like the prudent choice."

Now that Abby had backup, she decided to go on the offensive. "Cameron, if you're so sure that I have some information that I used to force my way onto the expedition, what do you think it is?"

Beside her, Roarke tensed.

Cameron gazed at her for a long time. "Oh, it could be something that would tarnish his reputation as a professor at NYU, or embarrass his family back in New York. They're very prominent back there, just as the Gentrys are in Portland."

"Well, there you go," Abby said. "You found me out."

Roarke laid a warning hand on her arm. "Abby."

"No, Roarke, we need to let Cameron know that he is right, because he'll keep digging away until he finds out. And God knows nothing ever dies on the Internet."

Roarke turned to stare at her. "The Internet?"

"I'm sure you don't want this told, Roarke, sweetie, but I need to get it off my chest." She turned back to Cameron. "Once I heard Roarke was out here giving lectures that embarrassed my grandfather, I sexted Roarke, and he—"

"What in the hell are you talking about?" Roarke's grip on her arm tightened. "You never—"

"I sent some nude shots of me, and Roarke responded very . . . favorably, I have to say. Before we ever met I had plenty of explicit e-mails from him, and they certainly weren't anything he'd want his family to see, or his department head at the university."

Beside her, Roarke was muttering under his breath, but when she glanced at Aidan, he gazed at her with something that looked like admiration.

"So you have these e-mails, then?" Cameron said.

"Oh, no. I deleted them all once I got what I wanted. Roarke stopped maligning my grandfather and took me on the Bigfoot search. Unfortunately, I didn't see anything that I could report to Grandpa Earl, but Roarke went off on his own, and maybe he has something to report. Do you, sweetie?"

Roarke opened his mouth, but all he seemed to be able to do was stare at her in amazement.

"Never mind that, now," Cameron said. "Roarke, did you save some of those e-mail exchanges on your Black-Berry?"

Roarke continued to gaze at Abby. "Nope. 'Fraid not."

"How convenient. Maybe it's a little too convenient." Cameron glanced at Aidan. "You're some kind of Internet guru, I hear."

Aidan shook his head. "Not really."

"Oh, come on, don't be modest. You're in charge of security for Wallace Enterprises, for crying out loud. Retrieving a few deleted e-mails should be child's play for you."

"Even if I could do that, I wouldn't invade my brother's privacy. If he and Abby have deleted those e-mails, then we need to let the matter go."

Cameron steepled his fingers and tapped them against his chin. "It's not easy to believe in stories that have absolutely no evidence to back them up."

Roarke stepped toward him. "Frankly, I don't care what you believe and don't believe. This poor woman is dead on her feet. I'm taking her back to her grandfather's place."

"I don't advise that," Cameron said.

"I don't give a shit what you advise or don't advise. We're done here. Come on, Abby."

"Roarke, I can't leave."

He frowned. "Sure you can. We'll just walk out of here. I'd like to see Gentry or any of his henchmen stop me."

"They have Donald shut up somewhere. I can't leave without Donald."

Roarke's jaw tightened as he glanced at Cameron. "So Donald Smurtz is still here?"

Cameron looked smug. "It would appear so."

"Why? He's just an innocent bystander in all this. Turn him loose."

"I have evidence that he was in the process of robbing me. I don't want to bother the police at this hour, so I'm keeping him here and I'll press charges tomorrow."

Abby touched Roarke's arm. "I need to stay so I can vouch for Donald."

"Right." He glared at Cameron. "Slight change of plans. I'm taking Abby upstairs. I give you my word that neither of us will leave."

"Good." Cameron turned toward Aidan. "I have a

room prepared for you, too, but I'd like to have a word before you go up. There are some family matters we need to discuss."

Abby guessed that Cameron wanted to talk about werewolf matters and probably about her and what she did or didn't know. But the jolt of adrenaline was wearing off, and she was too tired to worry about a discussion between Cameron and Aidan. She thought Aidan was on her side, but she couldn't be absolutely sure.

She allowed Roarke to guide her up the marble steps to the second floor.

"Sexting," he murmured. "How in hell did you come up with that?"

"I don't know, but I thought I should give Cameron something."

"I'd like to give him something, all right."

"Roarke, does Aidan know that I know?"

"Yeah."

"And what does he think about it?"

Roarke sighed. "Abby, could we not talk about that right now?"

She wrapped her arm around his waist and leaned into him as they walked down the hall. "Consider the subject dropped. Listen, earlier Cameron was bragging about his pillow-tops and thousand-thread-count sheets. Does he have those?"

"I suppose he does. I never thought about it." He pulled her closer as they continued down the hall.

She laughed. "But you're thinking about it now, aren't you?"

"I shouldn't be. We're both too exhausted. So have you ever sexted someone for real?"

"No. Want me to start with you?"

"Hell, no. I could never be satisfied with a picture after experiencing the real thing."

"So no e-mail exchanges, then?"

He hesitated, as if knowing that it wasn't the simple question it might sound like. "No e-mail exchanges," he said.

"I figured." Her heart twisted, but it was a small pain compared to what she'd be in for later on. Once they parted, they'd have no contact whatsoever. And that was going to hurt more than she could ever imagine.

Chapter 22

Roarke wanted to make love to Abby more than he wanted to breathe, but he had something to do first. And he would accomplish it better as a wolf. Yet as a wolf, he would have limitations that a human could overcome. He needed Abby's help.

The moment they were inside the room, Abby sighed with longing. "This is gorgeous." She walked over to the bed and threw back the covers. "First I want a shower, and then I want a nice, long, slow session in bed with—"

Roarke groaned. "We can't yet."

"Why not?"

"We need to go check on Donald."

"But how? Not that I don't want to check on him, because I do. He was incredibly brave when Cameron and his goons showed up. He'd promised you he'd watch out for me, and he did his best. But how could we find him?"

"I can find him. And this is how we'll get to him without alerting Gentry." Roarke walked over to a section of the wall and pushed against the revolving panel.

"It's a secret passage!" Abby walked over and peered

into the blackness beyond the opening. "Stairs and a secret passage. This is like something out of Nancy Drew."

Roarke had never read Nancy Drew, but he was glad to see that she was excited instead of freaked out. "There's a whole system of tunnels under the house, and if we work together, we can find Donald."

"Then let's go." She started to walk out through the opening.

"It's not that simple. I smelled him earlier, but this is a huge place and I was frantically looking for you. I don't remember which stairway it was. I could *probably* find him again as a human, but I'd be much more efficient if I shifted and searched as a wolf."

She glanced up at him. "Then shift."

"Once I do, we won't be able to talk. I can understand you, but I can't speak. So my idea was that I'll use my sense of smell to find the bedroom where Donald is. It will be very dark, so you'll need to hold on to my fur as we go. When I find him, you can go through the revolving panel and reassure him that we're here and we'll take care of him. But he can't see me and can't even know I'm there."

She nodded. "Of course not."

"He might want to come with you, but you can't let him do that. In fact, he has to stay in the room. We can't have him wandering around in the tunnels. It's risky to contact him at all, but I can't let him think we've abandoned him."

"Do the tunnels eventually lead outside?"

"Yes, but Gentry has posted a guard there. He'd report on anyone who tried to escape. I've given my word that we won't, and besides, I'd never go and leave Aidan holding the bag. Warn Donald not to try to leave by way of the tunnels or he'll be caught."

"Okay." She flapped her hand at him. "Take off your clothes, Roarke. Hurry."

"God, I wish you were saying that because we were about to jump into that big bed."

"Later."

He nudged off his shoes as he backed toward the bathroom. "I'll shift in there."

"Shift out here. I don't care. I've already seen you do it."

"I know, but . . . I'll be right back." He stepped into the bathroom and closed the door. He wasn't willing to believe she was as nonchalant about his shifting as she pretended to be. But this would be a test of sorts. They would have to interact while he was a wolf.

Folding his clothes, he left them on the counter and stretched out on the floor. The mansion's bathrooms were generous, so he had the room. He was aware of Abby waiting right outside the door, and it affected his concentration. But eventually the shift began to take over, and at last he rose from the floor and shook.

The second shift had given him another dose of healing power, and his paws felt almost normal. But he'd closed himself in the bathroom with no way to get out. Feeling like an idiot, he scratched at the door.

"Just a minute." Abby hurried to the bathroom door and opened it. "Wow." She hesitated. "This is intense, Roarke. But I want to get to know you like this, too."

Kneeling in front of him, she buried both hands in his ruff. "You're one gorgeous wolf." She leaned forward. "I even like the way you smell."

He touched his nose to her cheek.

"I like you better as a human, of course, but this is kind of cool." She wrapped her arms around him and gave him a hug, then straightened. "All right. This is getting a little bit too *Ladyhawke* for me. The sooner we do this, the sooner you can shift back and we can hop in that gigantic bed together. Lead the way."

Roarke started down the steps. Dried blood marked where he'd been earlier.

"I'm right behind you," Abby said, "and once my eyes have adjusted I'll close the . . . God, what's that on the steps? Is that *blood?* Wait, Roarke. These are paw prints." She gasped. "They're yours, aren't they? You ran until your paws were bloody. Oh, Roarke."

He whined to indicate his impatience.

"All right, we'll go. But these bloody prints tell me a lot about you. Go on down the stairs. I'll meet you at the bottom."

At the foot of the stairs he looked up and watched her push the panel closed. During the short time light streamed out the opening, it created a halo around her red hair. Aidan had called it. Roarke was falling for her, whether he wanted to or not.

"I'm here." She grabbed a fistful of his fur. "Take me through these tunnels. But don't go too fast. I'm only human." Then she chuckled. "A little joke, there."

His heart swelled in admiration. She was quite a woman. Any man would count himself lucky to spend a lifetime with her. Any werewolf, too, he silently acknowledged. Aidan had told him to listen to his heart, and it was talking to him now as Abby walked trustingly beside him down the narrow tunnel, her fingers buried in his ruff.

He paused at the first set of stairs and pulled away from her so he could climb them. Nothing. He returned and shoved his nose into the palm of her hand. She reached blindly for his ruff and they set off again.

On the fourth try he found Donald. Returning to Abby, he nudged her toward the stairs, and waited in tense silence as she felt her way up in the darkness. She stumbled once, but didn't cry out. Good girl.

When she pushed open the panel at the top of the stairs, the room beyond was dark. Roarke reminded himself that it was nearly five in the morning and Donald was probably asleep. Roarke counted on Abby to wake him up without sounding the alarm.

She was gone for what seemed like forever, but at last she came out, pushed the panel shut, and slowly descended the stairs backward, feeling her way to each step. When she reached the bottom, Roarke moved in close so she could find him.

"Oh, Roarke, I'm so glad we did this. Donald was feeling alone and scared. But he's better now. I told him everything you said—that we would make sure we got him out, but that he shouldn't try to escape, especially not through the revolving panel." She hesitated. "Just to be sure of that, I said there were snakes down here."

He nuzzled her hand. She'd done well.

"I hope there aren't, though. I don't mind snakes, but I like to be able to see them, and it's very dark down here." She took his ruff firmly in her right hand. "Let's go, Roarke. I'm trying not to think of you as my service dog, but it's beginning to feel like that. I'm eager to lay eyes on your manly self again."

He didn't blame her. But she'd done an incredible job of dealing with him as a wolf. He didn't want to put too much importance on that, but she'd handled the experience with a calm acceptance that made him start to dream a little.

Once they found the stairway leading back to the room he was using, she made the trip up with a little more confidence and opened the panel. On impulse, he held back and stretched out on the stone floor of the tunnel. Then he commanded his body to shift again.

"Roarke?" She called to him from the opening in the wall. "Roarke, are you all right down there?"

Slowly the wolf disappeared and the man emerged. Before meeting Abby, he would have said he preferred his wolf shape to his human one, even though he spent far more time as a human. The wolf felt more majestic to him, and he gloried in the physical strength and the heightened senses.

But Abby had changed that. His human form allowed him to communicate with her, and until tonight he hadn't realized how important that was to him. He'd been frustrated listening to her talk and being unable to respond. And, of course, he could make love to her in human form.

Heart beating in anticipation, he climbed the stairs.

Abby quickly figured out that Roarke had decided to shift before coming into the room. He was shy about transforming in front of her, and she didn't want to push him. Truthfully, she wasn't sure how she'd react to witnessing the act firsthand. Before getting to know Roarke, the transformation might have bothered her.

Now she didn't think it would. Spending time with him in wolf form had been strange at first, but she'd soon become used to it. Although he couldn't talk to her, he'd managed to let her know what he wanted her to do. And he was a most magnificent wolf.

But as he walked into the room and closed the revolving panel, almost godlike in his naked glory, she forgot all about the beauty of the wolf as she contemplated the majesty of the man. She could see traces of the wolf in his dark blond hair and green eyes. His lithe movements suggested extreme athleticism, which made sense when she thought about the distance he'd covered tonight in order to find her.

Once again she remembered the bloody paw prints and wondered if duty had driven him to such great lengths or another emotion, the same one she was battling every time she looked at him. He'd said back in the forest that he was growing attached. But she was *attached* to any number of things—her hybrid car, her cute little apartment in Phoenix, her favorite Mexican restaurant.

He turned to her. "You were terrific."

"You've been pretty terrific, yourself." She glanced at his hands, although to do that she had to ignore another part of his anatomy that held great interest for her. "By rights your hands and feet should be all torn up."

"One of the benefits of shifting is rapid healing. I've shifted twice since my run through the forest, and all I have are a few red spots." He held up his hands, palms toward her, and sure enough, they were practically healed.

"Thank you for getting here so fast."

"I had to."

That sounded like the call of duty to her. So maybe he felt lust and a great sense of responsibility, and logically, after all they'd been through, he felt *attached*. She, on the other hand, was falling in love. With a werewolf.

"Grandpa Earl is the one who told Gentry I was with you, Roarke. I'm so sorry about that. Gentry said he got suspicious about the trip and went over to talk to my grandfather, who was so proud of our expedition that he bragged about it."

Roarke sighed. "That's my fault. I should have told him not to tell anyone, but I didn't imagine that Gentry would go over there."

"I think we all underestimated Cameron Gentry."

"Yeah."

"But did you find the Sasquatch pair?"

"I did, and they're holed up in a cave waiting for me to come and help them board a helicopter."

"That's wonderful, Roarke."

"Maybe not. It was supposed to be Gentry's helicopter, and I'm not sure how that will work now."

"Oh." She had to admit having Gentry turn into a smarmy kidnapper changed things.

"And there's another thing. I said I'd come as a wolf so they'd recognize me. If I lead them out to the helicopter that way, it takes Earl out of the running as an observer."

She tamped down a rush of disappointment. "He'll never know what he missed, anyway. If I can see them, he'll be thrilled. It's way more validation than he ever dreamed of." She shrugged. "But at this point, we don't know what's going to happen. We have to get out of this mess first."

"Yeah, we do." Roarke glanced at the pile of camping gear in the corner. "I should have told Gentry to send your stuff up here."

"Good thing you didn't or the person bringing it might have found us missing when we went to visit Donald."

"True."

"My stuff's not important."

"Guess not." Roarke gazed at her, his expression guarded. "Look, I know what we said we'd do after finding Donald, but you must be wiped out. We don't have to—"

"But I want to. It'll probably be our last chance."

Regret flashed in his green eyes. "Probably."

"But I desperately need a shower first." She began stripping off her clothes.

"I could wash your back."

"To hell with my back." She tossed her underwear on the floor and headed for the bathroom. "If you're climbing in the shower with me, pay attention to the good parts, please."

Laughing softly, he followed her. "Yes, ma'am."

After only a few minutes in the shower with him, she could vouch for his ability to take direction. She'd never been washed so thoroughly or enjoyed it more. He chose not to bother with a washcloth and used his talented hands instead. After her second climax, he hoisted her up against the shower wall and pinned her there with one firm thrust of his cock.

On yet another adrenaline high, she watched the water cascade over his powerful back and run in rivulets through his wet chest hair as he pumped, driving her inevitably toward another climax.

He held her slippery body easily and she never gave a thought to falling. His display of strength was a turn-on she never would have expected, perhaps because he wasn't vain about it. He used his physical abilities for good . . . and this was *very* good.

When she came again, her cries echoing off the marble walls, she thought he'd take his pleasure, too. Instead he simply held her. A muscle in his jaw tightened, which was the only indication he was under any sexual stress.

As her tremors subsided, she gave him a questioning glance. "Roarke?"

"Soon." Slowly he withdrew and eased her feet to the shower floor. His cock quivered as he turned to shut off the water. Grabbing one of the large towels hanging beside the shower, he wrapped her in it before scooping her up, towel and all, and carrying her into the bedroom.

He didn't seem to mind that he was still wet, although holding her towel-wrapped body in his arms soaked up some of the drips. Then he laid her like a precious package in the middle of the bed. It was a king-sized bed, so she could only imagine the upper-body strength required to place her in the exact center.

She was not a small woman at five-nine, and no man had ever made her feel dainty until now. No man had ever made her feel cherished, either. Maybe it took a werewolf to do that. Climbing into bed, he unwrapped the towel.

Once again she had the image of being a gift that he treasured. "How do you do that?"

"Do what?" He smoothed back the white terry-cloth towel and began to kiss her, starting with her cheeks and moving to her throat.

"Make me feel precious."

"You should feel that way." He dotted her shoulder with more kisses. "You are precious."

"But I've never thought I was."

He placed soft kisses on her other shoulder before moving to her breasts. "Then you were in bed with the wrong guy."

And now she was in bed with the right guy . . . one last time. She wanted to be able to enjoy this without thinking about the inevitable parting, but the more he kissed her as if memorizing her body, the more emotional she became.

Finally she pushed him away and sat up. "Damn it, why do you have to be so good at this?"

He sat up, too, and gazed at her. "If you want me to stop, then—"

"Of course I don't want you to stop!"

He reached for her, and she backed away. He sighed and scrubbed a hand through his wet hair. "Abby . . ."

"It's just not fair. You're the perfect guy, and you're . . . you're a *werewolf*." She hadn't meant to cry, but it had been a very long day and an even longer night. The more she tried not to cry, the faster the tears came.

Roarke reached for her again, and she jumped off the bed, still crying. "I'm ruining this," she choked out between sobs. "And I can't seem to help it. I'm ruining our last time together, and you didn't even get to come, and . . . I *hate* this, Roarke!"

"Maybe I should go."

She stared at him through her tears. "Maybe you should. I thought when you left camp yesterday that was the end, but it wasn't. Here we are again, and you're making beautiful love to me . . . again. It's like pulling a bandage off bit by bit, drawing out the pain, instead of ripping it off all at once."

He nodded. "I know exactly what you mean." Leaving the bed, he walked into the bathroom. "I'll get dressed."

She swore she heard the crack of her heart breaking, but instead it was the sound of the revolving panel opening about two inches. She grabbed the towel off the bed and wrapped herself in it. "Roarke! Someone's—"

"It's me, Abby."

She recognized Aidan's voice as Roarke charged out of the bathroom with his shirt half-buttoned. He pushed open the panel. "What the hell are you doing here?"

"Busting you out." Aidan stepped into the room. "If you were having sex, I apologize, but we need to get the hell out of this house. Gentry is crazy."

Chapter 23

Roarke glanced at Abby, whose eyes were huge with distress. "It'll be fine," he said gently. "Just get some clothes on and we'll go."

"Not without Donald."

"No, not without Donald. We'll get him out, too."

"Okay, then." She scooped up the clothes she'd so recently taken off and hurried into the bathroom.

Roarke rounded on Aidan. "Could you have maybe done that without the drama? You scared her to death."

"She needs to be scared. Gentry's sure that she's cracked the werewolf code and his solution is to put her under permanent house arrest for her protection and ours."

"The hell with that shit."

"He's lining up support, Roarke. He's consulted with several pack alphas and they all believe that he has no choice. She's a security risk. Even our own father has reluctantly agreed that something has to be done, and this is the temporary solution until a better one can be found."

"Gentry couldn't get away with keeping her prisoner.

Her grandfather would move heaven and earth to find her, and he'd start here."

"He's already been here."

"What?"

"He showed up early tonight. Gentry wasn't here, of course, because he was out collecting Abby and Donald, but the housekeeper reported that Earl was worried that he shouldn't have been so free with the information about your trip with Abby."

Roarke blew out a breath. "That was my mistake for not telling him to keep it quiet."

"What's done is done, so don't beat yourself up. Anyway, Gentry called Earl once he returned with Abby. Got the guy out of bed with the news that the two of you had abandoned the Sasquatch hunt and eloped to Vegas."

Roarke laughed. "Earl's too smart to believe that."

"It seems that soon afterward, you sent him an e-mail confirming it."

"I couldn't have. My BlackBerry was in the . . ." Roarke crossed quickly to the pile of camping gear, but after rummaging through it twice he had to conclude that his BlackBerry was in Gentry's evil clutches. "Okay, so he might be able to fool Earl for a while, but Abby has a bunch of family members in Phoenix. When she doesn't get back when she's supposed to, they'll start investigating."

"Not if they get e-mails from her BlackBerry saying that she's in love and she's flying with you to New York to meet her new in-laws. He has her BlackBerry now, too."

Roarke wanted to throw something. "Doesn't he know I won't let him keep her locked up?" Or worse. Roarke could imagine Gentry arranging for an accident to befall Abby while she was under his "protection."

"He's counting on pressure from the rest of the Were

community to keep you in line." Aidan studied him. "Unless you'd like to lay claim to her yourself, and settle this?"

God, that was tempting, but he would never coerce Abby like that. "And then what? Hold her prisoner in New York instead? That's still wrong. You fought for Emma's freedom."

"Because I knew, from all that I'd learned about her, that she was trustworthy. I'd had her under surveillance for months, remember? You've known Abby a matter of days."

Roarke realized that was true, and yet it seemed he'd known her far longer. Logically, Aidan had a point, but in his gut Roarke knew he could trust Abby. Convincing Aidan wouldn't be easy, though.

"Couldn't we just tell Gentry that we're taking Abby to New York and we'll accept responsibility for her?"

"Number one, he wouldn't just let us go because he doesn't trust us to do the right thing. He doesn't approve of the freedom the Wallaces have given Emma, let alone an unknown person like Abby. Second of all, if you took Abby back home, our father would put her under lock and key, too. He doesn't have any more reason to trust her than Gentry does."

"Except his son's word that she won't betray us."

"In order to get that blessing, you'll have to take her back there, and I'm telling you, Gentry won't just let her go. We'll have to force the issue."

Roarke gazed at his brother. "So what is going to happen after we bust her out of here?"

Aidan met his gaze. "I'm leaving that up to you."

Roarke realized that although Aidan didn't have reason to trust Abby, he was willing to trust him. That was a hell of a lot of responsibility. He took a deep breath. "Thanks, bro."

"Roarke . . ." Aidan hesitated. "We could make this escape a lot better as Weres."

"Yeah, but Abby and Donald couldn't keep up with us."

"I'm not thinking of the running part. I'm thinking of the fighting part."

Roarke glanced at the bathroom doorway. "Don't tell Abby there might be fighting."

"I won't, but we both know it could happen."

"We can't shift. I've promised Abby we'll get Donald out, and he can't see us in wolf form."

Aidan looked at him. "So we'll blindfold him."

"And we'll tell him we're doing this because . . ."

"Because . . . it's the only way he's getting out of here and he has to trust us that it's the best thing."

Roarke frowned at him.

"Hey, don't expect me to come up with all the answers. Maybe Abby will have an idea."

"For what?" Abby walked out of the bathroom dressed in her rumpled hiking clothes.

Roarke turned to her. "Giving Donald a good reason why we need to blindfold him."

"Why blindfold him at all? That'll create a serious problem for the poor guy."

"Because Aidan and I will be most effective for this escape if we operate as wolves. Our senses will be sharper."

Abby stood with her hands on her hips, her gaze thoughtful. "All right. I'll tell Donald we're making our escape with the help of two very large, very protective dogs, which are . . . part wolf. That way you don't have to blindfold him."

Roarke wasn't crazy about masquerading as a domesticated dog, but losing the blindfold would mean they wouldn't be leading Donald around all the time. "And where did these *dogs* come from all of a sudden?"

"They're mine, but Grandpa Earl's been keeping them up here for me until I had a place big enough for them in Arizona. They dug under the fence and tracked me here."

Aidan nodded. "It's flimsy, but it might work, and I have to admit it's an improvement over the blindfold. Abby, if you don't mind turning around, I need to take off my clothes."

"Wait, bro," Roarke said. "We don't have a plan."

"Sure we do. We shift, use the tunnels to get Donald, and leave."

"On foot? Or in our case, on paws?"

"Of course not. I rented a Town Car, which is sitting in the circular drive. We sneak around to that and make our getaway—people in the front, wolves in the back."

Abby glanced at the dim light filtering through the curtains. "We're running out of darkness to sneak in."

"I know," Aidan said. "But that can't be helped."

Roarke stared at her bright red hair. "I wish you had a hat. That hair is like a beacon."

"Well, I don't, and borrowing Donald's neon-green hat isn't going to help matters." She looked at Aidan. "I'll drive the Town Car. Donald will be a nervous wreck by then."

Aidan reached in the pocket of his slacks and handed her the keys. "I hope you're as cool under fire as you appear to be, Abby Winchell."

"Don't worry. I am."

"She absolutely is." Roarke took off his watch and gave it to her. "I don't want to leave this."

"Good point." Aidan took off his and handed it to Abby as well.

She looked at Aidan's watch. "I suppose yours is as pricey as Roarke's."

"Not quite, but close."

"So I'm going to be carrying two timepieces with a combined value of a million and a half smackers?"

Aidan nodded. "Close enough."

"Cool." She put one on each wrist and pulled her sleeves down to cover them.

"Oh." Aidan handed her his BlackBerry. "If you'll keep this for me, too, I'd appreciate it."

"Sure thing." She tucked it in the pocket of her jacket.

"I just thought of another complication," Roarke said. "There's the not-so-tiny matter of the Sasquatch. I left them in a cave and they'll stay there until I come to get them."

"That's handled," Aidan said. "I contacted the Seattle pack and they're sending a helicopter to the Portland-Hillsboro airport. The pilot will await our instructions."

Roarke wondered if he'd ever truly appreciated the strategic skills of his older brother before. "I owe you one, Aidan."

"And never doubt I'll collect. Okay, we need to move out. Abby, if you wouldn't mind turning your back, I'm going to strip."

"Hold it." Irrational though it was, Roarke rebelled at having Abby in the same room with any naked man other than him. "Go into the bathroom. I'll shift out here."

Aidan shrugged. "If you say so." He went into the bathroom, but didn't close the door all the way.

Roarke took note. Aidan had more experience at shifting in front of humans than he did. Aidan could teach him some things about conducting human-werewolf love affairs. But that would only be necessary if Roarke pursued such an activity.

Abby stood there watching, obviously waiting to see how he planned to handle this. "Are you going to make me turn my back?" she asked.

Roarke began taking off his clothes. "Maybe, under the circumstances, I should give you the choice." Anxiety gripped him at the thought of shifting in front of her, but she deserved to make that decision.

"Then I choose to watch. I've seen you as a man and a wolf. I want to know what happens when you go from man to wolf. And vice versa, when it comes to that."

"All right." He hesitated in the act of shucking his clothes as he thought of something he needed to say. Soon he wouldn't be able to talk to her. "I want you to promise me something."

"Depends on what it is."

Roarke sighed. She was so damned independent, but then, that was one of the things he lo— Nope, wouldn't use that word. "Here's the deal. No matter what happens while we're trying to escape, just worry about yourself."

"I can't promise that."

He glared at her. "I mean it, Abby. Aidan and I will be fine. Donald's a survivor and Gentry doesn't want him, anyway. You're the target. Get away the minute you—" Roarke paused as the bathroom door swung open.

His brother came out, and the look in his golden eyes needed no interpretation. Clearly Roarke was holding up the show. Aidan's dark, silver-tipped fur seemed to glow in the light from the bedside lamps as he moved toward Abby and Roarke.

Abby's eyes widened as she stared at Aidan. "Amazing. Truly amazing."

Roarke chickened out and headed for the bathroom now that it was available. This wasn't the time to put on a demonstration for Abby, especially with Aidan there.

She might freak out and they didn't need that. Or more precisely, *he* didn't need that. His nerves were stretched thin as it was, because he wasn't convinced Abby would do everything possible to save herself. Lying on the bathroom floor, he initiated the shift.

Aidan led the way through the tunnels, pausing every few feet to sniff the air. Abby buried her fingers in Roarke's thick pelt and held on as they navigated the dark passageway. Touching his warm fur helped ground her and reminded her that this wasn't a crazy dream.

She'd wanted to watch Roarke change into his wolf form, but maybe that was best left to a more private moment, assuming they had another one of those. If she had anything to say about it, they would. Two people—or rather, a person and a werewolf—who shared such intense experiences couldn't just break off the relationship and go on as if they were nothing to each other.

Roarke might not want to mate with her because of her handicap of being human, but she thought that was a highly prejudiced viewpoint. If she could overlook his shape-shifting, he could overlook her lack of ability to grow fur at will. She was prepared to tell him exactly that once he was in a form that allowed for proper discussion.

For now she was grateful for his strong, calming presence in this subterranean maze. The tunnels were cold and damp, but the wolf padding next to her radiated warmth and protection. She figured that he and Aidan were using telepathy to communicate, because Aidan seemed to know where to find Donald's room.

Aidan sniffed the floor, too, as if retracing Roarke's earlier trail. When Aidan stopped and sat, Abby figured they'd reached the right set of stairs.

She could barely make them out in the darkness, so

she used her hands to feel her way up as she had the first time. As she climbed, she rehearsed the big fat lie she was about to tell Donald. She was counting on his fear to make him willing to believe anything that would promise him a way out of this spooky place.

Rapping softly on the revolving panel, she heard a little yelp of fear from inside the bedroom. She pushed the panel open a couple of inches. "Donald, it's me. Can I come in?"

"Abby!" The panel flew open and Donald dragged her into the room. "How's your leg? I should have asked that before."

"Much better. The antibiotics really helped. The bleeding's stopped and the swelling's down. I can walk fine."

"Good, good." Donald was fully dressed and every light in the room was on. "Abby, I have a theory about the people living in this place. Gentry and the rest."

Her pulse skittered. Now was not the time for Donald to get smart. "You do?"

"Yeah. You may have figured it out, since Gentry seems to think you know something you're not supposed to."

"Yes, but I really don't know anything." Abby groaned inwardly. She hadn't anticipated Donald stumbling onto the truth.

"Okay, then I'll tell you what we're dealing with, so you're prepared." He lowered his voice to a whisper. "They're vampires."

"Vampires?" Abby almost laughed, she was so relieved.

"Keep your voice down. You don't want them to think we suspect. But it all fits, with Gentry being so secretive and staying up until all hours of the night. I'll bet the tunnels are filled with coffins." He looked very proud of himself for coming up with that.

"I don't know if you're right or not," Abby said, "but I think I can get us out of here, if you want to make a run for it."

"God, yes! I don't want to be their next meal, do you? I mean, snakes are scary, but vampires are worse."

"Just so you know, I haven't encountered a single snake in my travels through the tunnels."

"That's good to know, but I'll go, anyway."

"Okay." Abby reviewed her story quickly in her head. "I'm not sure if you realize that the Gentrys and my grandfather are neighbors."

Donald's color started returning. "You mean we could escape to your grandfather's place?"

"Maybe."

"Would we be safe there?"

"Temporarily, at least, until we decide what to do. Anyway, here's my idea. We use my dogs to help us get out of here."

"You have dogs?"

"Yes. I've been keeping them at Grandpa Earl's until I had a place for them in Phoenix. They dug out of their enclosure and tracked me over here. They got into my room through the tunnels."

"Wow. Smart dogs."

Abby nodded. "Big dogs. They're part wolf and they're very protective. With those two dogs to guard us, I think we can find our way out of here and make a get-away."

"On foot? I'm not a very fast runner."

She realized this was where the story got really dicey. "I managed to get the keys to a Town Car that's sitting out in front of the house."

Donald didn't bat an eye. "Excellent."

She relaxed a little. Donald was scared shitless and wouldn't question anything she told him. "So, let's go."

"Wait. What about Roarke? Is he still here? We can't leave him. I know he's a big strong guy, but vampires have superhuman strength. He'd be no match for them if they decided to sink their fangs into his neck."

She admired Donald's loyalty, but wished he hadn't started thinking again. "*Uh* . . . Roarke's going ahead, to clear the way for us. He told me to take the Town Car, you, and the dogs. He's meeting up with us later." She gazed at Donald hopefully. *Please don't question that unlikely scenario.*

Thankfully, Donald nodded. "Just so you two have it all worked out. Roarke's a good guy, and I would hate to see him drained by a bloodsucker, or worse yet, be turned into one."

"We won't let that happen. Ready to go?"

Donald straightened his shoulders. "Let's blow this taco stand, kid."

"Follow me. My dogs are waiting at the foot of the stairs. And close the revolving panel after you. We need to be as secretive as possible." She started down the narrow stairs backward, so that she could feel for each step with the toe of her hiking boot.

Donald came after her, his feet slipping on the stone. "Vampires don't have trouble with these stairs because they can see in the dark."

"Guess so."

"What are your dogs' names?"

Her brain stalled. Of course her cherished pets would have names, and she couldn't very well call them Roarke and Aidan. Whatever lame choice she made, the Weres at the bottom of the steps would hear and probably hate whatever she picked.

No point in agonizing over it. "Spot and Rover."

Muffled groans came from the two wolves waiting for her.

"I hear them down there." Donald edged down the stairs on his hands and knees. "This is like those old Lassie movies, you know? Where the dog saves little Timmy who's trapped in the well."

"Uh-huh." When she reached the bottom of the steps, the tunnel seemed very dark after being in Donald's room. That might be a good thing, because she couldn't see the look Roarke probably was giving her as he stood and shook. She took hold of his ruff. "Hey, Rover, how're you doing, boy? Ready to lead us out of here?"

Roarke let out a martyred sigh, and despite the desperate situation they were in, Abby wanted to laugh. She didn't, because Donald wouldn't get the joke.

Donald reached the bottom of the stairs and fumbled around until he made contact with Aidan. "I've found one of your dogs. Which one is this?"

"That would be Spot."

"He feels pretty big. How much does he weigh?"

"I, ah, haven't taken him to the vet recently. Maybe around two twenty, two thirty."

"They're really serious dogs, *huh*?"

"Why do you say that?"

"Well, I'm holding on to Spot, and he's very quiet, even when I scratch behind his ears. I don't think he's even wagging his tail."

Abby doubted that Roarke or Aidan would oblige with some doggie tail wagging. "It's the wolf part of their breeding. They're too cool to do that."

"I can't feel a collar or tag, either."

"I keep telling Grandpa Earl to put those on, but he knows they don't like them."

"Dogs should wear collars and tags, in case they get lost."

"Yes, I know." Abby tried not to be impatient. Obviously dogs that had found her locked up in Gentry's house weren't going to get lost. But since the whole thing was made up, it wasn't worth pointing that out to Donald. They were legitimate comments and she had to keep up the dog charade or risk Donald finding out he was in the tunnel with two werewolves. "But since these dogs don't have collars on, just grab Spot's ruff and he'll lead you toward the exit. If he stops to sniff the floor or the air, let him do that."

"O-kay. Spot has a really nice coat." Aidan started off towing Donald with Roarke and Abby following behind.

She wondered what Aidan and Roarke were saying to each other telepathically. No doubt they were griping about being called Spot and Rover. Maybe they would have preferred Thor and Hercules, but it was too late now.

Thinking about dog names helped keep her from giving way to panic, because this was damned scary, walking slowly through the dank tunnels. Although she'd only seen movies about night patrols during war, this felt like those moments in the film where soldiers crept along, knowing the enemy was all around them, and at any moment a flash of light would—

Aidan growled.

Abby's knees trembled as Roarke pulled away from her and moved up beside Aidan, shouldering Donald out of the way.

Donald retreated to stand very close to Abby, and his voice shook. "What is it?"

"Don't know."

"They sense something they don't like."

"Yeah."

She strained to see into the darkness ahead of them. A grinding, squeaking sound made her jump, and then light filtered into the tunnel from some sort of doorway.

It was pale, early-morning light, and the air that blew in was scented with mint and rain.

But the door hadn't opened by itself. Roarke and Aidan stood, shoulder to shoulder, hackles raised, growls rumbling low in their throats. Slowly they advanced, stiff-legged, heads down, ears back.

Abby followed, but a quick glance to her left told her Donald was still back there. She turned around and motioned him forward.

"Maybe we should wait," he said.

"That's the way out, Donald. The dogs are going to help us get through it." She didn't know how they'd make it, but if Roarke and Aidan were advancing, so was she.

The escape route beckoned them, but when they were almost there, a shadow moved across the opening. A wolf stood silhouetted against the early-morning light.

Donald pulled back with a moan of fright. "It's . . . another . . . d-dog."

Abby didn't answer. Instead she focused all her attention on Roarke and Aidan. She could almost feel their hindquarters bunch. Snarling, they leapt in unison.

"Now!" Grabbing Donald's arm, she hurtled after them.

Chapter 24

The first wolf was easy. Of course it was Gentry, grand-standing with that silhouette-in-the-doorway routine. But once Roarke went for his throat, Gentry backed away and let his thugs move in. Two came at Aidan from the side, and Roarke had just enough time to see his brother fend them off before two more leapt at Roarke.

He might not be able to defeat them all, but he could draw the fight away from the opening. Dodging and weaving, he managed to move the contest to the right side of the stone doorway. Aidan, obviously of the same mind, did the same with his two opponents on the left.

It was an odd place for a werewolf fight. The formal gardens in the back of the mansion were meticulously groomed, with hedges in geometrical patterns and marble statues dotting the well-tended flowerbeds. The scent of crushed flowers filled the air as Roarke struggled to hold his own and keep the wolves busy so Abby and Donald could escape.

But that struggle might be for nothing if Abby didn't get her butt out here. Gentry was making his way back to the door, and soon he'd close it again, sealing her in.

Roarke was so busy watching for Abby that one of the wolves got his teeth into Roarke's thigh and pain shot through his leg.

Damn it, where was Abby? Then he saw her shove through the opening. She was practically dragging Donald. That little traffic cone was way more trouble than he was worth. *Let him go, Abby!*

Just then Gentry leaped at Abby, and Roarke pulled away from his assailants to stop him. But to Roarke's amazement, Donald threw out an arm and blocked the wolf. Whether it was reflex or courage didn't matter, because Donald had the element of surprise on his side. Obviously Gentry hadn't expected any trouble from Donald and he went sprawling backward into a hedge.

Once again, Roarke had allowed himself to be bitten by one of his attackers, this time on his right hind leg. But when he saw Abby and Donald sprint for the front driveway and the waiting Town Car, he turned and threw himself into the fight in earnest. Thank God. She was getting away.

He, however, was weaker due to his wounds, and a quick check of his brother's situation wasn't all that encouraging, either. Aidan was a strong wolf, but so were his attackers, and there were two of them.

Roarke had even less going for him than Aidan. He'd expended most of his energy running through the forest to get there. He wondered if Gentry would allow his thugs to kill both Wallace heirs. Maybe. Gentry could always claim that the Wallace boys had put the werewolf community at serious risk and thus deserved to die.

As Roarke tried in vain to throw off his attackers, he noticed that Gentry was up and running to the driveway, too. If Abby had been on foot, Gentry would have caught her, but by now she should be in the car on her way down the drive. She might have to smash through the gate, but the Town Car was built like a tank.

But wait, why was Gentry reversing course and running back this way? The roar of a powerful V8 echoed against stone walls as the Town Car rounded the building right behind the racing wolf. If Gentry hadn't leaped out of the way, Abby would have run him down.

And she kept coming, plowing through manicured hedges and knocking statuary right and left. The wolves working Aidan over glanced up as the car bore down on them with a redheaded maniac at the wheel. They ran, and Aidan staggered to his feet.

The car kept coming, roses and forsythia tangled in the front bumper and multiple scrapes and gashes in the glossy black hood. The rental company wasn't going to like this. But Roarke loved it.

As his attackers bounded away, Abby and Donald each leaned over the seat and popped open the back doors. Roarke made for the right side and Aidan leaped for the left. They were both still scrambling for purchase on the leather seats when Abby took off again, the doors swinging wildly.

"Watch your tails, guys!" she called out. She yanked the steering wheel to the left as they rounded the other end of the house. The car went up on two wheels and the right door slammed shut. She made a hard right around a giant spruce and the left door banged into place.

Roarke glanced over to see how Aidan was doing. He'd braced himself against the seat in an attempt to stay as stable as possible. He had several wounds and had smeared about as much blood over the leather upholstery as Roarke had.

"Hang on!" Abby yelled. "We're going through the gate Donald, are you sure those air bags are deactivated?"

"Yep."

"I hope you're right, because here we go!" She smashed into the gate, and although the hood buckled, the gate popped open.

Donald punched a fist in the air. "Yee-haw!"

Abby swung the car out on the main road and it lumbered along as if it had at least one flat tire, maybe two.

Roarke looked at Aidan. *Luckily for you, Abby's in the insurance business.*

If you think I'm putting in a claim, you took one too many blows to the head, little brother. So far as the rental company knows, this car disappeared without a trace. I'll write them a big check, and everybody will be happy.

Roarke looked out the window for the first time and noticed which direction Abby had chosen. She was heading toward her grandfather's place.

Hey, Aidan, we didn't script this part.

Guess we'll have to sit tight and trust that your girlfriend knows how to handle it.

She's not my girlfriend.

Then she's done a terrific imitation of your girlfriend. For God's sake, Roarke, the two of you have risked life and limb for each other. What more evidence do you need?

Shut up, Spot.

Just try not to be a complete butthead, Rover.

Abby pulled up in front of Dooley's General Store because she didn't know what else to do. Yet she couldn't let her grandfather, or Donald, for that matter, find out that she had a backseat full of werewolves. If she left them in the car, they could shift, but then they'd be naked, and a backseat full of naked guys wasn't a whole lot easier to explain.

Maybe they'd shift and disappear into the woods, but

she didn't want that, either. They needed clothes and medical attention. No matter what Roarke said about their healing abilities, she'd feel better if she could watch over them.

She turned to Donald. "I need to let my grandfather know I'm okay. Come on in with me." Then she turned toward Roarke and Aidan. "Both of you, stay. I'll be right back with . . . stuff."

Donald looked doubtful as he glanced back at Roarke and Aidan. "Are you going to just leave them here? They're wounded and bleeding."

"I know, and because they're part wolf, you have to be careful with them when they're injured. If we leave them alone to lick their wounds, they might allow us to tend them later on."

"But—"

"I know my dogs, Donald. The kindest thing we can do at the moment is leave them to nurse their wounds. If we could provide them with a cave, they'd be that much happier."

"If you say so. All I've ever had is cocker spaniels."

"Way different."

"Guess so." Donald opened his door and stepped out.

Abby turned to Roarke and Aidan again and lowered her voice. "I mean it. Don't slink off into the woods with no means of helping yourselves. I'll get clothes for you somehow."

She had no idea if they would go along with her plan or not, but she hoped they would. She'd rescued them, and she wanted them to stay rescued. But she had to admit the whole shape-shifting angle made things more complicated.

With one last glance at her two charges, she got out of the Town Car and walked with Donald up to the front porch of her grandfather's store. Before she got totally in the door, Grandpa Earl met her and pulled her into a bear hug.

He put his mouth close to her ear. "I found the flash drive."

She went still. No, this couldn't be happening. If he'd found the flash drive, then he was in danger, too, and she couldn't have that. Why in hell had she left it in a place where he could find it?

Her grandfather released her and bestowed a big smile on Donald. "So, who's this?"

Donald stuck out his hand. "Donald Smurtz, Mr. Dooley. A fellow Bigfoot seeker."

"Indeed, indeed. Well, you look as if you've been rode hard and put away wet, Mr. Smurtz."

"You have no idea. Your neighbor, Cameron Gentry, kidnapped us and was trying to say we'd stolen from him. And he had these vicious dogs that attacked Abby's dogs. She left them out in the car, but I'm worried about them."

Earl nodded and glanced sideways at Abby. "Right. Abby's dogs. I'm sure you are worried."

"They'll be fine out there for a little while," Abby said. "Thank goodness you've been keeping them here for me, though, Grandpa Earl. Those dogs rescued us from the Gentrys."

"Speaking of your neighbors," Donald said. "Do you have any garlic around? Or wooden stakes?"

"I'm not sure what you mean."

"I wouldn't say this to just anybody, Mr. Dooley, but if you're convinced that Bigfoot exists, you might not think I'm crazy if I tell you that I think your neighbors are quite possibly . . . vampires."

"Is that right?" Earl looked properly amazed and impressed. "Well, that would explain a lot."

"Exactly! And now that we've escaped, we should be safe until dark, but we have to take precautions."

"I'm sure we do. But how about a cup of hot chocolate and a cheese Danish while you're sitting in front of my woodstove in the back of the store? Doesn't that sound good?"

Abby barely heard any of the conversation. She was still processing the disturbing information that Grandpa Earl knew that Roarke was a werewolf, and he wouldn't have much trouble figuring out that this entire mess was about werewolves, not the vampires that Donald kept babbling about. How could she protect her precious grandfather from being embroiled in this debacle?

She heard him setting Donald up with hot chocolate and a Danish. Earl suggested Donald take his shoes off and warm his feet by the fire. With the kind of night Donald had been through, he might even fall asleep back there, which would be a huge help.

"Let me go check on my granddaughter," Earl said loudly enough that Abby could hear. Then he walked quickly between the shelves of merchandise and ushered her over into a far corner of the store. "Are the dogs in the car werewolves?"

"Yes. Roarke and his brother, Aidan. Donald thinks they're my dogs you've been keeping for me because I didn't have room in Phoenix. My story was that they dug out of their pen and came to the Gentry estate looking for me."

"So Donald has no idea that they're—"

"No, thank God. He's hung up on his vampire theory. But Roarke and Aidan need to shift back into human form, and then they'll need clothes and possibly medication for their injuries, but I'm not sure about that. Apparently they can heal more quickly when they . . ." She looked at Grandpa Earl. "You really saw the pictures I took?"

He nodded. "When I got that ridiculous story late last night from Gentry, I—"

"What story?"

"He told me you and Roarke had eloped to Vegas. Then I got an e-mail from your BlackBerry confirming it. But the e-mail didn't sound like you, so I got suspicious."

"My BlackBerry." Abby remembered having it on the hike, but she'd tucked it away when she'd realized there was no reception out in the woods. "He must have taken it when he dismantled our camp. I was too worried about being kidnapped by werewolves to think about something like my cell phone."

"I got a call from your folks. They got a message from you saying that you were flying from Vegas to New York to meet your new in-laws. They didn't think that sounded like you, either. So I started rummaging around in your room, and remembered the box with the secret compartment."

Abby sighed. "I shouldn't have left the flash drive in there. It's one thing for me to know and have to deal with the fallout, but they don't want their secret to get out, Grandpa. Anybody who knows becomes a suspicious person to them." She glanced up at him. "Let's pretend that you never saw it, okay? I won't tell, and if you don't tell, then—"

"But you're in trouble, Abby. If I know what's happening, I'm in a position to help you. Don't worry about me. I'm an old man. They can't do anything to me."

She considered that for a moment. "I'm not saying I agree with you, but I do need help with something. They're injured, and if they shift it helps them heal. But they need clothes."

"That's easy enough." Her grandfather moved to the

shelves of folded sweatshirts and sweatpants. "What size is the brother?"

"About the same as Roarke."

Earl pulled down two generic gray sweatshirts and two pairs of sweats. "Let's go over to the counter and take the tags off." But as he was doing that, he looked up. "This won't work. I assume when they're dressed they'll want to come into the store."

"I guess so. We have to figure out what to do next."

"Then what am I supposed to say when they walk into the store wearing my merchandise?"

"Oh."

Earl frowned in concentration. "Can they understand what you're saying to them when they're wolves?"

"Yes."

"Then here's what you told me. They were in a fight over at the Gentrys, and their clothes are so ripped and mangled that they were afraid to walk in here like that and asked if I'd sell them something to put on. So you came in and got these things."

Abby considered the explanation and hoped it would work. "I just don't want them to know that you know."

"Give that story a shot, and if it doesn't work and they suspect I know, oh, well." He finished removing the tags and refolded the clothes. "In any case, I'm glad I have something those boys can wear temporarily."

She shook her head in bewilderment. Her grandfather was referring to a couple of werewolves as *boys*. Apparently their shape-shifting ability didn't change the fact that they were young men who had been hanging out with his granddaughter, so that made them boys.

"They need something for their feet," he said. "I think flip-flops are the answer for now. I'll get a couple of pairs." He headed toward the rack at the far end of the store.

When he returned, his eyes were bright. "My strategy worked. Donald's asleep in his chair."

"Grandpa Earl, I don't know what I'd do without you."

"You're pretty important to me, too, kiddo, but I have to ask—did you see the Sasquatch pair?"

"I didn't, but Roarke did."

Her grandfather sighed happily. "I knew he would! I knew he had the right stuff for the mission." He clipped the nylon string holding the flip-flops together and placed both pairs on the stack of clothes.

"Thanks, Grandpa." She scooped up the clothes.

"No problem. I want that boy back to his human form as soon as possible so he can tell me all about the Sasquatch." Then he rolled his eyes. "Listen to me, being so self-centered. He probably has other more important things to do, but I would really—"

"I'll make sure you get a full report, Grandpa." She hurried back out to the car. How she longed for her grandfather to see the Sasquatch pair board the helicopter. Having a wolf accompanying them wouldn't surprise him now, but he wasn't supposed to know about that.

She briefly considered smuggling him to the spot without telling Roarke but knew she couldn't do it. Roarke had trusted her with far more information than he should have, and no doubt he'd catch hell for it with his pack. If she betrayed him in any way, she wouldn't be able to live with herself, even if he never found out.

Roarke and Aidan were both lying in the backseat, and when she opened the back door and saw the amount of blood, both on them and on the backseat, she gasped. "I need to get you some towels, and probably a first aid kit, and—"

Roarke growled softly.

"You don't want those things, do you?"

He growled again. Then he reached up and put a paw on the clothes she held in her arms.

"Right. The clothes." She hoped that she'd become a convincing liar because she had to look into those green eyes and make him believe her. She repeated the story her grandfather had concocted.

Roarke's unwavering gaze unnerved her. She was afraid he could tell exactly what she was thinking.

She broke eye contact. "Okay, then. I'll leave the clothes, and once you've shifted, we'll talk. By the way, Donald's asleep in front of the woodstove, so you caught a break there. I can tell him I tucked the dogs back in their kennel. You can give him whatever story you want when you see him and I'll go along with it."

She put the clothes on the floor of the car, away from the bloody seats. "Oh, and, Roarke, I told Grandpa Earl that you'd seen the Sasquatch pair, and of course he's dying to hear the details." With that she closed the car door.

Then she realized they might want to leave the car before shifting, and she opened the door again. After leaving it propped open about two inches so they could choose which way they wanted to accomplish their shift, she left.

Technically, she could have hung around and watched through the car window if she'd wanted to see them shift. But it wasn't a private moment with Roarke this time, either, and she had no desire to embarrass herself or Aidan by catching him in the nude. His wife might not like that much.

Or maybe Aidan didn't consider Emma a wife. Maybe calling her his mate was more inclusive, more permanent, and—truthfully—more thrilling. Abby walked back into the store thinking about that. The concept of becoming Roarke's mate, instead of his wife, was actually pretty damned exciting.

She would have to accept the idea that their children could end up in either camp. Was that so horrible? If they couldn't shift, then she'd teach them how to live in the Were community as nonshifters. If they could shift, then Roarke could instruct them in the finer points of werewolf etiquette.

Parents often had to take those kinds of roles depending on the temperament of their children. Or grandparents did. She wondered how she might have turned out if she hadn't had Grandpa Earl, the man who understood fanciful children, to depend on.

One thing was for sure, she never would have fallen in love with a werewolf. She only hoped that werewolf hadn't been able to tell she'd just lied to his face.

Chapter 25

Aidan heaved himself up from the leather seat. *Her grandfather knows.*

Yes. Roarke hated that, but it couldn't be helped now. *And if she told him, she had a good reason.*

Well, that clinches it, little brother. Once again, you're leaping to her defense. You're falling in love with her.

Roarke had no reply, because Aidan was right. Roarke was falling in love with Abby. He believed that she might be falling in love with him, too. But that didn't change the fact that they were from two different worlds and that made falling in love a questionable idea.

Aidan picked up a pair of sweats in his teeth. *I'm doing this in the forest. I'm sick of this damned car.*

Me, too. Roarke grabbed the other pair of sweats and followed Aidan through a misty rain into a wooded area out of sight of the road. By the time they returned to the car, barefoot and shirtless, they were no longer bleeding, but Roarke still had a limp.

Aidan reached for a sweatshirt and pulled it over his head. "Seeing as how you're a lovesick fool, I'd better take charge of this operation. We need to isolate both Abby and her grandfather."

"Once you do that, Gentry will know that Earl's involved."

"Gentry's going to think that no matter what we do. Better to take the precaution now."

Roarke put on the other sweatshirt and reached for the flip-flops. "Okay, we all need to get out of town, anyway. I don't know if Gentry will try anything else, but he might."

"We definitely need to leave, and soon." Aidan glanced at the trashed Town Car. "But this thing—"

"We'll get Earl to drive us all to the airport in his truck. Abby and I will ride with Earl in the front, and you can ride with Donald inside the camper. That way I can discuss the security breach with Abby and Earl."

Aidan nodded. "Then we'll have to get Donald home, wherever he lives, by private plane. The poor guy can't fly commercial until he replaces his ID and credit cards."

"Don't feel too sorry for him, Aidan. He needed to be scared straight. He's a potential menace to Sasquatch everywhere, but he'll be so grateful to us for saving his ass from the vampires and sending him home at our expense, that if we ask him to stop hunting Bigfoot, he'll do it."

"I see your point."

Roarke took a deep breath. "Long story short, I'm with you on the isolation plan. Besides that, I owe it to the folks to take Abby and Earl back to New York and sequester them there, at least for a while. I'm sure Gentry's raising a stink and Mom and Dad are taking the brunt of it."

"I'm sure Gentry's doing exactly that, and I see him as a guy who carries a grudge. If he gets his hands on Earl's land, he might leave Earl alone, but Abby's another matter. I don't see Abby being able to resume her normal life anytime soon, if ever."

Roarke had been wrestling with the same problem. He didn't want to keep Abby a virtual prisoner on the Wallace estate, but how could he let her go back to Phoenix where he couldn't watch over her? "I could hire a bodyguard for her when she goes home to Phoenix."

"There's another solution, Roarke."

Roarke glanced at him. "I don't know that Abby would want that solution. It would involve a lot of sacrifices on her part."

"Take some advice from your older brother. Don't assume she's not willing to make them."

Roarke gazed at Aidan and nodded. "Okay, I won't. Ready to go in?"

Aidan shoved his feet into the flip-flops with a grimace of distaste. "God, yes. The sooner we wrap this up the sooner I can put on shoes that don't make me look like a surfer dude."

The moment Roarke and Aidan stepped into the store, Abby knew that her lie hadn't fooled either of them. They knew that Earl knew. The only clueless person seemed to be Donald, who was overjoyed to see Roarke and meet Aidan for what he thought was the first time.

"Vampires." Donald stood warming himself by the woodstove as he sipped another cup of hot chocolate. "There's a houseful of vampires over there." He glanced at Earl. "I'd sell out and move if I were you."

"Funny you should say that." Earl glanced at Abby. "My granddaughter's been pestering me to sell, and I'm about ready to give in. Whether they're vampires or not, the Gentrys make terrible neighbors, going around kidnapping people."

"If they weren't vampires," Donald said, "Abby and I would press charges. Right, Abby?"

"Absolutely. But I like Grandpa Earl's solution better. We all just leave."

Aidan pushed away from the wall where he'd been leaning as if nonchalantly listening to the conversation. "I'd like to suggest we start putting that plan into action. Earl, if you're willing to drive us all in your truck, we should head for the airport and get out of town before the Gentrys regroup."

Donald glanced toward the front of the store. "Would they come over here?"

"They might," Aidan said, "once they have a new plan. We need to leave before that happens. Donald, I realize you've left your belongings and ID behind, but I can arrange for a private plane to get you safely home."

Donald's eyes grew wide. "You guys have a lot of money, *huh*?"

"Some." Aidan glanced at Earl and Abby. "You might want to pack a few things. We'll be taking the corporate jet."

Donald gasped. "Whoa! Which way are you guys headed? 'Cause I'm just down in San Jose, and I'd love to ride in the corporate jet."

"We can stop off there," Roarke said. He seemed to be deliberately ignoring Aidan, who was making slashing motions across his throat. "It's not much out of the way."

"And what is our direction, Roarke?" Abby asked. She thought she knew, but she wanted to make sure.

"For safety's sake, Aidan and I are taking you and Earl back to the family estate in New York."

"I see." She liked the idea that he was concerned about their safety, but she wished he looked a little happier about taking her home to meet his parents. Despite all they'd been through, she still might not be mate material, and that was depressing. "I'll go pack."

"Wait!" Donald called after her. "What about your dogs? You can't leave Spot and Rover."

"Oh, right." She turned to her grandfather and delved into her imagination for yet another story that would pass muster. At least Donald was easier to fool than Roarke.

"Grandpa! Could you ask your cleaning lady to feed the dogs until we can make other arrangements?"

"Of course!" His eyes lit with mischief. "Good old Bianca! She'd love to do it! I'll definitely leave her a note about . . ."

"Spot and Rover," Abby said.

"Yes, of course. Spot and Rover. Terrific dogs. Bianca will be happy to watch out for them. I'll ask her to take them home, in fact. She has a huge yard, and a big fence, and—"

"That will be perfect." Abby stopped him before he got them both into trouble by elaborating too much.

"Perfect." He gave her a conspiratorial smile.

Abby didn't dare stay in the room any longer or she was liable to start laughing. Twenty minutes later, when she walked out of her room with her suitcase in hand, Roarke was sitting in her grandmother's old armchair using Aidan's BlackBerry.

He glanced up as she came to stand in front of him, and he kept his voice low. "Gentry has my BlackBerry, obviously, and I need to contact the helicopter pilot who's taking me to the Sasquatch pair."

"Not the Gentry helicopter pilot, I hope."

"No, although the Seattle Trevelyans are distant cousins of the Gentrys. There was a split a long time ago, and I gather there's no love lost between the families now. George Trevelyan's son Knox is bringing a chopper to the Portland-Hillsboro Airport. Handling the Sasquatch situation will delay us some, but I can't leave those creatures waiting in the cave."

"Of course not."

"They're not safe anywhere near Gentry. I wouldn't put it past him to shoot them." He clicked a few keys on the BlackBerry and sent the e-mail.

Abby shuddered. "Me, either." It was the first private moment she'd had with Roarke, and there was something she needed to say. She gazed at him. "I'm sorry I lied to you about the clothes."

His expression tightened, but he didn't say anything.

She hated knowing she'd hurt him with that lie. "I foolishly thought I could hide the fact that Grandpa Earl had found out, but of course you saw right through me."

He powered down the phone but didn't look up. "When did you tell him, Abby?"

She winced. Roarke thought she'd offered the information, and yet still he hadn't blamed her. That spoke volumes. "I didn't tell him," she said softly, so glad she could erase that misconception. "He found the flash drive."

Roarke relaxed and blew out a breath as he glanced up at her. "I figured if you'd told him, you had a good reason. But I feel better knowing that he found out on his own."

"I shouldn't have left the flash drive where he could find it, but at the time . . ."

"I know." He stood. "You weren't sure you could trust me."

"I have the pictures and the flash drive in my suitcase. I'll give them to you when Donald's not around so you can destroy them."

Gratitude flickered in his eyes. "Thank you."

Yesterday he would have used this moment to kiss

her, but that was before she'd bounded out of his bed early this morning and told him she couldn't handle their long good-bye. Now he was probably reluctant to reach for her, in case she still felt that way.

"We should probably get going," he said.

"Wait." She had one chance to make her request before they joined the others. "Please take Earl with you in the helicopter when you relocate the Sasquatch, Roarke. Surely you could squeeze him in."

He frowned, clearly not comfortable with the idea. "You know I'm going as a Were."

"Yes, but now that he knows you can shift, that wouldn't matter. It would be the thrill of a lifetime for him."

"I suppose, but I— They're really smelly."

"He wouldn't care. Please, Roarke. He's dreamed of these creatures all his life."

Roarke massaged the back of his neck. "Abby, you're the only human I've interacted with as a Were. I've adjusted to that, but to deal with Earl while I'm a wolf . . . I just don't know."

And then she understood. Her big, strong hero was reluctant to interact with a human who'd never seen him in wolf form. Riding in a helicopter with two huge smelly creatures didn't sound like her idea of fun, but for Earl to be there, she would need to be there, too, for Roarke's sake. "Do you have room for both Earl and me?"

His expression warmed, but he shook his head. "You don't want to go."

"Sure I do."

"No, you don't." His gaze held hers and he smiled. "But you'll go if you think that will convince me to invite Earl." He reached out and stroked her cheek. "You may be really sorry you offered, because I'm going to take you up on it."

"Good." She was thrilled for her grandfather, and she'd survive just fine. The original plan of watching from a distance had been far more appealing, but she was beginning to understand that for Weres, who'd been hunted for generations, appearing as a wolf to a human was loaded with anxiety. "Thank you, Roarke."

"You probably won't thank me when everything you're wearing stinks like the spray from a thousand pissed-off skunks."

She laughed, and that brought another smile. He'd been way too serious recently. She stood on tiptoe and gave him a quick kiss, because it was obvious he wouldn't kiss her. The touch of his lips was achingly familiar, but she didn't allow herself to linger there. "It'll be fun," she said.

Roarke longed to remind her of that statement two hours later as they rode in the helicopter, skimming the tops of the trees in search of the cave where Roarke had left the Sasquatch pair. But Roarke could no longer communicate in words. He had his nose out the open window, and when the stench rose from a spot below them, he glanced back at Abby. Sure enough, she was wrinkling her nose.

Earl, seated beside her and looking like a kid going on his first roller coaster ride, didn't flinch at the smell. He'd been glowing with excitement ever since Roarke had invited him to go on this trip. Earl had been driving to the airport at the time, and he'd almost swerved off the road.

But he'd pulled himself together and had been extremely cooperative about everything ever since. He'd promised that no matter what he saw and heard on the relocation trip, he would never discuss it with any human other than Abby. His voice had trembled with sincerity, and Roarke believed him.

Once at the airfield, Roarke had shifted inside the helicopter before Earl and Abby boarded. Then Earl had climbed into the helicopter, greeted Roarke with quiet dignity, and taken his seat.

But Roarke couldn't imagine this trip without Abby. Earl obviously was trying to treat his first werewolf experience as no big deal, but he looked a little nervous. At first Roarke had been incredibly self-conscious with Earl there, but Abby's calm acceptance of the situation had done the trick. Gradually Roarke had relaxed.

Knox Trevelyan, the pilot from the Seattle pack, obviously wasn't happy to be transporting two humans with knowledge of the Were community, but he'd been reasonably polite to Earl and Abby. Other than the unhappy pilot, the arrangement had worked out well.

While Earl, Abby, and Roarke tended to the Sasquatch problem, Aidan had sent Donald to San Jose aboard the corporate jet, thus eliminating another take-off and landing for the queasy Aidan. Roarke pictured his brother relaxing in a comfy chair somewhere, sipping a vintage wine, if that was available, and talking to Emma on his BlackBerry.

Aidan liked his creature comforts. Roarke couldn't imagine Aidan trekking through the jungle or riding a camel across the desert. But he could imagine Abby doing both. Her sense of adventure matched his. She might not be eager to take part in this Sasquatch relocation, but that was common sense. Only a Bigfoot nut like Earl would think this was the experience of a lifetime.

Roarke glanced over to see if Knox had caught the scent. Obviously he had, because he'd begun scanning the terrain for a decent landing spot.

The moment the chopper started its descent, Roarke sent a telepathic message to the Sasquatch pair. He offered them support, but he also alerted them to the presence of two humans who would ride with them in the helicopter. He promised that they were good humans.

Blades whirling, the helicopter rocked gently as Knox set it neatly down on a grassy spot in a small clearing. Roarke envied Knox his flying ability and made a note to ask about taking lessons from him someday in the future. Roarke was almost ready to solo in the Learjet, and the chopper would present a great new challenge.

Knox backed off on the controls, but kept the blades turning slowly. Then he leaned over and opened the door for Roarke. Once Roarke was out, Knox would go back and open a cargo door in the rear to accommodate the sizable bulk of the Sasquatch.

All that assumed that Roarke could get them in this machine. He glanced back at Abby and Earl. Earl looked fine, but Abby appeared ready to puke. Yet she met his gaze and managed a weak smile.

Roarke had seen Abby in many situations—hiking through the rain while her muscles cramped, enjoying orgasms in a lantern-lit cave, laughing with him inside a tiny tent, and driving like a maniac to save his ass from some ferocious Weres. He'd loved every one of those moments, but in this moment, he loved *her*, the woman who'd willingly braved this awful smell to give her grandfather the experience she knew he desperately wanted.

Roarke vowed to tell her of his love at the first opportunity. His love wouldn't come with any strings attached, though. She wouldn't be required to do anything as a result of his declaration. But to love someone the way he loved Abby and never tell her would be a crime against nature.

Leaping from the helicopter, he set off to bring back the incredibly odious Bigfoot pair. One thing comforted him, if only a little. Abby's sense of smell wasn't as finely developed as his, so maybe, just maybe, she'd suffer slightly less.

Chapter 26

Grandpa Earl reached over and squeezed Abby's hand. "I don't think I've ever been this excited about anything. I take that back. Waiting for Olive to walk down the aisle—I was pretty damned excited then, too."

Looking into Grandpa Earl's sparkling eyes, Abby felt as if she'd swallowed a gallon of sunshine. Thank God Roarke had agreed to bring him. Earl would cherish this for the rest of his life, and so would she, provided that she didn't spend the entire time barfing.

Her grandfather turned to watch Roarke climb the wooded incline leading to the cave. "Roarke's quite impressive as a wolf, isn't he?"

"Yes." Abby admired Roarke's fluid grace as he moved toward the cave. "He's impressive as a man, too."

"He is, at that. When Gentry told me you two had run off to Vegas, I had a tough time imagining that you'd do that without telling anybody, but I wasn't too upset because I think he's the right guy for you."

"I don't know, Grandpa." Abby was all too aware of Knox Trevelyan, who was able to hear every word. Knox had left the pilot's seat momentarily to open the cargo door, but now he was back.

After meeting several Weres, Abby couldn't help looking at the dark-haired, dark-eyed Knox and wondering what he'd look like when he shifted. She'd estimate he was about the same size as Roarke and Aidan, and if his dark hair was any indication, he'd transform into a wolf black as the night.

Obviously sensing her scrutiny, Knox turned to her. "I brought a bandana along for myself, but you can have it instead." Pulling a blue-and-white patterned square from his pocket, he held it out.

The scent of mint wafted toward Abby, and she was sorely tempted to take the bandana. "That's very generous, Knox, but I begged my way on this trip at the last minute, and taking that would be so unfair to you."

"Would you rather have a barf bag?"

Abby lifted her chin. "I won't need that, either."

Earl turned from the window to look at her. "Take the bandana the young man's offering, Abby. It's a gentlemanly thing he's trying to do, and your color isn't so good right now."

"But yours is fine," she said. "Doesn't the smell bother you at all?"

"Oh, I can tell it's bad, and I'm sure once they're in the helicopter it'll be quite overpowering. But, Abby, I'm about to be within a few *feet* of a mated Sasquatch pair. The stink means nothing to me when I realize that."

"Yes, but Knox isn't looking forward to that experience. He deserves the bandana."

Knox reached back and dropped the bandana in her lap. "This will be bad, but walking into the cosmetics section of a department store is worse for me, believe it or not."

"I don't believe it."

Knox shrugged. "It's true, though. These two will stink, but at least it's an organic smell. It doesn't burn my lungs like a big dose of perfume."

"They're coming out! They're coming out!" Earl practically bounced in his seat.

Abby turned toward the window, and sure enough, Roarke descended the slope followed by two enormous, apelike creatures covered in long, unruly hair. The larger Sasquatch was a dark brown color, and the smaller one, who had a definite baby bump going on, was more reddish.

They seemed prehistoric, and yet strangely familiar. Their foreheads protruded in the same way Abby pictured cavemen and cavewomen must have looked. She'd worried that she'd be afraid of them. After all, they were capable of crushing her with a single blow.

But when she saw them coming down the hill, her fears evaporated. They were walking hand in hand.

Beside her, Earl kept muttering, "I can't believe this" and his lanky body quivered with excitement. He gulped for air. "Look at them, Abby. They're actually right there. Right *there.*"

"I know, Grandpa. It's amazing."

"I knew they had to mate and have babies. I just knew it, but no one has ever . . . Okay, I'm blown away by this, but believe me, I'll never breathe a word of it."

Keeping her gaze on the Sasquatch, Abby reached over and patted his knee. "I know you won't. Roarke wouldn't have brought you if he thought you would tell."

"I owe that boy so much. I swear, he could ask me to do anything—*anything*—and I'd do it in a heartbeat. Oh, God, they're hesitating. Look, Abby, they're pointing at the helicopter."

Abby held her breath as Roarke turned back to the Sasquatch pair. They faced each other for what seemed like forever, but might have been only a couple of minutes. The Sasquatch couple put their heads together as if conferring. Then the female patted her tummy and took a big breath before motioning to her mate that they should continue. After another long pause, he took her hand again and they began walking toward the helicopter.

Emotion clogged Abby's throat as she realized the courage required to climb into what must look like a monster machine to these creatures. But the combination of Roarke's gentle persuasion and the pair's devotion to their unborn child had won the day.

Abby didn't remember the bandana in her lap until the creatures were only a few feet away. She'd been so caught up in the drama that the smell had become secondary. But once they were this close, the smell was all she could think about.

She tied the mint-scented bandana over her nose and mouth like an old-fashioned bank robber and made a silent promise to do something nice for Knox Trevelyan if the opportunity presented itself. Even with the bandana offering some protection, she fought her gag reflex as the Sasquatch couple boarded from the rear amid various grunts and groans.

The helicopter rocked with their weight and Knox hopped out and ran around to the back hatch. Abby had to assume Roarke got in, too, but she was so focused on not barfing that she didn't turn around to look.

Knox had left the helicopter's windows open, but that didn't help much. When he climbed back into the pilot's seat, Earl leaned forward and tapped him on the shoulder. Good old Grandpa Earl didn't seem fazed by the stench.

"I don't want to frighten them by staring," he murmured. "Is there a possibility I will?"

"Just glance back there every once in a while and smile," Knox said. "They might find that reassuring. Smiles are a universal language among humanoids."

Earl nodded. "Good advice. Thanks."

Knox raised his voice. "All set back there?"

Roarke gave a short yip, which Abby interpreted as an affirmative. Knox must have interpreted it that way, too, because he revved the engine.

Both members of the Sasquatch couple began to howl in obvious terror. The eardrum-splitting sound, added to the horrible smell, created Abby's version of utter hell. She clapped her hands over her ears.

Once again Knox dug in his pocket and extended his hand back to Abby. In his palm rested two foam-rubber earplugs. She took them without protest and stuck them immediately into her ears.

The earplugs muffled the sound and slowly her tense muscles relaxed. She glanced over at her grandfather, but he was involved in giving the Sasquatch pair reassuring smiles and didn't seem to notice the racket any more than he'd noticed the odor.

When the helicopter lifted off the ground, the howls grew louder. Abby wondered if Knox had a parachute in his pocket and if he'd offer her that next. Roarke had said the flight would take about an hour, and Abby wondered if they'd all have permanent hearing loss by then.

But instead, miraculously, the howls tapered off and eventually stopped. Abby took out her earplugs to make sure she wasn't imagining things, but all she could hear was the rhythmic sound of helicopter blades slicing through the misty air.

Earl nudged her. "Take a look back there."

Abby turned around in her seat. The Sasquatch pair

sat on the floor of the helicopter, their legs out in front of them. Sandwiched between them, looking for all the world like the Sasquatch family dog, was Roarke. The female was gently stroking his fur.

Knowing how reassuring that thick pelt could feel, Abby wasn't surprised that the howling had stopped. Roarke was providing comfort to them in the same way he'd provided comfort to her in the tunnels under the Gentry mansion. But when she looked into his green eyes, she was glad to be wearing a bandana over her nose and mouth, because his miserable but resigned expression made her grin.

The hour passed more quickly than she'd expected. Knox circled a wooded area and set the chopper down near a small waterfall that fed into a rocky stream. Then he hopped out and opened the door for the Sasquatch pair.

Abby turned to watch their departure. They clambered out of the helicopter much faster than they'd climbed in, and then they stood, obviously waiting for Roarke. Abby hoped they hadn't decided to keep him.

Roarke jumped out, too, and trotted around the clearing as if pointing out its advantages. He sniffed at a bush, and the female came over to rip off a few leaves and munch on them. When she sat down next to the bush and continued to eat, the male came over to join her, and soon they seemed to be enjoying lunch together.

For a while Roarke stood watching, but then the female glanced up and made a shooing motion with her hairy hand. Roarke trotted back to the helicopter and once he'd leaped inside, Knox shut the door. Within seconds the helicopter was airborne.

Abby turned around, wondering if Roarke would come up to the front again now that the Sasquatch pair was gone. Instead he stayed far back in the helicopter, his head on his paws. She could imagine why. After such close contact with the creatures, his fur must stink to high heaven.

Earl plastered his face to the window for several minutes and then finally settled back in his seat with a sigh. "Wow." Then he turned to the back where Roarke lay. "Thanks, Roarke. I'll never be able to repay you for that."

Lifting his head, Roarke whined softly before settling back down.

That soft whine did it. Abby unbuckled her seat belt and moved to the back of the helicopter. Then she pulled off her bandana and sat down next to Roarke, who did indeed smell like a thousand pissed-off skunks. "I'm not letting you stay back here by yourself."

He looked at her as if she'd lost her mind and tried to scoot away.

"Stop that. I'm sitting by you, and that's that." Moving right next to him, she used the bandana to wipe his face. "This should help."

Roarke sighed and rested his head in her lap as she continued to stroke his head with the bandana.

"Isn't that better? It smells like mint." She couldn't read his mind. Only another Were in wolf form could tune into his thoughts. Still, she did know what he was thinking as she stroked him with the bandana.

It smells like you.

When they landed at Portland-Hillsboro, Roarke waited until Earl and Abby left before shifting and putting on the clothes he'd stashed in the back of the helicopter. Knox had jumped out immediately, too, probably to get his first real breath of fresh air. The poor Were was going to have to fumigate both the chopper and himself.

Once he was dressed, Roarke climbed out of the helicopter and glanced around. Knox stood nearby, but Abby and Earl had walked over to meet Aidan. Aidan was keeping his distance from them, though. Everyone who'd been in the helicopter carried the Sasquatch stink.

Roarke approached Knox and stuck out his hand. "Thanks for doing that, Trevelyan. I know it was a challenge."

Knox returned Roarke's firm handshake. "It was, but I'd never seen a mated pair before. When they came down the hill holding hands, I thought that was sort of touching."

"I thought so, too."

Knox gazed at him. "Your friend Abby seems very fond of you. Not many humans would have gone back there. You must have smelled awful."

"I'm sure I did. Abby's . . . special."

"You know Gentry's put out the word that she's a major threat to all of us."

Roarke nodded. "That's why I'm taking Abby and Earl back to New York."

"Is that your brother standing over there, the one who mated with a human?"

"Yes." Roarke started to add that he wouldn't be following in his brother's footsteps. But he was no longer sure of that. He wanted Abby desperately, and if he thought she was willing to make the necessary sacrifices . . . Could he ask her to do that?

Trevelyan gazed at him with a hint of disapproval in his dark eyes.

Roarke had a new appreciation for how Aidan must have suffered during Roarke's lectures on the subject of Weres mating with humans. He cleared his throat. "Listen, if I could make it out here for a visit, would you consider giving me flying lessons?"

"I could do that."

"Great. Well, I need to shove off. Sorry about the stink in your chopper."

"I'll deal with it. See you, Wallace."

"That's a given. I want to learn to fly one of these eggbeaters. Thanks, again." Roarke turned and crossed the tarmac to Abby and Earl. "Are we ready to go?"

Abby waved a plastic rectangle that looked very much like a hotel key. "We're driving to the Marriott first. Aidan refuses to let any of us into the Learjet until we've showered and changed."

"That may be possible for you, since you each packed a suitcase, but I don't have any clothes other than this." He motioned to the gray sweats and sweatshirt Earl had contributed.

Aidan held a handkerchief to his nose and moved slightly closer. "I've had some time to kill, so I picked up some clothes for you, stud. I figured you'd come out of this stinking up the place. Go to the service entrance and they'll let you in that way, so you don't contaminate the lobby. Then all of you just leave your dirty clothes in the room. Housekeeping has instructions to burn them."

Roarke shrugged. "I won't argue with that. Let's go."

Earl spent the short drive to the hotel raving about his Sasquatch experience. "I have to get it out of my system with you guys," he said, "because I won't be able to tell anybody else."

Roarke decided not to mention that Earl wouldn't have a chance to talk to other humans for a while, anyway. Better not put too fine a point on that.

When they reached the hotel, Roarke expected them all to be sharing the same room and shower. Instead he discovered that Earl had his own key to the room next door.

"See you in a few," Earl said with a smile as he walked into his room and closed the door.

Abby had the key, so Roarke waited while she opened the door. But he wasn't quite prepared for her to grab him by his shirtfront and haul him inside before slamming the door again.

Then she got right in his face. "Listen here, Roarke Wallace! I may not be able to shape-shift, but if that's the only reason you won't choose me as your mate, then, as much as I love you, I'll have to label you prejudiced and narrow-minded. So there."

He blinked. "You love me?"

"Of course I love you! Isn't it obvious? Would I have held your head in my lap when you smelled like a thousand pissed-off skunks if I didn't love you?"

He grinned. The scent of Sasquatch might just become his favorite aroma. "Guess not." Ah, sweet heaven, she loved him! The tightness in his chest eased as he accepted that love as the greatest gift he would ever receive.

She put her hands on her hips. "So, what do you have to say for yourself?"

He cupped her beloved face in both smelly hands and surrendered to the joy that washed over him as he imagined a lifetime with this incredible woman. "I have this to say: If you can forgive this prejudiced, narrow-minded fool, I'm the luckiest Were that ever lived."

Her expression went from fierce to gentle in an instant. "Of course I forgive you."

He sighed and leaned his forehead against hers. "Thank God. Because I love you beyond all reason, and if you'll have me, I want you for my mate, Abby Winchell."

She swallowed. "Are you sure, Roarke? Because our children might not be Were."

He brushed his lips over hers. "That's not the most important thing in the world. The most important thing for kids is that their parents love them and love each other. And we'll have that in spades."

She wound her arms around his neck and pressed her sweet body against his. "Oh, we will, Roarke. We certainly will."

He groaned. "I want to make love to you. And we don't have time. Aidan is expecting us to—"

"He's expecting us to spend the night in this hotel room, Roarke, and fly back to New York tomorrow. That is, if— Wait. Allow me to quote him exactly: 'We can fly back in the morning, Abby, assuming Roarke gets his head out of his butt long enough to realize what he has with you.'"

Roarke laughed, happier than any Were who'd screwed up so thoroughly had a right to be. "Seems like I did."

"Yeah." She smiled up at him. "I think you did."

"You know Aidan will never let me live this down."

"Do you care?"

Roarke shook his head. "After the grief I gave him over Emma, I deserve whatever he dishes out."

"I'm looking forward to meeting her. And the rest of your family."

"They're going to love you." He hesitated. "But I'm afraid your job as a claims adjuster in Phoenix isn't going to—"

"Are you kidding? I'm so ready to move on. I've even thought of something I can do for you."

"I can think of several things you can do for me, and they all involve getting naked."

She rolled her eyes. "This is work-related, you sex maniac. When you're doing fieldwork and you find indigenous populations who need financial help, I'll come along to administer those programs. I'd be good at that."

"Abby, that's brilliant! God, there are so many times

I could have used someone to figure out the details. It's a great idea."

"So I'm hired?"

"I'd be a fool not to hire you, and I've vowed to stop being a fool." He searched her gaze for any hesitation, any misgiving about the path she'd chosen. He found none. "We're going to be very happy, Abby. It won't always be easy, but we're going to be happy."

"Absolutely. But I do have one question."

"Only one?" He nuzzled the tender place behind her ear.

"For now. If I'm going to be your mate, I should probably know what your middle initial stands for."

"It stands for Adolph." Giving in to the lust he could no longer keep at bay, he urged her toward the bed. "Which means wolf, Little Red Riding Hood. And I'm warning you, I'm very hungry."

She laughed as they fell onto the bed, stinky clothes and all. "So fairy tales do come true."

"I don't know about all fairy tales, but this one will. We, my delicious Abby, will live happily ever after, starting now." And he proceeded to show her how.

Read on for an excerpt from
the next fun and sexy Wild About You novel
by Vicki Lewis Thompson

A Werewolf in Seattle

Coming from Signet Eclipse in June 2012.

Colin MacDowell was one jet-lagged werewolf. The trip from Scotland to Aunt Geraldine's private island off the coast of Washington State hadn't seemed this arduous the last time he'd made it. Apparently a seventeen-year-old pup could take more travel abuse than a thirty-two-year-old Were.

A dark-haired werewolf named Knox Trevelyan had greeted Colin at SeaTac International on this balmy June afternoon and had escorted him to a private helipad. Knox operated an air taxi service, one of many businesses owned by the powerful Trevelyan pack in the Seattle-Tacoma area.

"I'm really sorry about your aunt," Knox said as he loaded Colin's suitcase and carry-on into the helicopter.

"Thank you. It was a shock." Colin was touched by the sincerity in Knox's voice.

Colin's Scottish Aunt Geraldine and her Vancouver-born mate, Henry Whittier, had avoided Trevelyan pack politics in favor of a quiet existence on their little island. Henry's death a few years ago hadn't made much of a stir in the local Were community, which was how Geraldine had wanted it. Colin hadn't expected anyone to mourn Geraldine's passing, either.

"I was there the night she died," Knox said.

"Really!"

"Yeah. Her personal assistant, Luna Reynaud, called me in the middle of the night. I flew over to the island with the best Were medical team in Seattle. They tried but they couldn't save her. Her heart just gave out. It took her before we got there."

"So it was you who made that emergency run." Colin held out his hand to the pilot. "I can't tell you how much that means."

Knox returned his handshake firmly. "I wish we'd been in time."

"From what her lawyer said, nobody could have made it in time. But considering how they'd avoided being part of the community, you went beyond what could be expected."

"They didn't have much of a pack mentality, but they donated generously to our environmental work."

Colin nodded. "I did know about that."

"Besides, Geraldine was a hoot. I'd pick her up every month or so for her recreational shopping trips in Seattle. Even after Henry passed away, she still loved hitting the resale shops for designer clothes and shoes."

"I'm sure she did." The thought was bittersweet. Geraldine had specified that the contents of her closet be donated to charity, so he'd see to it while he was there. She'd willed a few pieces of jewelry to the female staff members, and he'd distribute those, too.

Knox sighed. "Damn shame. Well, might as well get you over there."

"Right." Colin climbed into the small chopper. Once he was settled in, his jet-lagged brain nudged him to do the polite thing and ask how the Trevelyan pack was faring.

"Quite well," Knox replied. "My father runs a tight ship, and all the various concerns, including my air taxi service, are showing healthy profits."

"Excellent." Colin remembered another bit of disturbing Were news that he wanted to check out while he was in America. "We got word over in Scotland about the Wallace pack—two brothers who each took human mates. Is any of that happening in your pack?"

"Not that I've heard. But I met Aidan and Roarke Wallace last year, and they both seemed happy with their choice. Maybe taking a human mate can work in some cases."

"Bloody reckless if you ask me." Colin had used those very words the last time he'd had an argument about human-Were mating with his younger brother, Duncan.

Knox shrugged. "Time will tell."

"It's a colossal mistake." Colin shuddered at the possibility of humans breaching the security of the Were world. Through the ages, werewolves had suffered horribly whenever humans had uncovered their existence, so secrecy was the only protection they had.

Humans could be business associates, perhaps friends, and occasionally even lovers. But they couldn't be trusted with the knowledge that Were packs controlled much of the wealth in major cities all over the world. Mating with a human risked losing everything, not to mention diluting the werewolf gene pool.

Knox reached for his headset. "You could be right, but at this point it's not a problem we're dealing with in Seattle." He turned to Colin. "Ready to go?"

"Yes." Or as ready as he'd ever be. The sound of the rotor sabotaged any further conversation, and he was happy to slip back into his jet-lagged stupor. Exhaustion coupled with guilt had sapped his desire for small talk.

Although he'd spent five summers on the island—

from the age of twelve until he turned seventeen—he hadn't been back since. What was done was done, and he couldn't change anything now, but regret weighed on his soul.

He could come up with a million excuses for why he hadn't visited. He'd been busy earning an economics degree. Then he'd dealt with his father's poor health, and eventually he'd taken over as laird of Glenbarra. But surely in the past fifteen years he could have spared a week or two.

Nostalgia gripped him as the chopper approached Seattle. The Space Needle rose like an exclamation point that would forever identify the city, and would forever remind him of the day he'd spent playing tourist with Geraldine. She'd treated him to dinner in the Needle's revolving restaurant, where he'd gazed endlessly at the lights that sparkled below them like the Milky Way.

Closing his eyes, Colin leaned back against the headrest and dozed. He roused himself as the chopper veered northwest and skimmed over Puget Sound, headed for the San Juans, an archipelago that included dozens of islands large and small. They all had official names on the map, but Colin had forgotten what his aunt's island was called. Now he just thought of it as Le Floret.

On his first visit, he'd told Geraldine that the island looked like a giant clump of broccoli rising from the sea. She'd promptly declared they would call it Le Floret from now on instead of whatever boring name the map showed. She'd laughed whenever she'd told that story. She'd had a great laugh.

As the pilot began his descent, wind from the spinning blades ruffled water bright as polished chrome. Colin blamed the glare for making his eyes water. Taking off his Wayfarers, he wiped away the moisture before settling the sunglasses back in place. Soon he'd walk into

Whittier House, and Aunt Geraldine wouldn't be there. That was going to be very tough.

A maverick to the end, she'd nixed the idea of a funeral. Her lawyer had read Colin her final instructions over the phone, and they were typical Geraldine. *Just dump my ass—I mean ashes—in with Henry's and sprinkle them on Happy Hour Beach while you toast us with a very dry martini. Make sure we're shaken, not stirred.*

Then the lawyer had dropped the bombshell. Geraldine had left all her worldly possessions—the island, the turreted, Scottish-style mansion Henry had built for her, and every valuable antique in that mansion—to Colin. It was an incredibly wonderful gesture, but he wished to hell she hadn't done it.

Much as he'd loved his irreverent aunt, he had no use for an island and an estate halfway around the world from Glenbarra. Sure, he had some fond memories of Le Floret and Whittier House, but keeping the property would be sentimental and impractical. As a new laird, he couldn't afford to be either.

Geraldine's lawyer had provided the name of a reputable Were real estate agent from Seattle, and Colin had contacted him before leaving Scotland. The agent would arrive the following afternoon, which would give Colin a chance to scatter the ashes and get some sleep.

That left the matter of the staff. That old codger Hector was still the groundskeeper, but the others had been hired since Colin had last visited. Perhaps the new owner would need them, but if not, Colin would hand the more recent hires a generous severance check and a letter of recommendation. He'd set up some sort of pension for Hector in recognition of his many years of service.

Selling a place that had meant so much to his aunt didn't make him particularly happy. Geraldine had probably hoped that he'd cherish the estate as she had. But he couldn't imagine flying more than twelve hours each way and dealing with an eight-hour time difference on a regular basis.

Logically, he had no choice but to unload what could only become an albatross around his neck. The proceeds would bolster the MacDowell coffers, and after years of his father's financial neglect and Duncan's carefree lifestyle, the coffers could use some bolstering.

The rapid beat of helicopter blades vibrated the crystal chandelier over Luna Reynaud's head and sent music and rainbows dancing through the entry hall. Tension coiled in her stomach. This Scottish laird had the power to ruin everything for her and the rest of the staff if he refused to consider her plan.

But he would consider it. He *had* to. She'd finally found a place where she belonged, and she wasn't about to give that up without a fight. The loss of Geraldine had been a cruel blow, and she grieved along with the rest of the staff. If, on top of that, she lost this precious haven, too . . .

Well, she wouldn't. No doubt Colin would arrive planning to sell the island. Although Geraldine had lovingly recounted tales from the five summers he'd spent here, he hadn't been back since, so how much did he really care about it?

It was impractical as a second home, or, in his case, as a second castle. Geraldine had called it a house, but no mere house had four towers, sixteen turrets, fourteen bedrooms, ten fireplaces, and twenty giant tapestries.

But if Luna could convince Colin that this old pile, as Geraldine used to call it, would make a fabulous Were vacation spot, half the battle was won. If he'd trust her to manage it for him, then, voila, an income stream for him and jobs for her and the staff. Most important of all, she wouldn't have to leave.

Also Available

FROM

Vicki Lewis Thompson

Werewolf in Manhattan
A Wild About You Novel

Emma Gavin writes about werewolves, but that doesn't mean she believes in them—not until a pack of real-life New York weres decide to investigate the striking accuracy of her "fiction."

When Aiden Wallace, son and heir of the pack leader, tries to sniff out Emma's potential informant, he discovers something even more dangerous—an undeniable attraction to her.

**Available wherever books are sold
or at penguin.com**

S0305

Also Available

FROM

Vicki Lewis Thompson

The Babes on Brooms Novels

Blonde with a Wand

Sexy witch Anica Revere has one rule: never under any circumstances get involved with a man before telling him she's a witch. Still, what's one silly rule? Especially when the guy in question is as cute as Jasper Danes. But when Anica and Jasper have a spat, she breaks an even bigger rule of witchcraft and turns him into a cat. Bad news for him. Worse for her...

Chick with a Charm

Lily Revere is free-spirited and fun loving—two dangerous qualities in a witch. Especially while planning her sister's engagement party, and she needs a date! She's determined to bring hot Griffin Taylor, but he's a divorce lawyer who claims his job has warned him off romance. He may pretend he's just not into her, but she knows better— he only needs a nudge in the right direction.

Slipping a love elixir into Griffin's drink may not be the noble thing to do—but it sure works! Lily's dreamboat drops all defenses and the two discover they're perfectly matched in every way. There's just one problem: Are Griffin's feelings the result of some truly good witchcraft—or is he really in love?

Available wherever books are sold or at
penguin.com